RECOVERED FUMBLE

BAYLIN CROW

Recovered Fumble by Baylin Crow

Copyright 2019 Baylin Crow

This is a work of fiction. All characters, locations and events portrayed in this work are either fictitious or are used fictitiously. Any similarity is purely coincidental.

The use of any real company and/or product names is for literary effect only. All other trademarks and copyrights are the property of their respective owners.

All rights reserved.

No part of this publication may be reproduced in any written, electronic, recording or photocopying without written permission from the publisher or author. The exception would be in the case of brief quotations embodied in the critical articles or reviews and pages where permission is specifically granted by the publisher or author.

Any images or models shown on covers are for illustration purposes only. The characters depicted and any texts expressed in this story are not reflective of any models shown.

Cover Design by Cate Ashwood

Proofread by Kathy Kozakewich

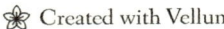 Created with Vellum

SERIES NOTE

While there is a real Sugar Land, Texas, the fictional city this book takes place in is simply that: fictional. Each story in the Sugar Land Saints Series will be semi-standalone and each will focus on a new couple. You can read them separately, but I recommend reading them in order. Characters from previous books in the series will make appearances and be referenced while new characters for future books will also be introduced.

To start from the beginning check out Quarterback Sneak (Sugar Land Saints Book One).

Hope you enjoy!

Baylin xo

ONE
RENDON
APRIL/NFL DRAFT

ACCORDING to the directions my brother had given me, the red brick duplex that belonged to Nash, one of Shaw's teammates, sat at the end of a long road lined with cars. As I eased between the rows, I searched for his blue sedan and came up empty. I parallel parked my old white hatchback between two trucks that had left enough space for my tiny car, snatched my phone up from the cup holder and tapped out a message to Shaw.

"Hey, I think I'm at the right place but I don't see your car."

I drummed my fingers on the steering wheel as I waited for the reply. The engine whined due to a loose belt so I shut it off and cracked my door open, prepared to climb out. When my brother had invited me for the weekend to roam the campus and possibly meet some people before I started my freshman year in the fall, I'd reluctantly agreed.

The trip from home where I lived with my parents wasn't too far, but it was long enough that turning around was just as unappealing as the view from my windshield. As

I glanced around at the cars and checked out the scene, I questioned my decision to stay.

Despite the fact that the sun still kissed the horizon, the party was well underway. I'd only been prepared for a small NFL draft watch party to see if Shaw's buddy made the cut. Yet the atmosphere seemed much more like the college parties I planned to avoid and not a few football players sitting around a big screen like I'd imagined.

Several people loitered on the front porch and from where I sat, held what looked like beer bottles. Music thumped from inside, gaining volume each time the door of the right-hand unit opened to let people come and go. I wondered what the neighbor thought about all the noise. The porch was partitioned by a large column, but no one seemed to respect the boundary and the whole space appeared to be fair game.

Parties weren't my thing. I'd never been to a real high school party either. That would have required being invited to one. And forget prom. I'd skipped that altogether.

My phone buzzed in my hand and I shoved my black wire-framed glasses up the bridge of my nose as I glanced down. *"Oh, shit. Sorry, I rode with Bishop and forgot to tell you. On my way outside now."*

I blew a raspberry and wondered if it was too late to change my mind. The front door swung open again and Shaw stepped out and waved.

As I climbed out of the car, a light breeze rolled over my skin and rustled the mature trees that towered above the homes. My brother, a Saints wide receiver, wore his usual comfortable t-shirt, cargo shorts, and tennis shoes. He dodged the people on the steps and met me halfway up the sidewalk.

Rethinking my ironed navy-blue short-sleeved button-up shirt and khaki shorts, I hoped I wouldn't stick out like a sore thumb. Six inches taller and much broader than my five-eight, slim frame, Shaw dwarfed me as he slung a heavy arm over my shoulder. Despite the difference in our height and weight, Shaw and I resembled each other with the bright green eyes and blond hair we'd inherited from our mother.

Shaw ruffled my hair and I batted his hand away and ran my fingers through the strands to fix them back into place. He chuckled. "How was your drive?"

"It was fine." My gaze was drawn to the house again when a few people stumbled onto the lawn and laughed as a girl fell on her hands and knees, giggling as she was helped up.

My brother released me and stepped back. "I swear we didn't plan on this many people showing up but word got out. Happens sometimes at these things." He shrugged. "It's mostly guys from the team, and some of their girlfriends. A few random people from school."

"A few?" My eyes widened.

"Okay, a lot. But this was about meeting people before you start in the fall and a lot of these people won't be around during the summer. Maybe it worked out for the best," he suggested with a hopeful smile.

I nodded but inwardly grimaced as the noise seemed to escalate. "His neighbor doesn't complain?"

"Nah. Most of the housing around here is for students and they don't care. Jesse is a cool guy. He was actually inside earlier, may still be." He pursed his lips then dismissed the topic. "Come on and I'll introduce you to some of the guys."

When I hesitated, he frowned.

"I don't think I'm going to fit in here," I admitted.

Shaw crossed his arms. "You might be surprised. They aren't bad guys, I promise."

Though I'd likely recognize most of his teammates from attending his games, I didn't know them personally so I'd have to take his word for it. And I couldn't tell him that after he'd left our hometown, my experience hadn't been the same as his. Being responsible for taking the football team to state year after year had given Shaw a get out of jail free card for being bisexual. No one had given him crap when he'd come out. Well, no one did it to his face anyway.

High school hadn't been fun for me. When I came out, I hadn't received the same pass. Maybe because I was gay and not bisexual, but I doubted it. They wouldn't have cared. Liking dick in any way was social suicide for a guy. Rumors and gossip followed my every step. My few friends vanished at the first whispers of any connection to the geeky queer boy. And a lot of it had been started by the hometown heroes wearing football pads and helmets on Friday nights. The moment I realized I could graduate a semester early, my full focus turned to that goal so I could escape the walls that echoed with taunts and made my life miserable.

I zoned back in on what Shaw was saying. "Most of them are watching the draft still so they are going to be preoccupied."

My brother's teammate, Rush, was the star center for the Saints and everyone expected him to be drafted. But if everyone was still watching, I wondered if it hadn't happened yet. At least one day of the draft had already come and gone. Selfishly, I'd hoped he'd go first round so I could avoid the party altogether and spend the weekend with Shaw and maybe a few of his closest friends.

I squared my shoulders and promised myself I'd keep an open mind despite my reservations. "Okay, let's go."

He turned and I followed him up to the porch where he paused. "I'm glad you agreed to visit. It'll be fine, you'll see. I wish I had known a few people going into my freshman year."

Shaw led the way inside the unit. There wasn't much of an entryway so we stepped straight into the living room where a black leather couch and two matching chairs were packed with huge guys rubbing elbows.

Girls sat in the laps of a few guys and the arms of the furniture were used as seats. Many more sat around on the carpeted floor. Some held beer bottles, others water bottles or energy drinks, and the scent of pizza and alcohol hung in the air. Plates were scattered across the wood coffee table laden with chips and uneaten crusts. The TV was at top volume so they could hear the draft over the music. I winced at the assault on my eardrums.

The open concept floorplan afforded a view of the small dining room to my left where four guys played cards and had started quite the collection of beer cans. The kitchen opened up off the dining room and was separated from the living room by a tall bar. Three raw-wood stools, each holding one of my brother's hefty teammates, matched the countertop. To my right, a short hall led to two doors, one open, to which I assumed was the bathroom, and one closed that must have been Nash's bedroom. And the back door was located directly across from where I stood.

Shaw was right. In the living room, other than a few girls messing around on their phones, almost everyone's eyes were glued to the huge TV mounted on the wall. And the others were absorbed in drinking games, poker and conversations. Not many spared us a glance.

"We have food if you're hungry." Shaw dragged me into the kitchen and motioned toward a huge stack of pizza boxes covering one half of the counter space. "Drinks are in the refrigerator."

With my brain screaming to make a break for it and run back to my car, the last thing on my mind was food. Still I managed a grin for my brother. "Thanks. I'm okay right now."

"Suit yourself, but it's there if you want it."

I followed him back out into the main room, but stood a step behind him.

"Hey, guys," my brother yelled, trying to gather everyone's attention. I wanted to find a hole to hide in rather than have so many eyes on me. "This is my brother, Rendon."

Three or four guys glanced up. I received distracted chin nods and careless waves. Brow raised, I looked up at Shaw as if to make my point. *Not my crowd.*

He gave me a sheepish grin. "They aren't always this bad. It's the third round and everyone is getting worried for Rush because he hasn't been drafted. It'll happen though. He's too valuable."

"I'm sure you're right." I scanned the room, searching for a quiet corner to settle in. No luck. While I wasn't claustrophobic, there were a lot of people packed into a small space and the tight confines put me on edge. I eyed the back door across the room and nudged Shaw's shoulder. "Does this place have a back porch?"

"Yeah, why?" Shaw cocked a brow.

"Just going to grab some air?" The statement had come out as a question and earned the suspicious look Shaw gave me.

He scrubbed a hand over his face. "You're uncomfortable and I feel like an ass now. I swear I thought it would be okay."

"No, it's fine. Just need to make a call," I lied. The environment was overwhelming and I needed to reset my expectations.

He narrowed his eyes and studied my expression, clearly conflicted on what to do. "I'll come with you."

"Oh, no. You go watch the draft. You'd hate if you missed it. I'll be back inside in a minute," I assured him and his expression relaxed.

"You sure it's okay?"

I scrunched my nose, causing my glasses to slip. I pushed them back into place. "Of course."

"Okay, but come find me when you're done with your call."

"Will do," I promised.

He crossed the room and plopped down on the carpet in front of the chair Bishop had claimed. I recognized Bishop from seeing him on the field. He was a huge guy that played defense. With striking black hair and eyes—and a matching dark disposition—he was intimidating and the opposite of Shaw in every way. I'd never seen the guy crack a smile, even when he made a highlight-reel play during a game.

Bishop's eyes stayed fixed on Shaw for a moment and my brother glanced up at him, wearing a dirty grin. Gross. I wondered if everyone was aware they were hooking up or if they were all completely blind.

Rather than crossing everyone's view of the TV, I slipped through the kitchen and slid by a group of girls laughing, one gesturing wildly with her hands mid-story, and snuck outside.

Like the front, the large connected back deck was split into two halves and divided by a column.

The last rays of the sun had disappeared and the temperature had dropped as night replaced day. The only light breaking up the darkness was provided by the indoor lights slanting through the windows.

Facing the acres of open field behind the fenced backyard, I leaned against the wooden railing that wrapped around the porch. Two sets of stairs, one for each unit, led down to the shared lawn where a few people milled around.

Tendrils of smoke curled up in front of my face at the same time the scent of a cigarette hit my nose. I glanced over and found there was a guy sitting on the top stair on the neighbor's side of the porch. He sat in shadow but his face was awash with the glow from the lights inside. Eyes dark and hooded stared back at me. His brown hair was shaved close, facial hair groomed and with only a white tank covering his sculpted chest, the dragon tattoo that wrapped around the full length of his arm was visible. His motorcycle boot-clad feet were propped one on top of the other as he sat back with stretched out legs. He was the epitome of a bad boy.

"Hi," I squeaked.

His lip quirked. "Hi."

He took a drag of his cigarette as his gaze raked me head to toe. The smoke left his lungs in a cloud. "Haven't seen you here before. You with Nash?"

The question was odd considering the number of people inside, but I shook my head. "Oh, no. I'm just visiting. My brother is on the team."

He continued to smoke but shifted his gaze up toward the dark sky.

After an awkward silence, I stepped away from the railing to go. "It was nice to meet you."

He glanced back at me and his lip quirked again. "I'm Jesse. And you are?"

Shaw had mentioned Nash's neighbor, so I recognized the name. "Rendon."

Jesse tossed his cigarette in a ceramic pot and stood. "Enjoy the party."

He crossed the deck to his unit and as the door closed behind him, I frowned at the strange conversation but pushed it aside. Minutes ticked by as I composed myself and prepared to rejoin the group.

I was in the middle of giving myself a much-needed pep talk when sudden shouts and the sound of utter chaos broke through my musings. Curious, I opened the door a sliver.

"I knew it!"

"That lucky shit. How'd he land Texas?"

"Damn, dude. I told you not to worry."

The voices rose as they continued to talk over each other, making it impossible to tell who was saying what, though it was clear Rush had made the draft. I found a spot against the wall and looked on while everyone huddled in front of the TV. Enough of the screen was visible that I saw Rush take the stage and pose for a photograph with his new jersey and cap.

After the first burst of excitement died, Nash stood in the center of the room, raised his hand and hushed the crowd. The music cut off and silence enveloped the room. "Pipe down. I'm calling them."

My stomach flipped as he flashed a wide smile at the people crowding around him. It was the first time I'd seen Nash up close and in street clothes. Seeing him on TV or from the distance of the stands on game day hadn't done him justice at all. He was tall—well over six feet—the ideal height for a top wide receiver. With short black hair, light brown skin pulled tight over sleek muscle and a voice like rich velvet, Nash was the kind of guy you couldn't help but notice. And I did. With my gaze trained on him, I bit my lip.

He shook his head and lowered the phone. "Voicemail."

"Give them a minute. They are probably busy and it's got to be loud," Shaw said.

Nash agreed but soon grew impatient. "I'm going to call Torin."

Torin was the Saints quarterback who'd also be graduating this year. And Rush's boyfriend.

This time Torin must have answered.

"Hey, T, ask your boy why he's not answering his phone. Is he too good to talk to his old teammates now that he's some hot-shot NFL player?" His playful tone negated his accusing words and then he laughed at whatever was said. "Let me talk to him."

Seconds passed and then Nash whooped. "Holy shit, Rush, you did it! You're in the NFL, not that we doubted you."

He listened for a moment and his grin grew. "Oh, yeah. We have quite the party going on as we watched the draft. Say hi." Nash switched it to speakerphone and held the phone up high.

Everyone yelled over each other but I made out my brother's voice. "Fuck yeah, man!"

"It sounds like more than Shaw and Bishop are there," Rush replied over the speaker with a laugh.

"Oh, the house is packed..." Nash glanced around and stopped cold when he spotted me.

His eyes were incredible—intense shades of green and yellow with dark brows that only highlighted the unique combination. His lids grew heavy and he sank his top teeth into his lower lip, mirroring my own reaction. There was no way that piercing gaze was locked on me. I glanced to my left and right and then swallowed hard when I realized I stood alone.

Nash took a step in my direction, shoving the phone at Shaw who barely managed to hang on to it. "Damn, who's that?"

Every muscle in my body locked up tight and my feet refused to move despite the adrenaline rush causing my breathing to speed up and my heart to pound.

Shaw growled and shoved Nash's shoulder. "Don't even think about it, Nash."

Nash's gaze scanned me from head to toe. Heat flooded my cheeks and my skin broke out in chills. He tilted his head, and without taking his eyes off me, he addressed my brother. "What?"

"Rendon is off-limits." Shaw narrowed his eyes, not that Nash would know. "Stay away from my little brother."

I hated when he called me that. It always made me sound like a kid.

"Hey, I had no idea." His words held no weight as he started walking again in my direction and a predatory grin crossed his face.

"Nash, where are you going? You better not be... We have to go"—Shaw spoke into the phone—"Congrats, Rush. We'll celebrate properly when you get home. I need to go kick Nash's ass real quick." He tossed the phone to Bishop and charged after Nash.

Now everyone was watching as two giant wide receivers stepped around people to get to me and I wanted the floor to open up and swallow me whole.

Shaw was blocked out by Nash's massive frame as he stopped in front of me. The scent of citrus and spice cologne invaded my space and I inhaled deep. He smelled amazing.

My gaze traveled from his trim waist to the wide muscular chest the sleeveless black shirt couldn't conceal, up his throat to his chin and holy... His lips. Lush and plump. I'd never reacted so hard to a pair of lips, but Nash had to have the most kissable mouth I'd ever seen. A slow grin spread across his face as he cleared his throat. My gaze jerked up to meet eyes that danced with humor. "Rendon, right?"

"My brother just told you that," I murmured.

He smirked and leaned in. With one hand against the wall over my shoulder, he caged me in. "I'm Nash."

"I know who you are." My voice shook. Why did he have to be so hot? He had to be messing with me, because there was no way he was interested in me.

"Yeah?" He cocked his head, and the small silver hooped ring in his left ear caught the light.

"Well..." I fought the stutter that happened when nerves got the better of me. "I come to my brother's games sometimes and recognize you."

He hummed. "How come I haven't seen you around?"

"I was going to school and don't visit the campus often," I offered when the obvious answer was because I was invisible up until about five minutes ago.

My brother stepped next to us and gritted between his teeth. "*High* school."

Nash frowned and took a step back, letting his arm fall to his side.

"I graduated early and start here in the fall," I blurted. I didn't know why the words flew from my mouth, but it was the truth. "And I'm eighteen."

Shaw cursed and Nash's grin grew again.

"No," my brother said, shaking his head with stiff movements. "Not happening."

Nash raised his hands as if in surrender but then held one out to me. I took it in my trembling hand and he shook it. He smirked before glancing at my brother.

"I hear you loud and clear, Shaw." His eyes latched onto mine again. Still holding my hand, he ran his thumb over my knuckle. I shivered and the hair stood up on my arms. "Well, it's nice to officially meet you."

"You too." *Lame.* For as well as I did in school, I'd hoped if the day ever came where I was hit on, I'd have a better response. Smooth and suave or something, but that wasn't me. Nope, I stood there like a deer in the headlights as his gaze dipped to my mouth.

My brother groaned. "Oh, for fuck's sake. Loud and clear, my ass."

"Shaw." Bishop's gruff voice grabbed my brother's attention, and he crooked his finger, beckoning him over. My brother's expression was conflicted and he huffed. Before he walked away, he glared at Nash again and then me. "The answer is no."

My brother and Bishop were so hooking up.

Nash chuckled and released my hand. When my brother was out of earshot, he winked and said, "We'll see if it's a no. Personally, I'm a fan of *yes.*"

As he turned and walked away, my gaze roamed over him, down to his butt filling out his shiny gray athletic shorts then to his exposed calves chiseled with muscle. His body was perfect, so unlike mine. Everything about him was hot as if put together straight from every fantasy I'd ever had. Why would someone like him want me?

I pressed my back against the wall while I regained my bearings. My heart thudded and my head swam. I'd never in my life been looked at like that and the feeling was heady. Once I'd calmed down, I scanned the room, content to keep to myself instead of being sucked into campus gossip or football-fueled conversations. Still I couldn't help but seek out Nash from time to time. Girls and guys flocked around him, and he hadn't so much as glanced in my direction again. I took it for what it was, a brief lapse in judgment, and he'd realized he had his pick of guys. Maybe girls too. I wasn't sure if he wasn't interested in them. My brow scrunched.

Some guy I'd never met handed me a beer and I stared at it with a frown.

"You look bored as shit," he explained. "Have some fun."

He'd grinned and it hadn't seemed suspicious or anything. But even if I were up to drinking, which I wasn't, I'd never drink something someone I didn't know gave me at a party. I shook my head and walked into the kitchen, moving around the crowded room to pour the wasted amber liquid down the drain.

A husky chuckle sounded behind me. "Not a fan of beer?"

Turning slowly, I found Nash gazing down at me with his hypnotic eyes and his lips tilted in amusement.

I scrunched my nose. "Sometimes, but I didn't know the guy who handed it to me and I'm driving."

"Smart." Nash turned around and squeezed past a group of girls with apologies, opened the refrigerator and retrieved a bottle of water. He returned, leaning his hip against the counter beside me and winked as he offered it to me. "Still sealed and everything."

"Oh, thank you." I uncapped it and guzzled a long drink. I wiped my mouth on the back of my hand. "It's warm in here."

"Small spaces with a lot of people tend to heat up quick. But the back deck isn't so bad now that it's dark." He paused and considered me. "Want to take a breather with me?"

I dipped my head to conceal my smile before glancing back up. "That sounds nice."

The grin he returned was boyish with a twist of cockiness that sent a jolt through my body. *I'm so not prepared for this.*

I followed his lead through the clusters of people and to the back door. Once we stepped outside, I half-expected my brother to come storming through the door right after us. Thankfully, that didn't happen.

"So"—Nash leaned his back against the wood column as I stood awkwardly to his side—"are you looking forward to the fall?"

The normal question caught me off guard. I was expecting more suggestive flirting, but not that. "You mean starting college?"

"Yeah." He took a sip of his beer wrapped in a black and gold Saints koozie. "What's your major?"

"I don't know, actually. I'm thinking history, but I plan to spend the first year trying to figure that out before I declare. Time to figure *myself* out away from home if that makes sense."

"It does." He nodded as if he understood. "You don't have to have it all decided right away."

It was my turn to ask a question. "Is it true you're headed to the NFL next year?"

He blew out a heavy breath. "If I'm lucky, yeah. It's been a dream since I was a kid."

"My brother said you were a sure thing." I peeled at the plastic label around my water bottle.

"Well, I don't like the idea of leaving my family if I get picked by a team on the other side of the country, so it's something I worry about. My dad's health isn't the greatest." He chewed on his lip and sighed. "I'd like to get an offer with Texas like Rush, but that would be a stretch so I try not to hope too much, ya know? I'd be happy with making it at all. If it happens, I just wish I could pack up my family and bring them with me."

"Oh." I hadn't expected him to share something personal with me. "I don't know what to say. I wish you could too."

He nodded then frowned.

"Did I say something wrong?" Leave it to me to ruin the situation.

"No." He studied my face. "Why do I want to tell you everything? It's weird, right?"

He didn't wait for an answer and I was glad because I didn't have one.

"Sorry, didn't mean to drop the heavy stuff on you." Nash set his beer on the railing. Digging his hand into his pocket, he pulled out a sucker, tore off the wrapper and stuck the trash back in his pocket.

"It's fine." I paused. "I'm glad you told me."

Nash glanced at me with a thoughtful expression and hummed. "Yeah, me too."

We stared at each other for a beat before I jerked my gaze away. His eyes were too much. I didn't want to end up embarrassing myself by throwing myself at him. Not like I had the nerve to do that, but it was possible I'd do something equally embarrassing. Like drool.

Nash popped the sucker in his mouth and spoke around it, his voice muffled. "It's an addiction."

The change in subject had me scrambling to keep up. "You're addicted to suckers?"

"Cherry suckers," he clarified.

I laughed. "Could be worse."

He pulled it from his mouth and licked his lips. "Truth."

The door swung open and Shaw stepped through. Late, but I'd called that one.

His gaze bounced to Nash before focusing on me. "Thought I might find you out here." His gaze swung back to Nash. "And I'm not at all surprised to find you, too."

Nash straightened. "We were just talking."

"I'm sure." He eyed Nash with mistrust.

When Shaw turned his back on Nash and leveled me with a look, I couldn't help but peek over his shoulder at Nash.

He rolled his eyes dramatically and then winked at me. Nash stuffed the sucker back in his mouth then ducked into the house, leaving me alone with my brother.

Shaw shoved his hands in his pockets. "I need to talk to you."

"Okay." I crossed my arms over my chest. "So, talk."

"Look, I know I said this would be a good idea to get to know people and stuff but...not Nash. Not in *that* way." He cringed.

I frowned. Nash was the only person who'd taken an interest in me and he was easy to talk to despite the nervous flutter in my stomach just being near him. "Why not?"

"Well, because it's apparent he's into you," he said, like that explained everything. It explained nothing.

It was exciting that someone noticed me. Especially someone like Nash, and somehow, I knew my brother was about to ruin it. "Okay, why's that a bad thing?"

Shaw hurried on. "It's a bad idea, Rendon. Nash is a good guy but...he doesn't do commitment. He's not a one-man or one-woman guy. I don't want you to get hurt."

My shoulders slumped. "How do you know?"

"He doesn't make it a secret, Ren." His expression was sympathetic. "He's notorious for hooking up. Guys and girls, not that it matters, but it's *always* one-and-done."

I frowned harder at the thought. Maybe it was good thing Shaw had interrupted what I had built in my mind as a special chemistry between Nash and me.

"So, he's a cheater?" I had zero experience with this stuff.

"No." He shook his head. "I didn't say that. To my knowledge, he's never been with anyone long enough for that to be possible."

I mentally kicked myself. "Okay, I hear you."

Satisfied, he nodded. "Are you about ready to head out?"

It was getting late and I was disappointed. Nash had been easy to talk to and I was attracted to him. Of course, he was a player. That made me feel stupid, and I wanted to head to my brother's dorm to bury my head in the metaphorical sand. "I'm ready."

"Okay, let me say some goodbyes. I'll catch a ride with you since I rode with Bishop."

"Whatever, that's fine." I waved him off.

"Give me a few minutes."

I followed him inside, losing sight of him as he disappeared into the crowd. On my way to the front door, I went through the less crowded kitchen and walked right by Nash. His arm shot out as he wrapped it around my waist. "Hey, you okay?"

When I glanced up at him, his gaze trapped mine, completely ensnaring it. Like an idiot, I wanted to ignore my brother's warning. "We are leaving. It was..." I swallowed hard. "It was nice to meet you."

He released me. "Yeah, you too, Ren."

We stared at each other for a minute, and he groaned. "Fuck it. I tried to do the right thing. You're going to get me into so much trouble." He shook his head. "Can I see your phone?"

A mixture of excitement, nerves, and worry exploded in the pit of my stomach as I pulled my phone from my pocket. "Why?"

He raised a brow as a slow smile spread across his face. "So I can give you my number."

I hesitated. My brother's words of warning echoed through my mind. But if it was a one-and-done thing, why did he want my number? I'd be going back home in a few short days. My hands shook as I handed my phone to him.

He typed quickly and handed it back. A chime went off and he pulled his phone out of his pocket. "Now, I have yours too."

There was no way I was telling my brother about exchanging numbers with Nash, and I was pretty sure Nash wouldn't either. The last thing I needed was another parental conversation with Shaw.

Nash reached out and ran a finger down my cheek and under my jaw. "I meant it. It was nice to meet you. I'm glad you came."

Neither of us moved away as we traded stares. Electricity crackled between us and his gaze dipped to my mouth. I licked my lips and he groaned.

"I better go," I whispered.

"Probably a good idea, young Wakefield." His gaze flicked back up to meet mine.

Slowly I retreated until I bumped into someone. I spun around. "I'm so sorry."

A big guy I thought I recognized as a Saints defensive player patted me on the head. "No worries."

Focusing on my surroundings so I didn't further embarrass myself, I went in search of my brother and found him outside standing close to Bishop by his car. The sleek black machine was parked on the opposite side of the road.

"Shaw, are we leaving?" I hollered.

"Yeah." My brother jerked away from Bishop. "Coming now." Bishop said something too low for me to hear and Shaw laughed. "Shut up."

When Bishop hopped in his car, Shaw jogged over to where I stood on the sidewalk and we made our way down the street until we reached my hatchback.

After we climbed in, he faced me with a serious expression. "I meant what I said about Nash."

I wondered if he'd seen us in the kitchen, but shook it off. He needed to mind his own business. He was trying to look out for me, but this was something I needed to figure out myself. If Nash was a mistake, it was mine to make.

Cranking up the car, I found an empty driveway and turned the car around. "What's going on with you and Bishop?"

He threw his head back against the headrest and laughed as I pulled out of the neighborhood, heading toward campus. "Well played, little brother. Well played."

My excitement dwindled with each day that passed after I'd come home from visiting my brother. There had been no call or text from Nash, and there was no way I was reaching out first. So, I waited. I checked my phone frequently, but after the second week, I gave up.

It shouldn't have come as a surprise. I *was* warned after all. I buried myself in extra shifts and overtime at the grocery store where I worked in the stock room to keep from thinking about him. Maybe it was for the best.

The more money I could begin college with, the better. My parents, Sarah and Phil Wakefield, weren't exactly swimming in cash. In fact, most months we struggled to get by. Dad was a mechanic at a small shop in town, and Mom had stayed at home with me and Shaw until five years ago when she had teamed up with a friend and started a house cleaning service to supplement income.

They were both hard workers and put in a lot of hours, but that didn't always equal great pay. Still, we were okay. But they weren't going to be able to help me out much financially once I began school. My scholarship would only go so far, so I'd been working since I graduated, saving as much money as possible.

Who needed a distraction like Nash anyway?

But a month after the party while I was taking a break at work, my phone buzzed. My entire body lit with nervous energy when I saw who it was from. *Nash.*

"Do you have any idea how impossible you are to ignore?"

What did that mean?

When I didn't respond he sent another text. *"I'm an ass. I'm sorry. I wasn't sure I should get in touch with you being my teammate's brother and all. And I had finals to study for, and then a short break with the family. But those are excuses. Forgive me?"*

I chewed on my lip as I mulled it over. *"So, why text now?"*

"Because it was driving me crazy not to?"

I grinned. Though it was a bad idea, I messaged back. *"Why?"*

"Fishing for compliments already?" He included a laughing emoji and my cheeks hurt from grinning as I responded.

"I wouldn't hate a few."

"Fine, I'll give you more than a few if you agree to come over. Not a party. I got the impression you weren't a fan of them, so just us two hanging out. Do I stand a chance?" This time he used the wink emoji and I could easily picture him mimicking the expression.

My hand tightened around my phone. Would he want to hook up? Was that what this was? If so, he was going to be sorely disappointed with my lack of experience and skill, but excitement thrummed in my veins. Even if it were only a hookup, my interest was definitely piqued along with a healthy dose of anxiety. My fingers hovered above the keyboard as I contemplated if I should go. Slowly I tapped out a single word. *"Maybe."*

The reply was instant. *"Ren, are you in?"*

I rubbed the bridge of my nose beneath my glasses as I tried to tell myself once again it would be a mistake. Who was I kidding? *"Yeah, I'm in."*

TWO
NASH
JUNE/SUMMER TERM

I'D BATTLED the urge to contact Rendon over the last month. It was critical to keep peace among the team so there wouldn't be tension that could disrupt our season and damage my chance of getting a first-round pick in the draft. Though I'd be happy to be selected at all, a top pick was almost a guaranteed spot on the roster with the longest contract option. Not to mention higher pay.

And that meant not pursuing the instant spark I'd had with Rendon. Even if he was the most tempting little thing I'd ever seen. So, I'd tried to stay away and then a few days ago I'd caved and texted him.

In my defense, I'd tried. I really had. But there was something about him that drove me to distraction and convinced me to do things I shouldn't. Like invite him over.

The thoughts were still swirling around in my brain as I hopped out of my shower and dried off before wrapping a towel around my waist. I ran a hand towel over the mirror to clear the foggy glass and checked out my reflection. I wasn't humble enough to doubt my sex appeal. The reaction I got from others had built confidence in my looks, particularly about my eyes.

All that self-confidence dulled when I thought of Rendon. How did he see me? Had he thought of me as much as I had him? He'd had my number and hadn't reached out...

I frowned. Why were those questions bothering me so much? Whatever. He'd accepted my invitation, hadn't he? I brushed my teeth and shot myself a winning smile. There was no way it was one-sided.

Rendon was due to arrive any minute and I still needed to pick up the place. I shut down those doubts and quickly dressed in a pair of comfortable black mesh shorts and a dark gray sleeveless shirt that showed off my arms and hugged my torso.

I'd just spritzed a light layer of cologne when the timid knock came at the door. In a rush, I ran around the living room, picking up a glass and plate I'd left out and darted into the kitchen to drop them in the sink. On my way back, I grabbed a pair of sneakers lying in the middle of the floor. I jogged to the door, but paused to toss the shoes in the entryway closet before I swung the front door open.

Rendon stood there with his hand poised to knock again. He lowered it as he gazed up at me with wide emerald-green eyes that sparkled like gemstones behind black wire-framed glasses. His light blond hair fell across his forehead and I itched to run my hand through it. From behind.

He was such a petite guy compared to my tall frame and cute as shit. He wore a pair of gray shorts and a white short-sleeved button up. I'd thought about his cupid bow lips many times and how much I wanted to have kissed that mouth. But I'd underestimated how I'd react once I faced him again.

Instead of the slow buildup I'd expected, my body responded instantly, my cock swelling in my shorts. I wanted to immediately take him to my room, throw him on the bed and show him how good I could make him feel. The image of swallowing his dick down my throat made me bite back a groan. But he was different than my usual one-nighters, and I got the impression I needed to take my time. I took measured breaths to calm down.

"Hi," he said with a sheepish grin.

"Hi, yourself." I flashed a wide smile and his cheeks bloomed pink. That blush of his was going to get us both into big trouble. I'd noticed it the first time I had approached him and hadn't been able to get rid of the memory. "I'm glad you came."

As I stared down at him, he chuckled nervously. "Are you going to let me in?"

With a laugh, I stepped aside and gestured him inside. As he brushed by, the scent of fresh linen floated in the air, and I inhaled deep, resisting the urge to yank him close and bury my face in his neck.

After I closed the door, I ushered him farther into the living room. "Make yourself at home. Do you want something to drink? I only have water and energy drinks." I scratched my chin. "I guess I didn't plan this out very well."

I should have asked him what he liked in advance. The belated idea showed me how little I knew about hanging out with someone I liked for more than the time it took to get off. And I did like Ren. He wasn't just easy to look at, he'd been easy to talk to.

"Water's fine. Thank you." He stood awkwardly in the middle of the room, and I studied him for a beat before I left to grab us some drinks.

When I came back, Rendon stood in front of the fireplace, scanning the framed family pictures crowding the mantle. The only other time he'd been to my place, the rooms had been bursting at the seams with people and I'd taken down all of my pictures and mementos so they didn't get broken.

I stepped next to him and held out a bottle of water. He took it and nodded toward the photos. "You have a big family."

"I do." I grabbed one with my immediate family. In the photo I was eighteen and about to start college. My family surrounded me, arms around each other. "This is my mom, Alicia, and dad, Marcus. And these two little brats are my twin sisters, Brooklyn and Jordan."

My mother's family was originally from Jamaica and she had skin several shades darker than mine, amber-brown eyes and long black hair. In contrast, my dad's family originated in Ireland and he had pale skin, auburn hair and green eyes. The two of them had produced me and my sisters, all with light brown skin and green eyes. Though if you asked, most people said they were yellow-green.

"Your sisters look young," he observed.

I glanced at my two favorite girls. "Yep, surprise babies. They're ten now."

"Oh, wow. That's a big age difference."

I set the frame back in its rightful place. "Yeah, but it keeps my parents young. You probably can't tell from the picture, but my dad played college ball too before he met my mom senior year." I took one last glance at the photo. My dad had lost a lot of muscle and was much thinner than he'd been during my childhood.

"Wasn't interested in going pro?" Rendon asked.

"Nah, he got a degree in business and marketing. When

he graduated, he started up a landscaping business and it took off."

He smiled. "Are they close enough to come to your games?"

Sighing, I popped the tab on my energy drink. "My dad doesn't travel well anymore so they haven't made it to a game in a long time. His side of the family is riddled with autoimmune disorders and he won the jackpot when it came to health issues. He had to stop working and now basically just runs admin from the house. The drive and navigating the stadium are too hard on him."

Rendon sucked in a breath. "I didn't mean to pry."

Grabbing his elbow, I steered him to the couch. "Oh, no, I love talking about my family. No worries."

Once he settled onto the cushion, I took a seat beside him, leaving some space so I wouldn't crowd him. I wasn't sure what he was thinking and what he wanted out of this. When I invited him over to hang out, I knew what I'd *hoped* would happen.

It was time to switch gears, but I figured I should approach the situation with caution. His stiff posture bothered me and upon closer inspection his hands were shaking slightly in his lap. I wanted him to feel comfortable with me, and it was clear he was nervous. If he just wanted to chill that would be okay. It might be torture to keep my hands to myself, especially because I was going through my first dry spell in years, but I'd live.

I covered his hand with mine and squeezed. "Hey, relax. We can watch a movie and order some pizza." I gave him an easy smile. "No pressure."

He visibly relaxed, shoulders dropping, and he sank further into the cushions. "Right, okay."

It was a reminder to pump the brakes and let him take the lead. "What kind of pizza do you like?"

"I'm pretty flexible," he said, and my gaze heated as I pictured just how flexible he might be.

My resistance, it would appear, was flimsy at best.

"I'm not that picky," he corrected himself. "You also have your mind in the gutter."

"It was a vivid picture. Sorry." I chuckled, and when he joined in, I shot him a wink. "Plain pepperoni it is then, if you don't mind."

"That surprises me. Don't you like, need to eat your veggies?" Rendon eyed my exposed biceps and I might have flexed a little. He rolled his eyes and I grinned.

"I do eat vegetables, but they aren't my favorite on pizza." I shuddered and was thankful he hadn't requested any. "Less talking about food and more ordering." I reached for my phone on the side table and then passed Rendon the remote. "Here. Go through the movies and pick what you want to watch."

As I spoke to the restaurant over the phone, Rendon scrolled through the channels, pausing from time to time. It was hard to keep my eyes off him when he moved his lips as he silently read the descriptions.

I forced myself to focus on the call and rattled off my address to the woman on the line. "Okay, great. Thanks." I hung up and turned to Rendon. "It'll be about twenty minutes. Did you decide on something?"

"Yeah, I think so. I haven't seen this one."

I glanced at the TV. He'd chosen an action film. "Perfect."

After I flipped off the light, I snagged the blanket from the back of the couch and draped half over myself and held the opposite corner to Rendon.

"Thanks." He smiled and tugged it over his body before snuggling beneath the quilted fabric. He turned back to the TV and he pressed play before passing me the remote to set on the end table.

It was hard to focus on the screen with him so close, but I did my best. And when the pizza arrived, the box sat untouched. Preoccupied by the space that grew smaller each minute as we moved closer to each other, I couldn't have told you what the movie was about. Rendon was equally distracted, glancing at me from the corner of his eye. I was aware because I was doing the same thing.

I paused the movie and shifted to face Rendon. "I'm sorry, you know."

He glanced over at me and the glow from the TV in the dark room cast parts of his face in shadow. "What?"

"For letting so much time go by without getting in touch."

"No harm. I didn't reach out either." He worried his lip. "But what changed your mind?"

How did I answer that? Nothing had changed other than my inability to stay away from him. Did that make me a dick? Probably. I hadn't even explained the problem to him.

"It wasn't only the fact that you're my teammate's brother." When his brow furrowed, I hurried on. "We talked about the draft, right? Well, as far at the pro teams are concerned, I'm only as good as my last season. I knew Shaw wouldn't approve of me pursuing you. He has his reasons," I mumbled. "So I worried if Shaw found out that I went behind his back, there would be friction between us and it would cause issues with the team.

"If I want to play the best ball of my life—and I have to if I want a chance to get drafted—it's not a good idea to do anything that could create a rocky season. I can't afford it. And I consider Shaw a friend, so I don't exactly feel great about what I'm doing. Am I making sense?"

Rendon seemed to contemplate what I said. "It makes sense, but doesn't explain why I'm here. I would think if anything you'd have not gotten in touch."

"Way to call me out," I teased then my voice lowered. "I tried not to. Drove me crazy."

He studied me in silence and then bit his lip. "I don't see why Shaw has to know about this. It's not his business."

"I feel like shit about it," I admitted but my gaze was trapped on the indents his teeth left on his lip. "But I want you and apparently have no self-control."

"Like you want to..." His wide eyes dropped to my lap where my cock was clearly hard, the stretchy material giving him an eyeful.

Slowly, while keeping my eyes on his, I nodded. "You have no idea what I want to do to you, but I'd be happy to show you. I don't know how much longer I can keep my hands off you."

"So, what do you plan on doing about it?" His voice shook but he held my gaze.

The bold question from such a sweet mouth made my cock jerk. "Would it send you running if I told you everything I wanted to do to you?"

He sucked in a sharp breath. "You just say whatever you want, don't you?"

"You asked, and believe me, I'm holding back." My gaze dropped back to his mouth. "I want to taste you so bad."

His ragged breaths came in short bursts. When I glanced back at him, Rendon's gaze was fastened on my lips and his pink tongue darted out to wet his.

A growl ripped free from my throat. "You keep staring at me like that and I *will* kiss you."

Rendon hesitated and swallowed hard. "Okay."

"Okay?"

He nodded and whispered, "You can kiss me."

When I leaned in, he held still except to grab ahold of my shirt. The barely-there brush of my lips against his fired off every one of my nerves to that single point of contact. With restraint I didn't know I had, I added the slightest pressure. When he didn't move, I pulled back enough to see that his eyes were closed, but his grip on my shirt tightened as if he wanted to hold me in place.

Angling my head toward his ear, I nipped the lobe. "Kiss me back."

"Oh okay." He panted as I placed open-mouthed kisses on his neck.

The stray thought about his possible lack of experience vanished when he tugged on my shirt, urging me back to his mouth. Placing one of my hands at the back of his head, I ran a finger lazily across the nape of his neck before I dove back in. Pressing firmer, his lips softened beneath mine and opened for me. My restraint crumbled as I brushed his silken tongue with mine. His movements were timid and lacked finesse and it drove me crazy.

I jerked one of his legs over my lap and ran a hand over his calf and then up his slim thigh, his shorts bunching as I stroked his bare skin. He shifted and kissed me deeper, his movements becoming surer as he moaned into my mouth. If my cock ached before, it was downright painful responding to the sounds escaping his mouth into mine.

"You taste fucking amazing," I murmured.

Rendon shut me up with a devouring kiss.

Things were quickly growing out of control, and I

yanked the leg draped over me until he rolled on top of me and straddled my thighs. He didn't seem to mind as he pressed against my obviously tented shorts.

Fuck, he was so hard. I gripped his ass as he rocked against me. Gone was any shyness. Rendon rubbed against me with frantic rolls of his hips. I itched to undo his button and yank down his zipper so I could feel him better. My hold on him tightened and trapped our cocks together. The only way we could possibly get closer was if we stripped naked. What I wouldn't do to see all that pale skin on display. I groaned and lifted my hips in a slow grind and pushed him down at the same time. He broke away and gasped.

"Oh, god." He panted as he rode my lap.

The temptation to get closer was too strong, so I jerked back and ripped my shirt over my head then reached for his, cursing at the inconvenient buttons. Working quickly, I slipped the last one though its hole and wrestled it off him. Before I got a proper look, he attacked me again. Our chests, skin on skin, worked up a sweat. He was so into it and I was losing my damn mind.

I pulled back and reached between us. With my fingers gripping the button of his shorts, I forced myself to pause. "Can I?"

Rendon gave a jerky nod, and I unclasped the snap and ripped down the zipper. I wrapped my hand around his brief-covered cock, and he jerked, crying out my name. Jesus, he was sensitive. I jacked him in short quick strokes as he writhed on top of me. He moaned as he chased his orgasm, and if he didn't stop dry fucking me, I was going to blow too.

I released him to yank down the waistband and damn near came at the first view of his pink tip. He was leaking and my mouth watered. I curled my fingers around his bare shaft and we both shivered. With my eyes locked on his dick, I tightened my fist. Three strokes later, he moaned and my gaze jerked to his in time to watch his mouth drop open in a silent *oh*.

Ribbons of come exploded against my abs and I groaned. *Oh, hell yes.*

Rendon's entire body spasmed as I milked the rest of his release. Reluctantly, I loosened my grip, and he sagged against me, resting his forehead against my shoulder. My cock still strained between us, demanding attention, but I anchored him to me, wrapping my arms around him and rubbing his smooth back. When he caught his breath, he leaned back and met my eyes. His glazed over when I ran one of my hands over my stomach, through the sticky mess and then into my shorts.

The first stroke over my cock was instant relief. With his wide, dazed eyes glued to my hand jerking my cock beneath the mesh fabric, it didn't take me long. I'd been on edge from the second I saw his tip leaking for me. I groaned and pulled my dick from my shorts as I came.

"Oh..." Rendon whispered in what sounded like awe.

I peered between the slits of my heavy lids. Rendon was staring at my cock, and though I'd just gotten off, it twitched under his scrutiny. "*Oh*," I repeated.

"I..." He seemed at a loss for words so I pulled him against me again. He went willingly, burying his face in the crook of my neck. "That was amazing."

Understatement.

"One of the hottest things I've ever seen," I mumbled and felt his smile against my neck.

After a few minutes passed, he sighed. "I need to tell you something."

"What is it?"

"This is embarrassing." His words were muffled against my skin.

Frowning, I rubbed his back. "Just tell me."

"Okay." He took a deep breath. "That was my first, you know."

Loosening my hold, I pressed him back so I could see his face. "Your first what? Hand job?"

He peered up at me with dazed eyes. "My first anything. Well, I mean I kissed someone once, but it was awkward and nothing like that."

My mouth opened and then shut. "Do you regret it? Did I overstep?"

Rendon shook his head fast. "I definitely don't regret it."

I relaxed, if only a little. "So, you're a virgin?"

He nodded this time. "Is that a problem?"

Shock held me mute, but I recovered quickly. How does that happen? Especially with someone who looked like Rendon. High school had been all about exploring for me. But there was a curious sense of satisfaction that no one else had touched him. Only me.

"No, Ren." I bit back a smile. Despite never have been the one to pop a cherry, I loved the idea I might be the one to do it. If I was being honest, it scared me too. "Definitely not a problem."

He gave me a small smile. "*Ren,* is it?"

I laughed and lifted him off my lap. "We need to get cleaned up."

He ducked his head as he found his balance.

Standing, I tucked my finger beneath his chin, encouraging him to look up and leaned down, nipping his bottom lip. "Stop being embarrassed. That was the single hottest moment of my life."

"Really?" He appeared skeptical.

"Oh, you have no idea." I took his hand. "Come here."

He followed me to the bathroom and I cleaned us up with a wet towel before returning to the couch. Now that I was aware he was a virgin, I set the idea of having sex on the back burner. No need to rush. If he agreed to visit again, and hopefully he would, there would be time for that.

Spent, Rendon curled against me, using my chest as a pillow as we calmed and watched the rest of the movie. Once the credits rolled, I glanced down and found Rendon passed out.

The unpleasant sound of a phone ringing woke me and I reached out to find my phone on the side table. My eyes slammed shut as the blinding light of the screen lit up the dark room. I turned down the brightness and eased open my lids. It was Shaw. *Shit.*

I glanced around and rubbed sleep from my eyes as the night before rushed back. When I could barely hold my eyes open, I'd coaxed Rendon to the bedroom where we'd both promptly fallen back to sleep. It was weird to share a bed with someone in a nonsexual way, but oddly I hadn't minded it. In fact, I'm not sure I'd ever slept better.

As the high-pitched noise continued, Rendon shifted on his pillow. I hit answer.

"Hello." My voice was raspy from sleep and trying to whisper.

"Get your ass out of bed," Shaw barked. "I need a workout partner."

I pulled the phone away from my ear. Did he have to be so loud? "Why? What time is it?" I checked the time on my phone. "Dude, we don't have to be there for another two hours. And where's your other half." I stifled a yawn.

"He's busy." Shaw sounded wound tight and agitated.

The fog cleared from my head and I was instantly alert as my gaze jumped to Rendon while addressing Shaw. "Everything all right?"

Rendon stirred again and grumbled. "Who's that? Tell them to go away."

Shit. I flipped on my side, facing him, and snaked my hand beneath the sheets and squeezed his thigh in warning. He didn't seem to register my meaning as he pressed his small firm ass into my morning wood. I held back a groan as I suppressed the urge to grind against him and his breathing grew even again.

"Give me twenty and I'll meet you there." I hung up before Shaw could respond. Had he heard Ren? Had he recognized his voice? Had he driven by and seen Rendon's car? *Fuck.*

I shook Rendon's shoulder lightly. "I have to go...but you can stay if you want." I didn't want him to think I was a complete asshole and giving him the boot. Anger at Shaw lit my insides. I didn't need drama, though having his brother over was a risk I'd already accepted.

He glanced over his shoulder with bleary eyes. "Huh? What time is it?"

"It's still early."

Rendon reached out and patted around him and I smiled. I grabbed his glasses from the nightstand on my side and handed them to him.

"Thanks." He slid them on. "Do you have my phone too?"

I gave him that as well. He glanced at the screen and

jumped out of bed like his ass was on fire. "Crap, I'm going to be late for work."

We both scrambled to get ready, racing around to get dressed. I tossed him a new toothbrush while brushing my own. Minutes later, I followed behind Rendon outside until we split directions to our vehicles. But my gaze stayed on him as he ran to his car parked on the curb and climbed in. When his engine cranked, I changed direction and hurried over to his driver side and tapped on his window. He glanced up and rolled down the window. "Did I forget something?"

I leaned down again and devoured his lips, chasing his tongue with mine. When we broke apart, he was wide-eyed and gasping for breath.

"No, I needed one last taste." My gaze locked on his as I backed away. Then with a wink, I turned and jogged back up the driveway.

My neighbor Jesse's black muscle car rumbled into the shared driveway and I gave him a quick chin nod before I hopped into the cab of my truck.

After Rendon pulled away, I backed out and headed for the athletic complex.

Shaw was leaning against his blue sedan when I pulled up next to his car. He was frowning and staring at the ground when I jumped out. "What's going on?"

"I need to clear my head." Without another word, he turned on his heels, and I hurried after him.

I followed him silently into the building and dressed out as he stewed over whatever was going on in his head. Meanwhile, I was still worried he'd heard Rendon, but if that was the case, he didn't say anything. Hell, he wasn't speaking at all.

He sat on a bench and I grabbed the one next to him.

We picked up our weights and began arm curls. When the silence was officially uncomfortable, I glanced over at him. "Do you want to talk about it?"

"No. Yes." He paused a moment before resuming his work out. "No."

"So why did you want me to join you?" I asked, puzzled.

He shrugged the opposite shoulder and his arm moved faster. "Don't you hate liars?"

He did know about Rendon. "Listen—"

"You think someone is being honest with you. They have your complete trust and then like a slap in the face"—he was pumping his arm so fast his face was turning red—"you find out they are lying."

I considered coming clean then and there, but this seemed bigger than me and his brother. "Wait, is this about Bishop?"

His silence was all the answer I needed. Bishop's and Shaw's relationship was the worst kept secret on the team. Everyone assumed Shaw was bisexual since they'd seen him with girls and guys. But the same wasn't true for Bishop. He'd never showed any interest in anyone. Ever. Except Shaw.

No one called the guys out because Bishop's dad was beyond rich and had many connections—connections that could ruin their future careers. And Bishop's standoffish demeanor didn't help. I personally didn't think he was as bad as most of the guys did.

Did it make me an awful person that I was relieved that this meltdown was about his relationship and had nothing to do with Rendon?

"Take it easy. You're going to overdo," I warned him, but

he didn't seem to hear me because there was zero reaction, only the rapid straining curling of his arm.

The weight room door creaked open and Bishop filled the doorway. His gaze landed on Shaw and his jaw clenched. As if he sensed him there, Shaw stiffened but didn't stop. He was going to hurt himself at the rate he was going.

"Yo, Bishop," I called out. Bishop spared me a glance with dark narrowed eyes and lips pressed in a tight line. "You'd better take that creepy ass look on your face somewhere else. Like the locker room and then come partner with Shaw. He isn't listening to me."

His eyes went back to Shaw and hardened.

"He's going to end up injured or something stupid. What the hell has gotten into him?" I set down my weights.

"Stop talking like I'm not right here." Shaw snarled, set down the dumbbell then glared at Bishop. "What do you want?"

The tension in the room thickened. And when the silence grew awkward, I opened my big mouth.

"Oookay," I interjected, prepared to make myself sound like a complete jerk, but enough was enough. These two were going to drive themselves apart if they didn't come clean and fess up about their relationship. And though Bishop was an asshole to most people, he and Shaw were good for each other. Everyone thought so.

My gaze flicked between the two. "Something is going on between you two. You both banging the same chick or something? Do y'all even bang chicks? Or, like, bang at all? You know, I never see either of you with anyone. Maybe that's the problem. You both need some pussy."

That got a reaction and it quickly became clear I'd gone

about it the wrong way. In my defense, I was still worried about Shaw knowing about Rendon and my judgment seemed to be off. I steeled myself for the blow that I deserved.

Bishop's face grew red and he snapped. "Shut the fuck up, Nash."

Realizing I'd asked for it didn't stop the sting. Bishop never talked to me or anyone like that. I scowled and stood, grabbing my water bottle I had snatched from the stocked fridge. "Well, that was rude. Seriously, what's up?"

"No, maybe he has a point." Shaw gave Bishop a defiant stare. "It's been a while. Maybe that is what I need."

Yup, I'd fucked up. Awesome.

Bishop fumed and whipped around and headed for the locker room. Shaw remained quiet as I moved to the stationary bike. Bishop was back in minutes, dressed out and prowling toward Shaw.

"Hell no," Shaw said when Bishop sat next to him.

Bishop raised a brow. "Yes—your favorite word. If I remember correctly, you said it several times last night."

I couldn't act like I hadn't heard that comment. "You guys are acting weirder than usual and I'm not dense. That sounded extremely sexual." I mashed my lips together and hesitated to continue. But they needed to know. "Maybe it's not the right time to bring this up, but that was a total joke about the chick by the way. Everyone knows you two are banging each other."

The look of shock that passed over their features as they looked at each other would have been laughable in a different situation. At least they didn't look ready to tear each other apart anymore.

"Don't look so surprised," I said. "Rush and Torin didn't hide it any better than you two. No one wants to say anything since you're possibly psychotic"—I glanced at

Bishop—"and have enough money and resources to ruin any one of our lives."

He scowled.

I winked. "True story."

"Damn it, Nash," Shaw snapped. "I'm sick and tired of y'all thinking he's some kind of bad guy."

"I don't." I shrugged and thought that Shaw's comment was off base considering his current attitude toward Bishop. "I think he's an asshole, and as of two minutes ago, I'm pretty sure you did too."

"He *is* an asshole," Shaw stated with a glare.

"I'm gay," Bishop announced without hesitation and out of nowhere.

I quirked a grin. Maybe I did know what I was doing. I mentally patted myself on the back. "Yeah, I got that when I said we all know you are doing the deed. Is this your official coming out party?"

Shaw's face whipped to the side to glare at me. "You're fucking my little brother!"

My eyes widened, and I stopped breathing, stopped moving. His accusation caught me off guard. I'd been lured into a false sense of security by the crashing storm between him and Bishop. My brain screamed deny, deny, *deny*. "What the fuck, Shaw? Why would you think—"

"Cut the crap. I heard him on the phone." Despite his words, I caught a glimpse of uncertainty. Like he knew, but he didn't *know*. I jumped on that seed of doubt.

"I don't know what you think you heard." I gave him the most innocent expression I could muster while thoughts of my shot at the NFL tanking soured my stomach. "But you're mistaken."

His eyes narrowed with suspicion. A swirl of guilt, worry and frustration about the situation clouded my brain.

Because from that one explosive statement, Shaw had proven what I'd expected. Getting caught with Rendon would be a season-ruining event.

Though he seemed only half-convinced, he powered on, conviction growing in his tone. "Really? Maybe I should call him and see what he has to say." He cocked his head and I read the dare for what it was. "What are you doing with him, Nash? He's my little brother. Not some fuck-and-ditch you're used to."

I held my hands up, refusing to come clean. As long as I didn't confirm it, he couldn't be sure, I reasoned with myself. "Fine, I'll stay out of your business."

Now if you'd stay out of mine, that'd be great.

"Yeah, you have your own shit and I should kick your ass for going near him," he said, but his tone lost steam.

I chuckled and shook my head as if he was nuts. Inside, I was consumed with frustration. The chemistry Rendon and I had was explosive and I wasn't ready to bail out yet. I imagined next year's draft. Could see it vividly in my mind. I wanted to be standing on that stage holding a pro team jersey. I wanted what Rush had.

Pedaling faster, I watched the timer and was relieved when Shaw's anger switched back to Bishop. They continued to argue and I picked up bits and pieces while I continued to convince myself Rendon was a bad idea. And he was. I'd already known that, but what if we were more careful? Then we didn't have to stop yet.

The burst of loud curses from Bishop broke through my thoughts and I whistled. "Not tryin' to pry but you may want to give him time to cool off. You too."

"Mind your own business, Nash." Bishop took the weights Shaw had abandoned and started his own frustration-infused reps.

I held up my hands. "It was just an idea."

"Well, you have your own issues to deal with." Bishop leveled me with a look that said he hadn't bought my denial. I swallowed and looked away.

"Truth," I muttered.

It was late by the time I got home from practice. After I took a shower, I sat on the couch and flipped my phone around in my hand as I stalled. I stared at it going around and around in my palm. I had to tell him, but then what? I sighed and pulled up our messages.

"Shaw called me out this morning. He heard you on the phone. Or he thinks he did, but I lied and said he didn't. I wanted to let you know."

As I waited for his response, I got restless. Setting my phone on the table, I went to find something to eat. I rummaged through the cabinets and ripped into a new box of protein bars. I'd just bitten off a hunk when my notification alert went off. I strode back into the living room and slumped back into my spot as I pulled up his message.

"I don't blame you. I was the one that said there was no reason for him to know."

So, he understood. Good. I typed again and hit send. *"Right. So, I don't know what to do."*

"You made no promises and I never asked for anything. We should end things before it creates problems."

I frowned as I read the message again. That was it? I thought he'd be on the same page and want to keep our... whatever it was...going somehow. At least for a little while. Was I that disposable? Even if he was right, my ego took a hit. *"You want to walk away?"*

The response was quick. *"It seems like the obvious solution. You were already taking a risk. Why push it when you know what will happen if we're caught?"*

I tapped my fingers on my thigh. Was that a trick question? *"You seem to have it all figured out."*

"My brother's already suspicious. I don't think you'd be able to lie your way out of another incident."

Why was he being so rational? I typed faster. *"I'd planned on asking you to come back next weekend."*

"It's not a big deal. You don't have to explain anything to me."

The whole conversation was twisting my gut. Why wasn't he upset? I wasn't exactly happy. Couldn't he express some regret at least? I'd never come as hard in my life as I had with Rendon and I was pretty damn sure he'd had a good time too judging by the loads of come he'd streaked across my stomach. And it wasn't even all about sex. Okay, a lot was, but I was also intrigued by him. Yet, walking away from me didn't seem to faze him.

Another message followed, salt to my wound. *"So, this is for the best. But thanks for everything. I won't ever forget it."*

Neither would I and that, I decided, was a problem. It was like getting to taste your favorite candy then someone took it away and scolded you for liking it because it was bad for you. Or something like that. I was getting bent out of shape and he seemed calm and collected, like no big deal.

Though I knew what he was doing was selfless because he had nothing to lose, I was still frustrated as I replied. *"We should keep our distance on campus."*

"I agree."

My jaw clenched at the quick response and I fired back. *"Piece of cake."*

"Yup, no worries here."

No worries? I growled. *"Same. I have ZERO issues with it."*

"Bye, Nash."

"Later, Ren."

Setting my phone on the coffee table, I leaned back and rested my head against the back of the couch. What had I been thinking with the childish texts? I immediately regretted them and my mood sank further.

Everything would be fine. Everything was as it should be. Everything would be *fucking peachy.*

THREE

RENDON

CURRENT DAY/FRESHMAN MOVE-IN DAY

"ARE YOU ALL DONE?" My mom, wearing a yellow, flowy summer dress, stood in the doorway to my room with her arms crossed. Her long, blonde braid rested over one shoulder as she checked my room.

I glanced around, scanning for missed items and going over my mental checklist. Boxes were scattered in no particular order across the old wood floor, with tape struggling to keep them closed. And I'd already stuffed my hatchback full of bags containing my clothes. "Yeah, I think that's the last of it."

"And you have everything you need?" She was nervous. The way she rubbed her arms and worried her lip were her tells.

"If I don't, I can always pick up stuff from the store." Working so many hours since graduation, I had more than enough money to begin school comfortably. I'd even sprung for a used tablet and phone, both newer models that gave me a sense of pride when I had them in my hands.

Mom shifted from one foot to the other. "Honey, I feel like we should be the ones taking you on your first day."

"They are already on their way." They being my brother and Bishop, Shaw's boyfriend as of a few months ago.

And Nash

When my brother said Nash had volunteered to use his truck for the move, I'd been hesitant to agree. But I couldn't refuse or Shaw would be suspicious. So now I waited, knowing I'd be face to face with Nash after months of no contact. After he'd agreed we should keep our distance.

So why would he volunteer? I frowned.

I'd been okay going our separate ways, because I had prepared myself for the probability of it being a one-time invitation when I'd agreed to visit him. Shaw's warning about him had left its mark and I'd been cautious.

But ending things had been hard despite having steeled myself for it. Especially when he'd said he planned on asking me to come back the following weekend. Nash had been everything I'd hoped for and it sucked it'd been over so quickly. But it was the right thing to do. The only thing I'd had to risk was my brother's disapproval, and I could handle him. Nash had much more at stake. But his last few texts had irritated me beyond belief. Jerk.

Now, I wanted nothing to do with him.

Shaking off thoughts of Nash, I gave my mom a reassuring smile. "This is easier than renting a truck and less expensive."

She sighed and rubbed her arms. "It's just—"

"Mom, it'll be fine. I checked in online and already grabbed my key. Please stop worrying." I crossed the room and pulled her into a hug. I wasn't much taller than her, not like both my father's and brother's large builds, so when I pulled back, I held her nearly at eye level and poured as much security into that connection as possible. "You'll be visiting soon for Shaw's first game, and my schedule is nothing like his. I can come home a lot more often on the weekends and during breaks."

She sniffed and swallowed hard. "Okay, no, you're right. I'm just"—she shook her head—"worried."

"I'd expect nothing less." I attempted to lighten the mood as I took a step back.

She huffed just as the deep rumble of an engine sounded outside the house.

I walked over to the window and peeked between the blinds. "They're here."

She wiped her eyes. "Well, then let's get this show on the road."

"Ready to be rid of me so soon?" I teased.

"Stop making fun of me." She cracked a small grin before disappearing from the doorway.

I checked myself out in the mirror over my dresser. My green eyes shone bright despite the lack of sleep I'd had the night before, thanks to a small dose of anxiety about the move.

About Nash.

My hair was messier than usual from packing, so I finger combed it enough that it fell over my forehead instead of all over the place. I pushed my glasses up and smiled to check my teeth. Finally, I sprayed a small amount of cologne before tossing the bottle into one of the boxes.

Just because Nash and I were finished didn't mean I was okay looking like a mess in front of him.

"Knock. Knock." A rap on my doorframe along with my brother's voice drew my attention and I smiled.

"Hey, thanks for coming."

"No problem. You should thank Nash for letting us use

his truck," he said nonchalantly and grabbed a heavy box full of necessities and toiletries. He lifted and shifted its weight, gaze drifting over my boxed belongings. "Is this everything?"

"Yup."

Two more giant football players entered my small bedroom. Bishop glanced at me briefly and gave me a chin nod. "Hey, Rendon."

"Thanks for helping." Since Shaw and Bishop had come out as a couple shortly after I'd visited in June, he'd eased up and was a pretty laid-back guy. For the most part.

"No problem." Efficient as ever, Bishop grabbed a box and maneuvered around the other tall, imposing figure in my room on his way out.

Nash stood still inside the doorway, and I refused to meet his eyes. That didn't stop the stupid flutters in my stomach, and I realized I was holding my breath.

"Grab a box, Nash, and let's get moving," my brother said, breaking the tension in the room.

I said a silent thank you to him as the breath rushed from my lungs.

From the corner of my eye, I observed Nash as he bent and grabbed a box before retreating.

Shaw hung back. "Hey, everything okay?"

I waved him off. "Yeah, everything's fine. Why?"

He frowned and studied my face. "For a moment, it seemed like you were uncomfortable with Nash."

"Nope." I let the word pop off my lips and adopted what I hoped was a confused expression. "Why would I be?"

"You'd tell me if there was a reason, right?" He continued to scrutinize me.

Bishop entered the room again, saving me from lying to my brother. Well, more than I already had. And I wasn't *uncomfortable* with Nash being here, I was irritated. So much for keeping his distance. Despite my annoyance, my body apparently didn't get the memo that we were done with Nash. My heart raced just being in close proximity to the jerk, and the way his muscles flexed as he lifted the box hadn't gone unnoticed.

Bishop turned Shaw around by the shoulders and pointed him toward the door. "You plan on helping?"

"I figured you'd do the heavy lifting," Shaw teased over his shoulder.

Bishop's voice lowered. "Oh, I plan on—"

"Right!" My brother interrupted something I didn't want to hear, I was sure. "Grab another load."

Bishop's raspy chuckle followed him down the hall and soon another body returned to my room. My space.

Turning my back on him, I faced my dresser, which was a mistake because when I glanced up at the mirror, he stood across the room. His gaze raked over me from behind before meeting my eyes in the glass. Memories failed to do him justice and I couldn't look away.

"You plan on ignoring me all semester?" Nash asked, and I hated the rich smooth tone of his voice. Hated. It.

I cocked a brow. "I thought that was the plan. Yet, here you are."

"Harsh." He chuckled.

"Whatever." I shrugged.

His grin grew and he winked. "I like you all sassy."

"I like it when you hold up your end of the deal," I retorted and winked back. "This isn't exactly keeping your distance, is it?"

He opened his mouth to respond, but the other two

reentered and gathered boxes, saving me from whatever he'd plan to say next.

"Nash, grab that one." My brother pointed to a box large enough to appear heavy but was only full of white towels.

Nash glanced at me once more, his gaze full of wicked promise, like the first time we'd met, and my stomach flipped. What was his game and why was he here?

Without a word, Nash bent down and grabbed the box before carrying it out. My brother followed behind him.

There was one last box on the floor filled with my favorite books that I was sure to read between classes, studying and work. I'd submitted applications for a wide variety of on- and off-campus jobs and had finally landed an interview as a barista a short walk from my dorm. I had a few days to prepare for it and crossed my fingers, because jobs seemed hard to come by with so many students vying for the positions and I *needed* the job.

I hefted the box with both arms and my knees wobbled. It was much heavier than it looked. My arms trembled as I carried it down the hall and through the front door. The guys were moving boxes in the bed of the gunmetal-gray truck backed into the driveway.

"This is the last of it," I called out and almost dropped the box again. I should have let the guys with arms the size of my thighs come back for it. My face heated with embarrassment as my arms quaked harder.

Nash ran over and quickly took the box out of my arms and raised his brows. "Holy shit, Ren. This weighs a ton. What do you have in here?"

"Books." I shook my arms out, and then adjusted my glasses since they'd slipped low. "And don't call me *Ren*."

His lips twitched and I glared.

With a low chuckle, Nash turned and carried the box to the bed of the truck where he slid it in with the rest of my belongings. While he and Bishop secured everything with the cords they'd brought, my brother approached my side and crossed his arms as he stared at the guys finishing up. "Are you excited about the move?"

I wrinkled my nose and brushed the hair off my forehead that had grown damp from struggling with the box. "Yeah, I guess."

He frowned at me. "You guess? I thought you'd be happier, brainiac."

"I am." I glanced back at Nash. "I just have a lot on my mind."

Like how I was going to get through the semester with Nash breaking the rules and messing with my head. Surely he'd leave me alone once we arrived on campus like we'd agreed. He'd probably flirt with the whole school then. Not that I cared.

The clang of the tailgate shutting signaled it was time to leave.

"We'd better say bye to Mom and Dad." Shaw bumped my shoulder. "Get ready for the waterworks."

I snorted.

"I heard that." Mom ambled across the lawn to where we stood, smudge marks under her eyes. "You boys don't understand now, but maybe one day you will. When you two drive off today, I'll officially have an empty nest for the first time in over two decades. It's a big deal."

"I'll drive down and visit," I assured her again.

"And you know I do when I can." Shaw pulled her slim frame into a hug and squeezed her tight. "One more year and then I'll visit so often you'll beg me to go home."

She sniffed and her arms tightened around his waist. "Never."

Shaw laughed and released her.

Mom turned to me. "Give me a hug."

I wrapped my arms around her and squeezed. My mom's light floral perfume clung to her skin, a familiar scent I'd miss. When she stepped back and wiped away a stray tear, my chest tightened, and the reality that I was actually leaving home set in. You'd think packing my things would have been when it sunk in, but it was the goodbye that tugged at my heart.

Bishop stepped next to Shaw and nodded at my mom with a small smile. "Mrs. Wakefield."

She waved him off and smiled. "Stop with that Mrs. Wakefield stuff. One day I hope you'll call me Sarah."

"What am I missing out here?" My dad's gruff voice came from the doorway. His gray hair was brushed down, a change from the frizzy mess of strands he didn't usually bother with. His blue eyes scanned the lot of us. "Are you boys about ready to leave?"

I nodded. "We just loaded the last box."

He ventured further into the yard and placed a large hand on my shoulder. "Be careful out there and let your brother know if you need anything at all."

"I will, I promise." After a quick hug, I left them standing there and crossed the lawn to where my car was parked at the curb. With one last smile and wave, I hopped in. I looked out my window to where Shaw still stood with my parents. My mom hugged her arms around herself but beamed when my brother kissed her cheek.

As the guys piled into the truck, I slowly pulled away until they followed. Worried about my mom, I glanced in my rearview window. My dad slung an arm around her and led her inside. As ready as I was to leave, I'd miss them both.

Turning up the music, I set the AC on high as I drove away from the home I'd shared with my parents my entire life. I was ready for a new start, and as I took the on-ramp for the highway a small smile slipped across my face.

FOUR

NASH

SHAW AND BISHOP sat together in the backseat with their heads together, whispering and laughing as we followed behind Rendon's car on the way back to campus. Meanwhile, my thoughts were all over the place.

Lie.

They were on Rendon.

I should have expected it. Offering to help with the move had been a test of my willpower. How would I react with the youngest Wakefield right under my nose on campus? Well, I had my answer in seconds of being near him.

I'd thought about him enough over the last few months and my right hand had become my best friend. Why? Because I couldn't fuck anyone else. It wasn't because I was hung up on Rendon. I wasn't. But no one else was doing it for me. Opportunities presented themselves often, but they were all wrong.

Not short enough. Not blond. Didn't have green eyes bright as emeralds. And why didn't more guys wear glasses, specifically black wire ones? I shook my head as I drove.

Whatever, I didn't need anyone to help me get off. Why should I when I had enough material from that single night with Rendon to handle it myself? But my dick was sore, and if I didn't do something soon, I was going to develop carpal tunnel syndrome.

So yeah, I wanted to see him and prove to myself that my little obsession with his cute ass was something in the past and I'd built our chemistry up to be hotter than it actually was. Then things could go back to the way they were before.

But my plan backfired. That feisty mouth of his... Where had that come from? Where was the shy nerdy guy that had my blood running hot?

In his place was a smart-mouthed, sassy guy in Rendon's body. And my blood fucking boiled—scalding beneath my skin. And it should with the fire blazing in his narrowed gaze. When I thought he couldn't get any hotter, he had to go and mess things up further.

So much for willpower.

I would get him back in my life and my bed. It was only a matter of time.

The situation with Shaw was still an issue. He was protective of his younger brother, and I couldn't fault him for his hang-ups over my reputation. But Rendon was capable of making his own decisions.

I'd been called a playboy more times than I could count and maybe I deserved it in the past. But the only one I wanted to play with now was Rendon and to put that smart mouth to better use. Or better yet, I could put mine to use and listen to him moan. Sexiest sound ever. The memory was vivid as if it hadn't been months since he writhed in my lap. The thought made me groan under my breath.

"Everything all right?" Shaw asked from the back seat of my super cab.

"Yeah, had something in my throat," I lied.

Bishop and I traded glances for a moment in the rearview mirror. He'd cornered me a few days after I'd offered to use my truck for the move. The conversation had left me wondering afterward if I'd made a mistake by putting myself in the direct path of Rendon, and I couldn't help but recall the exchange.

"WHAT ARE you planning to do with Rendon?" Bishop had ambushed me in the locker room while I changed back into my t-shirt and shorts.

His tone was calm, but the stoic defensive player was eyeing me as if I'd kidnapped Rendon and had him handcuffed in my non-existent basement.

Glancing around for Shaw, I spotted him with Logan, waiting by the exit. I lowered my voice as I leaned toward Bishop. "What are you talking about?"

"Shaw is still on the fence over whether he believes you and Rendon had a thing going, but you and I know you did." Bishop's posture remained relaxed as if we were discussing the weather.

"If that were true and you could prove it—which you can't—I'm sure you'd have already told him."

"You're right I would have, but I'm not asking you to admit it. It's over and done, right?" When I didn't respond except to clench my jaw, he checked over his shoulder where Shaw still stood with our teammate before facing me again. "What I don't understand is why you volunteered to help."

"Can't I just be nice?" I shrugged and sat on the bench to put my shoes on.

"My opinion? No, you can't. Not with Rendon. And I think it's only a matter of time until you crack."

Having had enough, I glanced up at him. "Bishop, I hate to break it to you, but some things aren't your business."

He shook his head slowly. "Shaw is my business, therefore Rendon is too. I don't want you to hurt him. It would kill Shaw if he had to choose between his brother and the team. And we both know he'd choose Rendon. With Shaw planning on a career as a sports journalist he needs the connections he makes by being on the team. You know he does. Whatever you're planning to do"—he took a step back—"just don't fuck up."

As he turned around and walked away, I leaned forward, elbows on knees and rubbed my temples as a headache formed. It would be easier if I could forget Rendon and move on. But so far, I hadn't been able to. I needed to see him. I needed to prove to myself it was nothing more than a bruised ego that was making me obsess over him.

Standing, I slung my bag over my shoulder and walked out to my truck where I sat and wondered what the hell I was doing.

A HORN BLARED at the car in the next lane, jerking me back to the present. I ran a hand down my face in frustration. Rendon was an addiction. And that was the problem.

Several times in the weeks that followed his exit from my life, a selfish part of me wondered whether he still had his v-card. Would it change things? No. But the thought of him with someone else sparked a bit of jealousy that made me grip the wheel tighter. What was I doing being possessive when he wasn't even mine?

Campus came into view so I pushed those thoughts aside. One thing at a time.

I pulled my truck into the dorm parking lot, claiming the space next to Rendon's hatchback, and threw the gear shift into park. Rendon wasted no time jumping out of his car, and with arms loaded down with bags, he headed for the entrance.

I rolled down my window. "Hey, what room are we looking for?"

"Two twenty-three," Rendon called back and I nodded.

The three of us climbed out and circled around to the bed of the truck, where I lowered the tailgate.

Each holding an oversized box, we followed Rendon's path toward the entrance with me leading the group.

Behind me, Bishop lowered his voice to Shaw. "I love you even when you're being creepy and staring at me."

Both Shaw and I snorted.

"I love you back." The smile in Shaw's voice prompted me to pretend-gag over my shoulder.

Adjusting the box in my hands, I opened the door and kicked it wide for one of the guys to catch. "That shit is still weird."

"You're welcome to mind your own business," Bishop growled out, prompting me to roll my eyes.

We turned the corner and climbed the steps.

"He's just jealous," Shaw said.

"Nah." I shook my head. "You know me. That's not my thing. You two are just disgustingly happy."

"Fuck you." Shaw laughed.

"Nah, you're not my type." *But your brother is.* "And even if you were, Bishop's ass would kill me."

They were silent as we arrived at the second floor and made our way down the hallway, glancing at the room numbers, searching for Rendon's.

A few doors down, Rendon stepped into the hall and waved us in, pausing when he saw me first. He jerked his gaze away and stomped off, reentering his room. The space was big enough but depressingly bare. Two of each—twin beds, matching end tables, dressers and desks—all which were institutional gray and tan. Boring as shit and nothing like Ren.

The air was stale since the room had been shut up for a while, and Rendon must have thought so as well as he lifted a window the few inches it allowed to encourage fresh air to circulate.

"Where do you want me?" More than a hint of suggestion crept into my tone.

Rendon whipped around and his gaze snapped to mine so fast I worried he'd crack his damn neck. He glared as he pointed to the left side of the room. "The *boxes* can go on the floor over there."

Probably digging my own grave, I couldn't help but chuckle. He was fucking adorable when he was feisty. Rendon didn't seem to appreciate it as his spine went rigid.

I was only going to make things worse if I continued to rile him up, so I set the box by his desk and gave him some space.

Shaw spoke to his brother and then faced Bishop and me. "Let's go grab the rest, guys."

After a few more trips to the truck, Rendon's half of the room was buried in cardboard and plastic sacks. I stood aside and was shocked that after thanking his brother and

Bishop for their help, Rendon turned to face me. His smile was forced. "Thanks for offering to use your truck. It made things a lot easier."

I grinned. "No problem, Ren."

"My name is Ren*don*." He pursed his lips.

Just as I opened my mouth to say something that would ruffle his feathers further, Shaw interrupted. "All right. You two can fight about your name another time. Call if you need anything at all," he told Rendon. "Our house isn't far and I can be here in ten minutes flat."

Rendon blew his shaggy blond bangs up, only to send them fluttering right back down, brushing the top of his glasses. "I know. You've told me, like, a million times."

Shaw pulled out his phone and glanced down at the screen. "We gotta run if we want to make it to practice."

Shit, I hadn't checked the time. I pulled mine out as well to see that we only had a few minutes to get there. The team was meeting to study film of our upcoming opponent's strategies from last year. With our season-opening game only days away, there was barely time to breathe between the first day of class and the first game.

"Better you than me," Rendon muttered as he untied one of the bags and began unpacking his clothes.

"We have a championship to win this year!" I whooped, already looking forward to Saturday. "Gotta be ready."

His shoulders stiffened. "So you told me."

Fact. I had.

Everyone froze and a nervous chuckle escaped me. Well, if that wasn't an admission we'd talked, I didn't know what was. It would take Shaw approximately point-five seconds to come to the same conclusion. Yes, he'd called me out on it in the past, but there had never been a definitive confirmation on either my or Rendon's part. If Rendon had confirmed Shaw's suspicion, I had no doubt I'd have known about it. Real quick.

I slowly turned toward Shaw and neither of us looked away for a moment. His eyes narrowed and I didn't quite know how to handle it. Did I come out and say it, blow the whole thing wide open? Or did I play it off and tell him I'd said something at the party, which *was* exactly where that conversation took place. I had a decision to make.

Averting my eyes to the wall behind him, I muttered, "So, practice? Yep, we're going to be late. Better hurry."

When I cast Rendon one last glance, he refused to meet my eyes, so I slunk out of the room and back downstairs.

Once I'd climbed back into the cab of my truck and settled onto the black leather seat, I dropped my forehead down onto the steering wheel. I hadn't had enough time to prepare what to say to Shaw. Bishop was probably gloating and ready to say *I told you so*. Or he would be if that was his style.

My fist clenched and everything that had happened with Rendon raced through my mind. It was time to decide whether to spill my guts and make a move with a possible extremely negative outcome. Or to leave it alone once and for all.

After cranking the engine, I checked the time on the dash and nodded to myself. We were going to be late, because with Rendon right under my nose, without a doubt I was going to pursue him.

The rear doors opened and the truck shifted beneath the weight of the guys as they climbed in the back.

When the doors thumped shut, I sighed in resignation and, surprisingly, relief. "Right, so I might have withheld the truth before. But you should know, I didn't walk away." I paused. "He did."

Glancing at Shaw in the rearview mirror, I noted the shocked expression he aimed at Bishop. Only moments passed before he slowly turned his head and narrowed his eyes at me.

"It's not what you think." As soon as the words left my mouth, I reconsidered. "Well, okay, it kind of is."

"Please explain then," Shaw ground out. "Because right now I'm thinking you're a liar." He angled Bishop a sharp glance. "I told you."

"Shaw, let him talk," Bishop said evenly as he eyed me with curiosity. I think I'd surprised him by coming clean.

"Well, first yes, I lied. But we—Rendon and I—decided that together. Actually, he was the one to suggest we keep it from you." I twisted around in my seat to face Shaw. "And I agreed because it wasn't your business."

"Like hell it wasn't," he bit out.

"See? This is exactly why we decided to keep it from you." I gestured to his rigid posture and clenched fists. "But after your tantrum that day in the weight room when you called me out—"

"That was *not* a tantrum," Shaw argued.

I rolled my eyes. "After that *non*-tantrum you threw and called me out, I told Rendon and he decided *for us* to end things. But I expected him to at least try to…I don't know… suggest we keep going and leave you guessing. But nope, he says *later, Nash* like I was just some disposable di—" I smashed my lips together before I said 'dick' and ended up decked by my friend. I considered a better phrase. "Like I was replaceable."

I wasn't. And I was going to prove it.

Turning back around in my seat, I slouched and leaned my elbow on the console.

The silence that followed was uncomfortable and prolonged, but then Shaw laughed.

Startled, my gaze flew to his in the mirror. What the fuck?

"Nash, the player, got bested by my little brother?" He swatted Bishop's chest. "Hear that, babe?" Shaw grinned with pride at his boyfriend.

I scowled. "Fuck off, Shaw. It wasn't like that."

"What?" He shrugged. "Come on, I'm allowed to be a little proud."

The rare sound of Bishop's raspy chuckle grated on my ears.

Spinning around in my seat, I pointed at him. "You too, you moody bastard."

Shaw barked another laugh and his shoulders shook as he leaned against his boyfriend.

"You guys are assholes." I popped open my center console and retrieved a cherry sucker. Wasn't he supposed to be pissed or something? Instead the situation was a joke and I was the punchline. My mood shifted from slightly nervous to determined. "I'm going after him. Just telling ya now."

Shaw grinned. "I wouldn't expect anything less from you."

"Good."

He scoffed. "More like *good luck*. I don't know what else you did to piss him off, but did you see the way he was looking at you?"

I growled, which Shaw apparently thought was hilarious. Yes, Rendon appeared irritated, but that was fixable now that Shaw knew about us. It had to be.

Shaw wiped beneath his eyes. Tears. Was it that funny?

No, it wasn't. I stuffed the sucker in my mouth and frowned.

He seemed to gain some self-control. "Seriously, how do you think Rendon feels?"

"Based on the daggers he was shooting at me with his eyes, I'd say he's open to the idea," I deadpanned. I'd have my work cut out for me for sure.

Shaw grinned. "You know, I thought if I ever found out without a doubt you'd hooked up with Rendon, I'd lose my shit. But I realize now you were helpless. He does come from good stock." He puffed out his chest before smirking. "This might be downright entertaining."

I frowned because fuck them. "We're late to practice."

"Then get driving, Casanova." Shaw winked.

For all I'd convinced myself that I'd worm my way back into Rendon's life and get him in my bed, hearing myself say it out loud, I had to admit, Rendon had me tied in knots. And I didn't have a single clue what I was doing.

FIVE
RENDON

SHAW HAD JUST LEFT when the door creaked open and a guy with pale skin and black hair, long enough to brush against his chin on one side and buzzed short on the other, bounded into the room. Shorter than me and slim, Tristan had a sharp jaw, small nose and high cheekbones. Black eyeliner surrounded his bright blue eyes and the skin at the corners crinkled when he grinned.

Tristan and I had emailed each other after receiving our roommate assignments and then exchanged numbers. When he was lazy, he opted to video call so I knew his face well.

He dumped two overstuffed duffle bags onto the ground. "Holy shit, those were heavy." He winced as he rolled his shoulders back and then crossed the room, holding out his hand for a fist bump. "Hey, Ren. It's nice to meet you in person."

"Yeah, you too." I awkwardly reciprocated the gesture, tapping my fist against his lightly. He smirked and a slight trace of cinnamon lingered in the air as he stepped away. "Do you need any help?"

"We're good. Thanks, man." He scanned the room and sat on the mattress closest to the door with a bounce. "This my side?"

My things were stacked next to the desk on the opposite side of the room. "It doesn't matter to me, but I'll take this side if it's okay. If not, I can move my stuff."

"Oh, no you don't. Please tell me you're not a people pleaser." He put his hands together as if in prayer and closed his eyes. They popped back open. "You're not going to move your stuff, Ren."

"I'm not a people pleaser." I leaned against my desk. "I'm just not picky."

"Neither am I." He grinned again as a woman and man, who appeared to be in their early to mid-forties, stepped into the room. They set down more bags and the man placed a box with a picture of a mini fridge on Tristan's desk.

Tristan snapped his fingers. "Did you bring towels?"

"Yep, they are in one of these boxes." I waved my hand toward them, my contribution to the roommate deal we'd made when discussing who'd pitch in with what.

"Awesome, we can run to the store and get everything else later." He reminded me of our plan as he dragged some of the bags out of the way. "Oh, Mom and Dad, this is Rendon, my new roomie."

"Nice to meet you." His mom smiled politely and his dad held out a hand.

I shook it. "Nice to meet you too."

They made several trips to their car to bring up the rest of Tristan's things while I continued to unpack my clothes. Then I made up my bed with the light blue sheets, matching pillows and royal blue comforter I'd brought from home, all the while listening to the commotion out in the hallway. Music of every genre played, excited students chattered as they met their new neighbors and frazzled parents' voices were caught in the middle of the chaos.

Once they'd finished, Tristan's dad had the mini fridge unpacked and plugged in next to his desk in minutes.

I busied myself unpacking while his mom fussed over him and his dad lectured him on safety and responsibility. I smiled to myself when Tristan groaned. "I know, Dad."

"Well, we worry..." His dad bit back his obvious concern.

Tristan sighed. "Ren already knows I'm gay."

There was an audible rush of air as if a massive load had been lifted from his dad's shoulders.

"All right," his mom cut in. "Let the boys have their space." She hugged Tristan. "You two have fun, but not too much. School first."

"Yes, ma'am," I replied at the same time Tristan sighed. "Of course, Mom."

Once they were gone, he turned to me. "Who was that leaving our room when I got here?"

"Depends on who you passed. My brother was the one walking out and his boyfriend Bishop—huge, dark hair and eyes, and looks like he's in a bad mood—left just before him."

"Oh, yeah. I saw him too." He waggled his brows.

"Stop. That's just weird." I paused. "And...Nash left first."

I bent down and opened the box filled with my books and started to stuff them onto the bookshelf. As I examined the shelf space, I frowned. There was no way they'd all fit.

"Let me guess, the one with crazy ass eyes and hot as fuck." Tristan pretended to swoon.

His comment gave me pause and I glanced up with a nod. "One of my brother's friends."

"I passed him on my way in." Tristan cocked a brow. "They all look like big jocks."

Shifting the box to the side, I sat cross-legged on the floor to work on the bottom shelf. "Yep. Saints football royalty."

"Sounds about right." He tilted his head. "So, you're into this Nash guy, huh?"

I dropped the book I was holding. "What? Why would you think that?"

"Your tone changed and you got this weird look on your face. Anyway, only a guess at first, but now I'm sure of it." He winked. "I don't normally like the athletic type but all three of them…" He hummed and unzipped a bag, pulling out his own bedding which was, unsurprisingly, black.

"Gross. One was my brother." I cringed.

He shrugged. "Well, he's not *my* brother. Did your parents come too?"

"No, they wanted to, but it was easier to let my brother and the guys help move me," I explained. "But my parents will be around sometimes. They come to the games and stuff."

"I don't have any siblings or I might have done that myself." He spread his comforter out on the bed.

"So, your dad was worried about what your roommate would think of you being gay?"

He snorted. "You have no idea. He tried to get the school to make an exception so I could live off campus for my freshman year but they denied him."

I frowned. "Why didn't you tell him about me? I'm out."

"Not my news to share and I didn't know you were like *out* out." He pulled the rubber band off a rolled-up poster.

"Speaking of sharing, what's the deal with you and that Nash guy? Unrequited crush thing?"

"Not exactly." Different entirely.

"Ah," he said as if he had figured it all out. The springs in his mattress squeaked when he hopped on his bed to tack up the large poster of a band I'd never heard of. They were all wearing black and were covered in tattoos and piercings.

"What do you mean *ah*?" I asked and shoved another book onto the shelf.

"I'm not sure what I meant." His expression twisted in amusement as he jumped down to the floor. "Well, I should mention that I'm not on the market then, so don't get any ideas. Bachelor life for the win."

"You didn't tell me you have an ego the size of Texas." I groaned.

"I'm sort of a catch. I mean look at me." His effort to not laugh failed with a weird snort. "Not afraid you'll develop a massive crush?"

"That's a no." I shook my head.

He chuckled. "Oh, right! You like them tall, dark and super strong. Big enough to hold you against the wall and—"

"Tristan!" The pillow I threw hit him in the side. "And here I was thinking I'd lucked out with my roommate."

"I'm messing with ya. And I do think we lucked out." He grinned. "It's going to be a good year. You and me, we got this."

"Now, I'm afraid *you'll* develop a massive crush on me." I shot him an amused grin.

He tilted his head and his gaze swept over me as I crouched in front of the bookshelf. "I don't know. Maybe. You're pretty hot."

I rolled my eyes. "Shut up."

"I think we are going to get along just fine." He laughed

and picked up the pillow I'd thrown, only to hurl it back at me.

We were almost finished unpacking the bulk of our belongings when I glanced up as he tapped the bottom drawer of his nightstand. "This drawer is off-limits."

"I would never." I adopted a serious tone and crossed my heart while suppressing another eye roll.

He winked. "Finish up so we can go meet everyone at the barbeque."

"Do we have to go? Maybe they won't miss us." I glanced from the box to the shelf and gave up trying to make them all fit. I'd find a place to put the rest later.

"Hell, yeah, we have to go. No way am I going to let you hang out in here with your books, even if it wasn't mandatory." He straightened up with both hands on his hips. "Besides, it will be good for us to meet people. How else will I know where the parties will be?"

"Okay, okay! I'm trying," I groused. "You keep distracting me."

Tristan shook his head. "I knew you'd develop a crush. We're doomed."

SIX
NASH

THE NEXT DAY WAS BRUTAL. Not only was I thinking of Rendon, but we were also preparing for our first game of the season on Saturday. I'd gone into the day with a plan. When practice wrapped up, I'd message him and try to get him to hear me out. Until then, my mind had to stay on football.

Easier said than done.

After watching film with the team, we'd taped up before gathering on the indoor field located in the giant Saints practice facility. Defense was sent to one side of the field while I followed the offense to the other, where the receivers were made to stand in a line to run fade route drills to improve our passing game.

Second in line, I stood behind Shaw who positioned himself next to Memphis, our starting quarterback and a friend of mine. Memphis was only a sophomore, but the guy had an arm like a cannon. He'd been a walk-on during spring camp and Coach had practically jizzed in his pants when he saw the guy's skill set.

Memphis grunted and the center hiked the ball.

Shaw burst into motion, his speed increasing as he followed the fade route to the sideline. Memphis floated a perfect throw and Shaw glanced back as the beautiful spiral drilled into his hands with seamless timing.

Stepping up to claim Shaw's vacated spot, I snapped my chin strap in place and shook out my hands at my sides, opening and closing them in my tight gloves as I readied to run.

Shaw trotted back with the ball and passed it to one of the staff members on his way to the end of the line.

"Ready! Set." Memphis grunted and I took off, stepping it into high gear half way down the field as the drill called for.

Another throw, flawlessly executed, hit me right in the breadbasket and I hung on tight. I gave Memphis a half-salute and he shook his head as he was tossed another ball.

Following in Shaw's footsteps, I carried the ball back and lined up behind Shaw. All of the receivers did this, rotation after rotation.

As time ticked down to the season opener in a few short days, adrenaline was running high and the whole team buzzed with the need for a win. So, we sweated our asses off, dug our cleats into the green turf and gave it everything we had.

Coach, who had been watching from the sideline, walked out to midfield and called us over to huddle around him. "Good job. Tomorrow we'll take practice outside. We start early so be ready and get plenty of sleep. It's going to be rough to get acclimated to classes on top of your athletic schedule. Anyone in need of organizational help, please meet me after warm-ups tomorrow so we can go over the programs we offer to help you stay on top of things." He eyed the younger guys. "True freshmen and redshirt freshmen, this is mandatory." Then he clapped once, a solid crack and addressed the whole team. "Get cleaned up and get out of here."

After putting my gear away, I stripped off the tape and showered the sticky residue and sweat from my skin. Ignoring the guys around me, I dressed in black mesh shorts and a Saints t-shirt and hurried out to the parking lot. Once settled in the cab of my truck, I grabbed my phone to text Rendon and let him know I was coming over to talk. With my fingers hovering over the screen, I changed my mind, cranked the engine and drove toward his dorm building.

There was a good chance he wouldn't be in his room and a greater chance that, if he was, he'd tell me to get lost. As far as he was concerned, I wasn't holding up my side of the deal to keep my distance, and his irritation was clear. But the game had changed with me telling Shaw about us.

I found a spot to park, hopped out and wove between the other cars to the door. When I entered the building, I took the stairs two at a time. The halls were mostly empty other than a few students milling around talking animatedly, enjoying their time before they'd be buried in studying and trying to cram in a social life between their class schedules and work.

Hearing the sound of music and a couple of guys talking on the other side of Rendon's door, I knocked. The voices quieted and footsteps shuffled toward the door.

I rubbed my hands together. *Here goes.*

The door swung open and a guy shorter than Rendon, also slim and giving off a hard emo vibe, smiled. But half a second later, his smile dropped.

"Uh, Ren." The guy stepped back and revealed Rendon lying on his bed holding his phone. "Nash is here."

My brows rose. How did he know who I was?

Rendon pressed a button on his phone and the music died. He swung his pajama-clad legs over the side of the bed and sat upright. "What are you doing here?"

"I was hoping we could talk." My gaze cut to who I assumed was his roommate but maybe Rendon had already taken an interest in someone. My stomach clenched. "I hope I'm not interrupting."

"You're not." The guy leaned against the doorframe. "I'm Tristan, the roommate."

"Hey, I'm Nash—which I guess you already know."

"Yup." He winked and I didn't know how to respond, so I glanced back at Rendon.

Rendon glared at Tristan and I hid a grin under the guise of scratching my nose.

I cleared my throat and Rendon's narrowed gaze swung to me. "Do you maybe want to go somewhere?"

"Oh"—Tristan bounced on the balls of his feet—"actually, I was about to go grab us some burgers, so the place is yours." He ran over to his desk and stuffed a wallet in the snug pocket of his black skinny jeans. "Just, you know, hang a sock or something if things get weird."

"Tristan," Rendon hissed and his roommate chuckled as I coughed out a laugh.

I was officially a Tristan fan, even if he seemed a bit eccentric.

As he moved passed me, Tristan patted my arm and whispered, "Good luck." Why did everyone keep telling me 'good luck'?

Rendon crossed his arms. "Well, are you going to come in?"

My lips twitched as I suppressed a grin and stepped farther into the room, pulling the door closed behind me. The room had lost the stale scent and now held an odd mix of fresh linen and...cinnamon? The combination of two polar opposites living in one space I guessed.

We both stared at each other.

"Are you going to stand there and gawk at me or did you want to talk?" He adjusted his glasses before re-crossing his arms.

Pulling out his desk chair, I took a seat. "You look good."

"You came to tell me I look good?" His tone still held a note of annoyance though he cocked his head and appeared curious.

Leaning back in the chair, I studied him. "Actually, I have a question."

"So, ask it."

"When you broke things off, I was frustrated with Shaw. But you seemed to not care at all. Seemed one-sided." I paused. "Was it?"

His brow furrowed and he nibbled on his lip. "It wasn't that I didn't care, but I'd gone into it knowing what I was signing up for."

Confused, I cocked my head. "And what was that?"

"I mean I was warned what you were like, so I don't know...a hookup." His voice squeaked the last two words. "I wasn't sure what to expect."

"Wait." I sat up straight and held my hand up as I struggled to understand. "You were warned?"

"Well, yeah. Shaw told me about your reputation." He squirmed uncomfortably.

"What exactly did he say?" My jaw ticced. Shaw was quickly landing on my shit list.

His cheeks flushed and swallowed audibly. "He...he said you only hook up once then that's it. Said you were notorious for it, I believe. Guys and girls, if I remember correctly."

My teeth ground together. I understood Shaw's position. I did. But I also had the urge to deck him.

Rendon cleared his throat and squared his shoulders. "Well, it's true, right?"

I sealed my lips and breathed through my nose, my nostrils flaring. Yes, it was the truth, but for the first time it bothered me because I didn't want Rendon to see me that way.

When I gathered a sense of calm, I relaxed back in the chair and answered his question with a question of my own. "Do the girls bother you?"

He scowled. "Girls may not be my thing, but it doesn't bother me. Who you hook up with is your own business. The *point* he was making was that you are a one-night kind of guy."

Based on Rendon's disapproving frown, Shaw had made his point loud and clear. "When did he tell you that?"

"At the draft party after you went inside. Why?"

Nodding, I fixed Rendon with a pointed look. "And still you came to my house when I invited you."

His flush spread down his neck and up to his ears, but he stayed mute.

I felt used and it sucked. In response, I could only repeat his words as they truly sank in. "You just came to hook up."

Confusion twisted his features. "Isn't that what you wanted?"

"Well, yeah. But..." I tugged at my bottom lip as I considered my answer. Of course I'd wanted that. But I also liked Rendon. He was different than the rest of my hookups. I hadn't realized that one night was all that was on the table.

"Then why do you look mad?" He chewed on his lip.

Why was I mad? Because he had flipped the roles. "I tell people what I want up front. You didn't say that," I accused.

"Neither did you." His set his lips in a firm line.

I leaned forward in the chair. "*Maybe* because that's not what I wanted."

"And *maybe* I'd have been okay with more. We'll never know because it's over." Rendon shook his head as if he didn't believe me and let loose a long breath. "Why are you here, Nash? We agreed it was best to keep our distance."

When I told Shaw I was pursuing Rendon, I only knew I wanted him in my life and my bed. But I was quickly realizing I hadn't given it enough thought. With zero experience in the relationship department, I was so far out of my depth and had no idea what I was doing. And why was I thinking the word relationship?

With a groan, I ran a hand over my face and muttered, "Things didn't go back to normal after you left."

"What?" He scrunched his nose.

Slowly I rose to my feet, stepped close and hovered over him. He tilted his head back, and I peered deep into those big bright green eyes and lowered my voice. "I'm rethinking the distance thing. Where we don't keep it. At all."

"That's not a good idea and you know it," he mumbled.

I shrugged. "I still want it."

Rendon sighed and rubbed his temples. "Spell it out for me. What is it you're really after?"

"To pick up where we left off." I bit my lip as I raked his body with my gaze. His little nipples poked through his shirt. With memories of what lay beneath the flimsy fabric rising to the surface, I held back a groan.

Rendon stared at me with wide eyes. "Like you want to

start hooking up again?" He shook his head. "I can't do that."

"Why? You said that's what you wanted from me," I said, though the words tasted sour in my mouth. I sat on his bed next to him, waiting for him to push me away. He didn't.

"Well, I don't anymore." His tone was firm, but his body leaned in toward mine.

We were hot together. Explosive. Even sitting beside him, I couldn't help but notice how sexy he looked, despite the tension or maybe heightened because of the tension. How could he not feel it? Unless... "Are you with someone else?"

His eyes widened and he jerked back. "What? No. Jeez, Nash. Even if I was, it wouldn't be your business."

"Then why?" I asked again. "You're not going to find someone who can make you feel the way I can. You won't find someone who can get you off as hard, willing to do anything and everything to your body. Everything you've ever fantasized about." Rendon shivered and I pounced. "See? No one else is going to set you off like I do."

Rendon's spine straightened and he glowered at me. "You are so arrogant, you know that?"

I did. But if I admitted it or pointed out he was now sporting a solid bulge, it wouldn't help my case. "What's wrong with being sure I can make you see stars?"

"You are so full of yourself. This"—he pointed at me and then himself—"is not happening."

"What did I do now?" I groaned. This was excruciating. No wonder I'd never wanted more than one night with anyone. But with Rendon, I couldn't seem to give up.

"Just...stop. Even if I could overlook your stupid cocksure attitude, I still wouldn't do it." He stood and paced the floor.

"Because?" I asked as he walked back and forth, wearing a path on the old worn carpet.

Rendon sighed with exasperation and rubbed his face and arms, fidgeting like hell. "One, because you are a jerk and said staying away from me was a *piece of cake* and you had *zero* issues with it."

"I lied," I admitted. "Though I wanted it to be easy."

"You seem to do that a lot." His stopped pacing and his eyes narrowed to slits.

"Believe it or not, I actually don't," I defended myself. "But things have been difficult with us. You know my reasoning. And it was your idea to keep it from Shaw."

"Whatever." He waved away my explanation. "But that brings up the other issue. You know, problems between you and Shaw...the team...your season. Ring any bells?"

"Well, that's part of what I wanted to—" My words were cut short when the door creaked open.

"There's no sock on the door so I guess..." Tristan glanced between the two of us and took a step back into the hall. "Oh, hey. I can come back later."

I shook my head and stood. "Nah, I'm not going to keep you out of your own room." As I neared the door, I paused and glanced back at Rendon. "What I wanted to tell you was I told Shaw everything yesterday." When Rendon's eyes widened, I bit my lip and ran my gaze down his body. "And I haven't been with anyone else since I met you."

Rendon's jaw dropped.

"And I'm not done with you," I added. "*We* aren't done."

Before he could reply, I walked through the door and

passed Tristan, who was carrying a couple of greasy bags and two drinks.

But Rendon's words drifted into the hall. "You don't get to decide that! Can you believe him?"

"Tell me everything," Tristan said with an excited tone and shut the door.

My feet pounded down the stairs. *Cocky. Arrogant. Full of myself.* So what? I wasn't allowed to be confident I'd rock his damn world? Because I would.

I waved at a few people I recognized on my way out, but I was thinking of Rendon. I hadn't lied. I wouldn't give up, because his body language didn't match his words. He was affected by me, and I wanted to give him time to think about what I'd said.

I'd come clean about us to my friend, teammate and his brother while knowing the risks. For him. That had to count for something, right?

Once I was in my truck, I sat behind the steering wheel for a few minutes, stewing. That had gone better than I expected but not as well as I'd hoped. He hadn't kicked me out so that was a win.

I pulled a sucker from my stash in the console and shoved it in my mouth. At least I could feed one addiction.

As I drove home, I contemplated my next course of action. With no clear answer when I pulled into my driveway, I decided I'd have to sleep on it. My headlights illuminated the front porch and I found Jesse sitting on his top step, holding a soda bottle and smoking a cigarette. He lounged against the rail in a pair of loose jeans and white t-shirt, eyeing me as I killed the engine and stepped out of my truck.

"Hey, man." I gave him a quick wave as I ascended the steps.

The wood boards creaked when Jesse stood. "What are you up to tonight?"

"Not a damn thing except face planting in bed." I slid my key into the lock and glanced back at him. His forehead wrinkled and he twisted his lips. "Everything all right?"

Finally he settled on giving me a tight smile. "Let me know if you want to hang out sometime."

"Sure, man." I tipped my chin and let myself inside.

After tossing my keys on the kitchen counter I headed for my room, set my alarm for the ass crack of dawn and crawled between my cold sheets.

SEVEN
RENDON

TRISTAN SAT on his bed eating a burger while I sat across from him on mine and dug into the paper sack, fishing out some fries.

"So, are you going to leave me on pin and needles here?" Tristan sucked down some of his soda.

"Nash..." I set the bag in my lap and lost interest in the fries, tossing them back in. "We have history."

Tristan cocked a brow. "Huh, so not just a crush. What happened?"

Where did I start? I sighed. "We met at a party in April and exchanged numbers, but he didn't call or text for weeks. I didn't either. Then one day out of the blue, he did and invited me over. I agreed and things...happened."

"You had sex with him?"

"No, but other things." I squirmed. Sharing the details was uncomfortable and personal.

"Oh, tell me more," Tristan said, his eyes big while he continued eating.

It was odd to tell someone about Nash. There had never

been anyone I could talk to about this kind of stuff before. As I explained what had happened, I found comfort in being able to confide in Tristan.

"After that, he said we should avoid each other on campus and when I agreed, he was like *piece of cake.*" I scowled as I made air quotation marks with my fingers. "And said other things that made it clear I didn't matter."

Tristan tilted his head. "What if he was just mad?"

"It was still a crap thing to say," I muttered. "But I agreed and said stuff I didn't mean because it struck a nerve. I hadn't seen him or talked to him until he showed up to help me move." I let out a long exhale. "There's nothing more to the story."

"Yeah, that's a douche thing to say. Why's he all over you now?" Tristan stuffed a giant bite of his hamburger in his mouth.

"You're going to choke. You know that, right?" I eyed him with disgust and he grinned, cheeks full as he chomped away.

"Nah, I have lots of practice." He winked and I groaned at the mental image I definitely didn't want.

"Anyway, when he was helping me move, he made some flirty comments which not only irritated me, but confused me. He's the most infuriating guy I've ever met." I crinkled the bag with my fists. "And then he shows up here and says he's rethinking the distance thing. Like I should just jump when he says how high."

Tristan paused with a fry halfway to his mouth. "What do you mean rethinking the distance thing?"

"You know..." My gaze darted to the dingy carpet before glancing back at him. "He wants to hook up or whatever."

Tristan's eyes widened as he wiped a napkin across his

mouth. "He came over to talk to you to see if you wanted to hook up?"

I nodded. "That's weird, right?"

He nodded in agreement. "Unless you made a lasting impression." He waggled his brows.

"Shut up." I opened the sack and threw a fry at him.

He swatted it away before it hit him. "What? That's the only thing that makes sense. And he wants seconds. Maybe thirds."

I groaned. "I don't know about thirds but he definitely thinks he can just waltz in and ask for seconds. My brother told me Nash is a one-time wham bam, see you later. Maybe he just wants to finish what he started and then after..." It made sense and he had said he wanted to pick up where we left off.

"You said no?"

"Of course I did," I snapped. "Because he's the most arrogant person I've ever met. He thought he'd just show up, turn on the charm and get me in bed. Most of the time when I think of him, I don't know what I was thinking in the first place."

"Oh, I know the answer to that one." He raised his hand. "Because he's smoking hot. There's nothing wrong with being attracted to guys like that. It's not like he asked you to marry him and it's not like you're in love with him. Hate sex is also superhot."

I scrunched my nose. I hadn't told Tristan I was a virgin and while hooking up wasn't something I'd done, I wasn't against it. This was college and I wanted to try things I hadn't had the opportunities to before. "I don't hate him, but it's still not happening."

He hummed. "Well, then he's going to be disappointed.

He wanted it bad enough to tell your brother. I wonder why he'd do that."

Trying to figure out Nash was impossible and giving me a headache. "I'll tell you if I ever find out. Probably so he can bug me without worrying if Shaw will find out. Well, whatever, it's a no and that's final. I'm sure he can find someone besides me to help him out in that area."

"I get it." He tilted his head and paused. "But...he said he hasn't been with anyone else."

Yeah, I'd definitely caught that and it had thrown me for a loop. But it wouldn't be the first lie he'd told.

"So?" I asked defensively. I didn't need Tristan messing with my head too. "You sound like you're on his side."

"No way." He shook his head vehemently. "I was just going to say he sounded sincere."

"You don't know him."

"You're right," he agreed. "And you are probably doing the right thing."

Probably. I huffed. "What sucks the most is I had looked forward to college because there weren't really options to meet interested guys where I lived. And then Nash came into the picture and I was flattered because he *was* interested. Of course he turned out to be a self-centered jerk. That's my luck for you."

Tristan held up a finger as he finished chewing. "Okay, so tell me if I'm hearing this right. You were hoping someone on campus would jump your bones. You're not interested in Nash anymore, so you're back on the hunt? Because if so, you're totally speaking my language." He balled up his wrapper, rose from the bed to shoot it into the trashcan and held up his arms when he *scored*.

Just because I was attracted to Nash didn't mean I was

interested. I wasn't. So I perked up at Tristan's words. "I'm all ears. Show me your ways, wise one."

"Well I can't just walk up to guys and ask if they want in my pants, obviously. I'm not trying to get my cute ass kicked. It's my best feature." He cocked a brow, apparently waiting for me to agree. I didn't and he frowned. "Anyway, I use an app. It's super easy. You set up a profile, say what you are looking for. Like if you just want to get off or actually date"— he rolled his eyes at *date*—"then you just say so."

We hadn't discussed Tristan's history with guys but it didn't appear he was in any rush to find a special someone. He seemed to find playing the field with whoever and whenever he wanted to his liking.

I scoffed. "I'm not that far behind on things. I know how the apps work, I just haven't used them."

"So, you just found guys randomly before?"

Pausing, I debated over admitting how inexperienced I was. "Ah, no, not exactly."

He crashed down on his mattress and lay on his side with his hand propping up his head. "Ren, I'm just going to spit this out. Are you a virgin?"

The fact that there didn't seem to be any judgement in his tone helped my words flow freely. "Yes. But I don't want to die a virgin and it's not like I wanted to wait. But...ya know. Lack of options. I'm not exactly a wet dream."

He snorted. "I can tell you at least one guy thinks you are and he happens to be walking sex appeal."

I groaned. "Stop."

"Fine." He sat upright and dug around for his phone that was twisted in his blanket somewhere. "Found it." He held it up proudly before tapping on the screen. "Here."

He climbed out of bed and joined me on mine, sitting cross-legged next to me.

"What's this?"

"The app I was telling you about."

"Oh." I leaned over to check it out. He showed me how to scroll through prospective fuck buddies. His words. And then showed me how to message someone and showed me some graphic examples of his conversations. Some things I did not need to know but he just shrugged. "Don't judge."

"I'm not. But there's something called privacy."

He looked at me like I had a third eye. "Anyway, so we should totally set you up a profile."

I chewed on my lip as I considered it.

"No pressure." He put his phone down.

"No. I think maybe I should." I nodded with conviction.

His brows rose in surprise. "Huh, I thought you'd shoot the idea down."

"Why would I?" I frowned.

"I don't know. Maybe..." He shook his head. "At least you'll know your options."

"Exactly," I agreed. "Now what do I do?"

His grin was full of mischief. "Grab your phone."

"Come on, Rendon. I seriously thought you were going to be rushing me to get ready. Not the other way around. I have a reputation to uphold." Tristan yelled through the door while I brushed my teeth. "I want to make sure we get good seats and aren't forced to sit on the front row. Ugh, can you imagine how bad that would suck?"

My first class was History. A mix of excitement and nerves made me jittery as I hurried through my morning routine. It was a nice distraction from thoughts of Nash. I hadn't been able to get the fact that he'd told my brother out of my head, and falling asleep the night before had been difficult. Why would he do that? He could have easily let the careless comment I'd made in front of Shaw go. I couldn't wrap my head around it.

I couldn't lie and say I wasn't tempted to accept his proposal. I knew it'd be good. Had solid proof from our first time. Frustrated with myself for considering it, I mulled over my conversation with Tristan and the app I'd downloaded. He'd helped me input my information, told me to upload a picture and that was that. I had a dating profile—if dating was the word that could be used. I wasn't looking for a relationship, not while I had Nash on my mind, but I wouldn't stay a monk forever.

I jammed my toothbrush back in the holder and then brushed my hair, blowing up my bangs when they continued to fall in my eyes. I needed a haircut.

When I came out of the bathroom, Tristan stood ready to go with his hands on his hips. I quickly pulled on a new pair of jeans and a heather-purple button up before sliding my feet into my white tennis shoes. I glanced at myself in the mirror mounted on the closet door to make sure my outfit was decent enough to attend the coffee house interview after my second class of the day. Smoothing my hand over my shirt, I decided it was as good as it was going to get.

"Oh! Almost forgot..." Tristan ran to the bathroom and came back out with a sleek layer of black eyeliner. "I can't believe you almost let me leave looking like that."

"And I'm the one slowing us down?" I arched a brow. "Are we ready?"

"I've been ready," he insisted as we grabbed our backpacks.

We ventured downstairs, grabbed a few muffins at the breakfast bar and ate as we powerwalked across campus to the History building.

The campus grounds had come alive with an eclectic mix of students, teachers, and staff in a hurry to get where they were going. The difference between college and high school, where everyone was trying to fit in, was shocking. Every type of clothing, shoes, makeup and hair—nothing seemed off-limits. I had never fit in anywhere and a calmness settled over me. Things would be different here.

The hike to class in the early morning humidity was nothing compared to what noon would feel like when the hot midday sun blazed through the sticky air. But I was still relieved when Tristan yanked open the door and a burst of cool air flowed over my skin.

"I don't know if I'm ever going to get used to the heat here and I've lived in Texas my whole life," Tristan mumbled as we followed the hall and then entered the large stadium style lecture room.

My gaze swung around the massive space. A huge screen hung from the ceiling at the front of the room where the professor—a short, balding man—was already arranging his materials on top of a lectern. The class was filling fast so we quickly snagged a couple of seats in one of the middle rows.

The instructor looked up briefly and nodded in approval to those of us who had made it in early. Other students continued to file in slowly and then in a rush as the clock struck the hour.

As copies of the syllabus were passed around, the professor spoke with a practiced voice. "Good morning, students. The books and materials you need for this semester are listed on the papers in front of you. Hopefully, you will enjoy History, but at the very least I expect your attention and civility."

Excitement filled my veins. This was what I'd worked so hard for.

"Stop smiling like a drunk chimpanzee." Tristan laughed.

EIGHT
NASH

THE FIRST TWO days after classes started were rough. I was getting back into the swing of things, balancing classes and football, but I had to admit the exhaustion was taking its toll. Our opening game was in less than twenty-four hours and we had to board a charter bus first thing in the morning.

The anticipation was the only thing that would get me through evening practice. Thankfully, it would be short as they always were the day before a big game, and this one was important. It would set the tone for the season and playing on the road was always more difficult.

The minute my second class of the day of was over, I packed away my laptop and sent the same message to Shaw, Bishop and Memphis. *"Lunch?"*

My stomach growled. The protein bars I'd put away after the morning's workout had worn off hours ago and I was craving a sub with all the fixings.

They agreed and planned to meet up at the sandwich shop across the street. When I opened the door of the small restaurant, the smell of baking bread and a variety of entrées made my mouth water. A head taller than most of the other diners, the guys weren't hard to spot. But as I approach the table, my gaze zeroed in on the shorter blond sitting next to Shaw.

The last to arrive, I slid onto the only open seat, beside Rendon. "Hey, guys."

He studied his menu, but muttered quietly to Shaw, "I thought it was just going to be us."

Shaw shot me a triumphant smile. He still thought I stood no chance with Rendon. We'd see about that.

"We were all hungry and Nash invited us," Shaw told Rendon and gave his hair a solid ruffle. "I thought you might want to join us since we haven't had time to catch up."

"Stop doing that," Rendon growled like a baby tiger and did his best to fix the mess of strands. He closed his menu and tapped his fingers on the table.

The waitress came over and since we'd been there so many times, she knew what we usually ordered and jotted them down along with Rendon's sweet tea, chicken sandwich and cheese fries. Scanning his skinny body, I wondered where all those calories went.

"So, how's college life treating you?" Shaw asked Rendon. "Classes going okay so far?"

"It's different from high school so that's already an improvement."

Shaw frowned. "I didn't know you were having trouble at school. Why didn't you tell me?"

"It wasn't a big deal. I had it handled." Rendon shrugged it off but I noticed the tension in his shoulders.

Shaw didn't seem convinced either. "Rendon, what kind of—"

"Save it, *Dad*. It was fine. Pinky promise." Rendon

flashed a smile that must have convinced Shaw, but I didn't buy it.

"Smart ass." Shaw quirked a brow. "When will you find out if you got the job?"

"What job?" I interrupted.

Rendon surprised me when he answered. "The coffee shop two doors down."

"Well?" Shaw asked.

Rendon grinned and his body relaxed. "They offered it to me on the spot."

"Hell yeah, congrats, baby bro." Shaw ruffled Rendon's hair again.

"Knock it off." Rendon scowled and batted his hand away. "I hate when you do that."

A piece was sticking up from being caught in his glasses. I reached over and untangled it and Rendon glanced at me. "You missed some."

He held my stare for a moment before ripping his gaze away, returning his focus to Shaw.

"When do you start?" Shaw reclined back in his seat but shot me a look with a hard glint in his eyes.

"Tomorrow actually. I have to get there early to get my uniforms but then I'll spend the weekend training before they saddle me with a permanent schedule."

"Nice," Memphis spoke up. "So free coffee, right?"

"I don't think they'll let me." Rendon gave Memphis an apologetic smile.

"Just kidding. I don't drink coffee." Memphis glanced at me, and then turned to Rendon. He winked and slipped a smile across his face that made his stupid dimple pop. "But I may have to start."

Memphis was an observant motherfucker and I had no doubt he was purposely attempting to provoke a reaction from me. Having become close friends with him over the summer, I'd been tempted to tell him about Rendon, but hadn't.

When Rendon blushed at the comment, it worked. Memphis and I were going to have a conversation because... not cool. My fists balled beneath the table and my teeth ground together.

"Your roommate seems interesting," I said, trying to regain his attention with casual conversation.

"What's that supposed to mean?" he snapped and glared at me.

"Nothing," I backpedaled. I actually liked Tristan. He seemed to be on my side. Maybe. "He's just a lot different than you, but you two seem to get along."

"We do." His response was short and left me grasping for a response. "You interested?"

I raised my hands and brows. "That's not what I meant. You know damn well who I'm interested in."

The smug smile on Shaw's face was annoying. He'd have to stop that shit.

"I meant when I stopped by the other night"—I purposely grinned at Shaw and he gaped with furrowed brows—"he seemed cool. That's all."

Shaw schooled his features as our food was dropped off. "Well, I'll have to meet this guy then."

"His name is Tristan." Rendon bit into a sandwich and glanced back at his brother. "And he thinks you're hot."

Bishop who had been quiet but attentive, growled.

"Easy, babe," Shaw soothed, but a twinkle of mirth danced in his eyes when he glanced back at his brother, knowing just as well as I did Rendon had poked at Bishop on purpose.

"He thinks you're hot too," Rendon told Bishop who

only grunted in reply, which made Rendon laugh. A soft, chuckle that I could get used to hearing.

Unfortunately, I never brought that side of him out and it bothered me.

Memphis stuck out his bottom lip. "I'm feeling left out."

"Well he hasn't met you yet." Rendon grabbed his drink and sipped from the straw.

"Damn right he hasn't," Memphis said with a cocky grin. "Or he wouldn't have even noticed these guys."

Rendon rolled his eyes and glanced at me. "Tristan thinks..." His mouth snapped shut.

"What?"

He dropped his gaze to the plate in front of him and snagged a cheese drenched fry. "Nothing."

I was too hungry to engage in another battle with him so I tore into my sub piled high with veggies, meat and cheese. I moaned with the first bite.

"I thought you didn't like vegetables," Rendon said and I almost choked when it brought up immediate thoughts of that night together.

Everyone else politely ignored the conversation.

"I said I don't like them on pizza." I took another bite to prove my point.

He rolled his eyes. "I thought you'd order a *piece of cake*."

"Rendon..." I started. If he wanted to do this with people around then fine. I had nothing to hide. "I've told you—"

"Oh, I know what you told me, you conceited—"

"I wasn't being conceited." A ripple of frustration swept through me. Why did he keep trying to deny what was between us? Maybe I was going about it the wrong way, but wasn't honesty the best policy? "What I told you was the truth and we both know it."

Shaw interrupted with an edge of steel in his tone. "Okay, you guys. Maybe another time would be better for this."

"Tell your stubborn brother to not be so...stubborn." *Really? That's the best I have?*

Rendon glowered. "His stubborn brother is right here and can speak and decide for himself."

"Oh, come on. You guys are acting like little kids." Bishop's deep voice cut across the table. "Let's eat or we are going to be late and you two obviously need to talk."

Shaw flashed a glare at Bishop. "They don't."

"They do." Bishop's voice was calm but firm.

"I'll remember that," Shaw threatened, which only made Bishop's psycho ass smile.

Rendon stood, pulled his wallet out of his pocket and tossed some bills on the table. "I gotta go, thanks for the invite."

"Ren," I started. "You don't have to go. I'm sorry."

"No problem. I'll catch you later," he said to Shaw before lifting his backpack and slinging it over his shoulder. He waved to everyone. Except me.

Shit.

"Smooth." Shaw snorted. "I almost feel bad for you."

"Fuck off."

The table broke out in a laugh at my expense. Jumping up from my seat, I grabbed my own bag and chased after Rendon. Behind my back, Memphis whistled. "Oh. He's got it *bad*."

No, I didn't. Fucking Memphis.

When I caught up to Rendon, I tugged on his elbow. "Wait up."

He spun around. "What do you want?"

I scrubbed my hand over my face. "You frustrate me beyond belief."

His shoulders squared. "And you annoy me, so why are you here?"

My gaze flicked down to the concrete sidewalk before locking with his. "Rendon, I'm sorry."

He deflated and a rush of air left his lungs. "I was a jerk too. I'm sorry."

It took me by surprise and I quickly masked my shock. "We can keep apologizing or we can talk." I figured he'd knock the suggestion but asking couldn't hurt.

He shuffled his feet and adjusted his backpack strap. "I hate you, you know?"

"No, you don't." I shook my head.

"No"—he shook his head back—"I don't, but why do you have to be so cocky and difficult all the time."

I shrugged. "If it makes you feel any better you have me second-guessing myself." Not that I'd admit that to the guys. Hell, I was just acknowledging it to myself.

He frowned. "What do you mean?"

"It means I don't have the slightest clue what to do with you," I confessed.

He opened his mouth then closed it again before sighing. "I'm going to be late to my next class, Nash. I gotta go."

"Yeah, okay. Maybe later we can talk?" I stepped back but he was the one to break eye contact.

"Maybe." He gave a bob of his head, which I took to mean I had a chance, before he turned to leave.

As he walked away, I watched his retreating form. I'd never met anyone as maddening at the same time equally tempting. Rendon Wakefield was going to make me lose my mind and I apparently had no say so in the matter.

A large hand clapped on my shoulder. "We gotta get a move on, Romeo." Memphis's blue eyes twinkled when I glanced back at him.

My mood shifted at his teasing tone. "You're lucky we need you as a QB."

"What did I do?" His eyes went wide before he smirked. "I was only having some fun. You couldn't take your eyes off him and haven't said a word to me about him. I'm hurt."

"There's nothing to tell. He keeps shooting me down."

A girl with tight red ringlets cleared her throat and I glanced over, realizing we were taking up the entire sidewalk. As we stepped aside, she ran an appreciate gaze over the two of us that made my skin crawl. I quickly looked away.

Memphis chuckled. "Oh, how the mighty have fallen."

I shoved his shoulder. "It's not like that. I just don't know what to do with him."

He nodded in agreement. "Don't ask me. I've got a history of dating the wrong guys. I'd be the worst to give advice."

We'd never discussed Memphis's history so I was naturally curious but too wrapped up in my own shit to voice it. "I'm not dating him."

"Well, then whatever you two are doing...you better be careful or it could blow up in all of our faces," he warned, concern written in his gaze.

"I'm fully aware. Trust me." Shaw and Bishop had made sure of that. It was no secret I was courting disaster.

"And yet you have no plans of stepping back." It wasn't a question.

I shook my head. "Nope."

He sighed but kept his mouth shut once Shaw and

Bishop exited the sandwich shop. Shaw ignored me as we all headed toward the practice facility.

I didn't see the headlock coming until it was too late. "Let me go before you choke me out," I gasped out at Memphis who chuckled as he attacked me on the sideline of the Bears Stadium.

He released me and slammed his giant paw against my helmet before I ripped the hard gold shell off my head. Even though I knew the pass I'd just caught would pad my stats, we'd already put that game away in the third quarter, leading by thirty-five points.

The play I'd just made showed up on the big screen lit up on the far side of the stadium. It had been a good catch but only because Memphis had sent a dart through a difficult window between two defensive players. His passing game was exceptional and we all knew it.

There was just enough time to kick off to the Bears and allow them one play, a Hail Mary pass that our defense batted down in the end zone.

There were more boos than cheers as the blue and orange clad Bears fans who filled the stadium voiced their disappointment. But I was riding a high from the first win of the season and an exhausted smile stretched over my face.

Led by Coach, we met the other team, staff and a host of reporters on the field for handshakes and a show of good sportsmanship among backhanded compliments.

The guy who had been covering me for the majority of the game found me and patted my helmet. "Nice job."

"Thanks, man. You didn't make it easy." We bumped

shoulders and I moved on to the next guy, slapping his palm.

Seconds later, I was pulled aside by a member of the Saints staff and led to a journalist. With a camera in my face, a woman with pristine blonde hair and makeup prattled on into a microphone.

"How is the team adjusting to the loss of Torin Hopkins this year?"

Torin had graduated last year and he'd been such a favorite with the reporters that the question didn't surprise me.

"We miss the guy but wish him all the luck in his future endeavors." I stuck to the general script we all gave the media.

"And the new quarterback, Memphis Hale. How has the team adjusted to a sophomore starting quarterback?"

"You saw him for yourself. He has more than proven he's up to the task. He's a vital part of our team and we're lucky to have him."

One of the Bears defensive line guys clapped me on the shoulder. "Good game."

I glanced over and we fist-bumped. "Yeah, you too."

As he walked off, the reporter regained my attention by asking another question. "Do you think the Saints are ready to face the better ranked Hawks next week?"

"Without a doubt." I nodded and flashed the camera a smile. "We practice hard. We play hard and we don't give up. It's all about motivation."

"Is that what drove you tonight to make those two touchdowns. Hopes of being drafted?"

Reporters always snuck in those questions, hoping to be the first to hear a confirmation I'd declare for the draft this year straight from my lips. I flipped once again to my default answer. "Winning motivates me. My team motivates me. And I push my limits regardless of the situation."

She gave me a wry smile. "Thanks for stopping by to talk to us."

"No problem." I jogged off as Coach took my place to answer questions. Around the field, players were being interviewed and others jogged toward the tunnel where I was headed.

Catching up to Memphis, I shook his shoulder pads. "Talk about a way to show up."

"Hey, we did it together." Memphis grinned. "I'm only as good as the guys blocking for me, catching and running the ball. And our defense killed it."

We whooped and the tunnel echoed with the voices of the Saints as we ambled down the concrete passageway on fatigued legs. Showers were quick and we barely had time to get dressed before we were hustled toward the closest restaurant, stuffed our faces and then booked it to the charter bus to take us back to Texas. We'd crossed into New Mexico for our first game so it was going to be a long trip home.

Exhaust fumes permeated the air as we reached the door and the rumble of the engine vibrated beneath my feet as I squeezed down the aisle where Memphis and I claimed two seats in the back.

Once the team was seated, the loud squeak and hiss of the hydraulic system closing the door announced our departure. Drained of energy and with full stomachs, we lazed in our reclining seats.

"What are we doing when we get back?" Memphis asked loud enough to include the guys up front.

We wouldn't get back until after midnight, so my ass was going to bed. Most of the team agreed.

"What about tomorrow? We should celebrate the season opener win. Come on guys, it's my first game," Memphis said and glanced at me for help.

"Bishop," I hollered. "Party at your place?"

"Definitely," Shaw answered for him and Bishop glared. But now it was Shaw's place too.

Shaw lowered his voice. "Come on, big guy, it'll be fun. Remember the last one? That worked out well didn't it?"

Since their relationship wasn't a secret anymore, several of the guys within earshot groaned and pretended to gag until Bishop leveled them with a dark look.

"Fine." His one word was all Shaw needed.

He climbed up onto the seat, perched on his knees. "Who's in?"

Exhausted agreements went up around us and I had to admit some pool time after spending the day beneath the sun and constricting pads and a tight uniform sounded amazing.

"Okay, so the party is on. If you don't have directions, just text me tomorrow." Shaw yawned. "In the meantime, I'm exhausted." He flopped back onto his seat and tilted his head. It was hard to see over the high back seats but he was definitely using Bishop's shoulder as a pillow. Rendon wouldn't even be able to reach my shoulder. My lips twitched at the visual.

Rendon. We'd left things unfinished. Or at least I had. I hadn't had a spare second to once again push my luck and attempt to convince him to give us a shot. *Us*. I shook my head at the word. It sounded foreign, but not wrong.

The trip was agonizingly long and my calves cramped and back ached. When campus came into view the whole team perked up.

I wasted no time once we were released to hop in my truck and drove straight home.

Once I dragged my tired ass inside, I tossed my gear by the door and blindly kicked off my shoes. After I peeled out of my clothes, I climbed into my king-sized bed and got comfortable beneath the black comforter draped over me. Leaning back on a stack of pillows, I pulled out my phone and texted Rendon. *"Did you watch the game?"*

It was late so I wasn't sure he'd get the message, or even reply if he did, so I was surprised when the response came before I could put my phone down.

"I did. Good game."

"Thanks, Ren." I included a smile emoji to match the one that crossed my face.

I reached out to plug my phone into the charger when it vibrated against my palm. Checking the screen again, a warm hum settled in my chest.

"You played great."

NINE
RENDON

"WHAT ARE you frowning about over there?" Tristan asked on Sunday as he reclined against his headboard.

It was noon and we both had slept in late because Tristan insisted on watching a horror movie that kept me up all night with dreams of creepy dead nuns. Why had I agreed to that? I was reminded of why I didn't watch scary movies which, of course, he thought was hilarious.

"Huh?" I placed my phone on the side table and then lay back down on my bed. "Oh, Shaw invited us over to their house."

"Like to just hang out?"

I yawned and stretched my arms over my head before flipping onto my side to face him. "A pool party to celebrate winning the game."

That grabbed his attention and he sat up straight in his bed. "You said yes, right?"

"I haven't responded, but it's for my brother's game. I think I'm required to go. What do you think?"

He looked at me as if I'd lost my mind. "I think yes! We have to go. One, yes, it's your brother and you'd be a terrible sibling if you didn't. Two, we're talking about lots and lots of half-naked, wet football players. What reason is there *not* to go?"

"I'm pretty sure your first point was an attempt at a guilt trip for your own advantage." I chuckled and pulled the covers up to my chin.

"Astute observation. That how you got your academic scholarship?" Tristan stuck his tongue out.

"You're not funny." I returned the gesture. "Speaking of my scholarship, I really need to study today."

"Oh, come on. You can do that tonight," he pleaded.

When I failed to give an immediate response, he proceeded to jut out his bottom lip, pouting.

I sighed as I realized as much as I didn't want to, I was going to give in.

His expression morphed as he grinned manically. "So, we're totally going, right? You have me too excited to say no now."

Running a hand over my face, I knocked my glasses out of place in the process and then readjusted them. "I'm not even all the way awake yet."

"Your eyes are open and you're talking. That's all I need for an answer." He bounced on the mattress, eyes wide and hopeful.

"You're like a dog with a bone sometimes, you know that?"

He nodded. "It's called persistence. One of my best traits."

I couldn't say I agreed. "Whatever. Yeah, we'll go."

"Sweet." He fist-pumped. "What time?"

"I'll find out." Grumbling under my breath, I reached for my phone again. I glanced at the time and then typed out a message to my brother. *"When should we be there?"*

Tristan cursed. "I didn't even bring swim trunks. We'll need to go shopping."

I hadn't brought any either. My phone went off with a reply from Shaw. "He said we have a few hours before everyone shows up. So we have time to go to the store."

"Okay, grabbing a shower." Tristan hopped off the bed and disappeared through the bathroom door. The water cut on and he started singing off-key at the top of his lungs. I buried my head under the pillow to drown out the assault on my ears.

Tristan's eyes widened as we entered the upscale neighborhood where Bishop and my brother lived, and he whistled when I pointed out their house as we approached it. "Pretty swanky for college kids."

"Yeah. It's pretty awesome. Bishop inherited it from his grandmother." I pulled in behind a car parked on the street. New swim trunks and beach towels in tow, Tristan followed me up to the impressive two-story home.

Dove-gray bricks were accented with white trim and large windows. Both the front door and the garage door were glossy black, and tall pine trees and aged oaks stood sentinel over the lush green lawn.

We seemed to be the last to arrive as the party appeared to be in full swing judging by the laughter and occasional shout or squeal coming from around the house. When no one answered my knock, we let ourselves in.

The house was mostly empty with the exception of a few people I didn't recognize in the kitchen and a short line to the downstairs bathroom. The back wall boasted huge windows that afforded a view directly to the large patio and free-style shaped pool. The backyard was swarming with people both in and out of the pool.

Next to me, Tristan was practically vibrating with excitement as he bounced on his feet. "I can't believe you didn't want to come. Hurry up and let's get changed so we can get up-close to all that man candy."

He grabbed my hand and dragged me across the living room to join the line to the bathroom and then we took turns changing. Emerging shirtless in navy and white striped trunks, I took our clothes and put them inside the shopping bag and tossed it in a corner where a lot of bags were already piled up. Tristan followed behind me in electric green bottoms and I glanced up, shaking my head. They suited him.

The dark hardwood floor had drops of water from people coming in from swimming and I nearly fell as I slipped on a slick spot.

Tristan grabbed my arm and balanced me. "Don't break your neck as an excuse to leave."

He smirked and I flicked his ear.

When we stepped outside, the distinctive smell of chlorine wafted in the air from the clear blue water. Scanning the sea of faces, I found my brother and Bishop cozied up on two loungers beneath the shade provided by the patio overhang. Neither had bothered to shave that morning and they looked completely comfortable together.

Bishop glanced up, shot me a small closed-lip smile and nodded his chin causing Shaw to follow his gaze. A wide grin spread across his face as he waved us over. "Hey, little bro, I'm glad you made it."

I rolled my eyes at *little bro*. "Tristan, this is my brother, Shaw, and his boyfriend, Bishop. Guys, this is my roommate."

"Nice to meet you." My brother sat up and bumped Tristan's fist.

"You too." Tristan beamed.

"The silent one is my boyfriend. Don't take it personal. I think he forgets to act like normal human being most of the time."

Tristan walked around the lounger to Bishop's side, and the brooding man cast him a wary glance, and when Tristan patted his dark head of hair in greeting, Bishop's brow scrunched and the corner of his lips pulled down.

I didn't bother to stifle my laugh as Tristan crowded his space. "Hi there, grumpy."

Shaw's laugh burst from his chest and he pinched Bishop's thigh. "Play nice and say hi."

Bishop glanced at Tristan and in a stiff voice said, "Hello."

Tristan beamed again as he made his way back to my side. "I think he likes me."

Bishop's expression was classic. Confused and uncomfortable, he looked to Shaw who only leaned into his side. "I'm so proud of you." When Bishop grunted, Shaw grinned, eyes full of amusement as he tilted his head at me and then Tristan. "Make yourselves at home."

When we left them, Tristan whispered, "He's a weird one, but I can see why your brother digs it. Kinda hot."

I bumped my shoulder into his. "You have no shame."

"Zero," he agreed as he made a show of checking out the scenery. "Look around, man. You almost deprived me of this display of half-nude men."

I had to admit the view wasn't terrible. As we passed the pool, a guy in hot pink trunks cannonballed and sent a spray of water over us making Tristan jumped back with a curse. The noise around us was a constant mix of chatter, splashes, laughter and somewhere music played a rock song that Tristan sang to in a low tone, thankfully sparing everyone what I'd had to listen to while he'd showered.

Motioning to a couple of free loungers, I hurried ahead. "Those two just got up. We'd better snag the chairs before someone else does."

After we claimed our spots, we spread our towels out and leaned back. While the sun beat down on me, I surveyed the party around us and clashed into yellow-green exotic eyes trained on me, lids hooded. My breath caught and lips parted as mixed feelings of annoyance and excitement swirled in my belly. Traitorous body.

Nash stood waist deep in the water on one side of the volleyball net, apparently teamed up with Memphis. My gaze dropped to Nash's throat and bare chest. Rivulets of water clung to his light brown skin then rolled down his perfectly defined muscles. I swallowed hard when Nash repaid the attention, stare coasting over my body. Most of the guys here were tall and muscular, so a wave of self-consciousness rolled through me. Tristan and I resembled a couple of beanpoles, minus the tall part, amidst the crowd.

"Oh, you are in so much trouble, Ren," Tristan whispered. "Nash looks like he's seconds from climbing out of the pool and dragging your ass to somewhere he can do dirty, dirty things to you."

"Whatever. He does not." Except he did so I tore my gaze away and closed my eyes as I tipped my face toward the sun, wishing I owned a pair of prescription sunglasses.

The sun was hot. Too hot. And after a measly ten minutes, sweat beaded on my forehead. I turned my head toward Tristan who lay in the same position, soaking up the sun. "Want to swim?"

Tristan's head whipped to the side and he stared at me in horror. "And mess up my eyeliner?"

"You wanted to come to a pool party and not swim?" I squinted.

He shrugged. "I'm not complaining."

"Then stay here and hold my spot." When he lazily waved me off and re-closed his eyes, I headed for the pool.

The cool water lapped at my chest as I sat on the second step, watching the volleyball match. No one paid me any mind. Except Nash. His gaze flicked to me from time to time and each glance burned hotter than the last.

Nash and Memphis won the game and were challenged to a rematch. Though I tried, I had a hard time keeping my eyes off Nash, especially since every time he volleyed back, his abs and arms flexed. My lip was near bleeding from biting it so hard.

Once my skin began to prune, I returned to our chairs and found Tristan had flipped onto his stomach and dozed off. I reclaimed my chair content with the heat on my now chilled skin and dozed off with him until my brother announced he was putting hotdogs on the grill. Translation, Bishop got up and did it.

Tristan turned over and sat up with a sigh. "He really loves your brother, huh?"

"They are stupid in love," I agreed. Under the annoying big brother act, Shaw was a great guy and I was happy that Bishop treated him like royalty. I wasn't sure there was anything Shaw could ask of him that he wouldn't do.

We quieted and soon the smell of grilled food overpowered the chlorine. Having skipped breakfast, my mouth watered and stomach rumbled.

When the food was ready, I was the first in line, grabbed two loaded paper plates then returned to our spot, passing one to Tristan. As I ate, I found myself scanning the crowd, ignoring the majority of people around us as I sought out one person.

Why did I have to be so attracted to Nash? And his admission that I'd made him second-guess himself weighed heavily on my mind. I didn't want that. What I wanted was for him to not act like he could have me with a snap of his fingers.

He sat at a square glass table with four tall chairs under a forest green umbrella. Memphis sat to his right, focused on his phone, and another one of his teammates I recognized as Logan Kelley sat to his left. The Saints offensive line player with auburn hair and deep brown eyes had a pretty brunette wearing a white two-piece in his lap. He dipped his head next to her ear and wrapped his arms around her waist.

Then there was a red-head sitting across from Nash with curves spilling from the black bikini that didn't leave much to the imagination. She leaned across the table top and touched Nash's hand. The now empty paper plate crunched as I squeezed it in my fists.

He shook his head and she yanked her hand back, shot off her chair and marched away.

I was only a little surprised when Nash glanced back at me, catching me staring. His gaze went hot and my stomach flipped.

Memphis leaned in and said something to Nash, snagging his attention as he showed him something on his phone. Nash peered at the screen and his laughter carried across the patio. Bits and pieces of the conversation drifted over between the noise.

"You know he..." Memphis said before his voice was drowned out. "If you weren't so wrapped around..." The words cut off again when a loud group started laughing from where they were gathered on towels on the hot cement. Memphis's voice rose over the noise. "Oh, shit." Memphis turned wide eyes on Nash, tilting the phone toward him again.

Nash's shoulders went rigid and his gaze swung to me once more. His eyes narrowed and his lips thinned into a tight line. Taken aback, I shifted uncomfortably. He'd never looked at me that way before.

Tristan who had silently been devouring his food and enjoying the view, elbowed me. "Why does Nash look like he's going to kill you?"

Before I could respond, the screech of Nash's chair as he pushed it back, rough and hard, startled me and garnered everyone's attention.

"Uh, oh," Tristan said as Nash stalked over. Behind him, Memphis shook his head and cast me an apologetic grimace. What was going on?

Looming over me, Nash's jaw ticced. "We need to talk. Now."

"Damn, bossy pants." Tristan whistled.

Despite his obvious anger, Nash changed his tone as he spoke softly to Tristan. "I need to talk to Rendon. It's important."

Rendon. Okay, he was mad but what reason did he have to be such an asshole. "What's the matter with you?"

"What's the matter with *you*?" He flung my words back at me, eyes blazing.

I scanned the crowded patio. So many eyes were focused on us. Standing, I forced him to step back. "Fine, let's go talk before you completely embarrass me."

"I'm not trying to embarrass you." His tone relaxed the slightest bit but it was clear he was still mad.

"Well, you are," I gritted through my teeth and then led the way inside. I saw Memphis and his guilty expression out of the corner of my eye.

Shaw had come to his feet, caught my eye and took a step forward. I raised my hand and he stopped but his eyes conveyed his message loud and clear. *Just say the word.* I gave him a curt nod.

Continuing my path, I dumped the crumpled plate in the trash and dodged the few people in the house while glancing around. There wasn't a good place to have a conversation when I had no idea what to expect, so I headed upstairs with Nash on my heels. My brother wouldn't care. In the hallway, I stopped and spun around to face him and snapped, "Care to explain why you just made a scene in front of everyone?"

He stared for a second then bit out, "Memphis found your profile."

"My profile?" It took me a minute to understand but then my eyes widened.

"You know exactly what I'm talking about."

Anger flooded my veins. "So? What right do you have to call me out about it? Lots of guys use it and I don't see what the problem is."

Nash's nostrils flared. "What happens if you meet up with some guy twice your size and he doesn't like it if you change your mind? Do you not—"

Though he might be worried, I also found it highly probable he was upset because I'd turned him down, and then had cast a net out to meet other guys. His ego couldn't take it.

I held up my hand, ticking off numbers with my fingers. "One, *you* are twice my size. And two, I can take care of myself. Three, it's not your business."

"Not my business," he repeated and slowly closed in on me. "You can keep denying it, but you *are* my business."

I sucked in a breath. "Says you."

"I do. And you know it's true. Why did you create that profile, Ren?"

"Same reason as most people. I'm in college and I want to experiment and I have...there's things I want just like everyone else." I felt so dumb saying that, but it was true. A sick thought occurred to me and more anger flooded my system. "Do you use it?"

His slowly shook his head as he stared at me. "Not since meeting you. I deleted the damn app."

My fire burned out. "Why?"

Before another word was uttered, he pinned me to the wall, swooped down and claimed my lips. The sudden pressure against mine caused me to gasp and he took advantage, slipping his tongue into my mouth. I moaned. I couldn't help it. Months without kissing Nash—missing it more than I realized—caused my body to melt against his. Pure instinct brought my hands to the back of his head and held him to me. He growled and with one hand planted on the wall, his other slipped around to squeeze my butt through my damp swim trunks.

The sounds escaping me should have been embarrassing, but I was hard and aching, desperate for relief. He pressed his length, long and thick, against mine. The world could end and I'd still be lost in the aggressive slick slide of his tongue against mine. In the way he ground against me while digging his fingers into my flesh.

His teeth tugged on my bottom lip, and then he was thrusting his tongue deep again. We pressed so close there wasn't an ounce of space between us. The friction was too much and I was close to coming in my trunks.

He pulled back and I gasped for breath as his gaze locked onto mine. "I'll say it one more time. You *are* my business. I will give you what you need. Just say the word and it's yours. It doesn't have to be more. If you want to experiment, use me. I'll make you come so damn hard and..." His gaze dropped to my lips again. "Fuck, I love your mouth."

The way he crashed his lips back onto mine before he could even finish his sentence, and the possessive way he held me, drove me crazy. Nash had full power over me with those soft, full lips and drugging kisses.

I moaned and pressed my hips into him harder. Gripping my butt hard, he lifted me until I stood on my tip toes.

"Fuck, I want you," Nash mumbled and groaned as I leaned in and nipped his ear, the tang of metal from his earring sparking on my tongue.

When I murmured my agreement, he slipped his hand beneath the elastic waistband and his warm palm caressed my flesh. He inched his fingers toward my crease and I squirmed, wanting and needing his touch there.

"Yes," I hissed into his ear as he spread me.

Feet pounded up the stairs, stopping halfway up. We froze.

Bishop's voice called in warning, "Your brother is worried, Rendon, so wrap up whatever you guys are doing."

The tension broke.

Nash pulled his hand from my trunks and stepped back.

"We'll be down in just a second," I called back as I fixed my shorts.

No response came but his footsteps retreated.

My gaze steadied on our bare feet. "That got a little out of control."

His silence met my statement and then his finger caught

the bottom of my chin, tilting my head up until I was forced to look into his eyes. "Deny it all you want, but this thing between us isn't going away. Please take that profile down."

At this point I knew he didn't have a right to ask me to do that, but I'd never even reopened the app. If I was being honest with myself, what I wanted was standing right in front of me, staring down at me with eyes that begged me to agree. But I needed to think. Still, I found myself reassuring him. "I haven't used it. I haven't even logged back on."

His grin was slow and cautious. "Not at all?"

When I shook my head, his grin grew.

"Good." His gaze heated and I swallowed hard.

"I didn't say I wasn't going to use it." When he growled, I let slip the grin I suppressed. "But I don't think it's for me."

I earned a swatted butt for that.

"So, you'll delete it?" he asked.

I nodded. "But not for you."

He opened his mouth and I covered it with my hand. "We better get downstairs before my brother comes to see if you murdered me."

When I moved my hand away, he grinned. He thought he had it in the bag, just like I knew he would. And hadn't I proved him right when he had me against the wall, begging him to touch me? I wished he didn't affect me so much. My dick had softened enough that I wouldn't embarrass myself, but Nash's bulge was still noticeable. His hand dipped into his shorts and adjusted himself. I ripped my gaze away before my body betrayed me once again.

He followed me downstairs and right before I stepped off the bottom step, he grabbed my elbow and leaned down to my ear. "Really think about what I said and let me know what you decide."

As if I could forget.

When I stepped outside, I headed straight for my brother and told him I was good. But Bishop had already apparently beaten me to it. I gathered Bishop had unfortunately heard enough to arrive at that conclusion. Shaw only gave me a relieved smile though his eyes narrowed when he took me in. I hurried off, thinking I probably should have stopped by the bathroom to check out the damage.

Then I found Tristan's curious gaze and made my way to the loungers.

"I was going to come check on you, but Bishop said you were good." He studied me and smirked. "I'd say he was right."

My skin had to be flushed, lips swollen and my hair a mess, but it was too late to fix now.

Taking my lounge chair back, I lay down and tilted my head to face Tristan. "Shut up."

"So?" he prompted. "Are you going to leave me hanging?"

Glancing over at him, I shielded my eyes from the sun. "I'm sure you can figure it out. You have a pretty vivid imagination."

He waggled his brows then closed his eyes with a sigh. "Yup. I think I get the full picture."

Shaking my head, I laughed. "Gross. You're such a pain."

He cracked his lids open, squinting. "Seriously, you guys put some insane chemistry out there. If you don't want him, you mind if I give it a go?"

"Yes, I mind." I glared.

He tossed his head back and laughed. "It's cute how possessive of him you are and don't even realize it."

"I'm not," I insisted, but the small spike of jealousy when he asked if he could *give it a go* disagreed.

"Sure you're not," he said with a mocking tone.

"You're annoying." But then, because I needed advice, I told him what Nash had said.

He sat up straight, swung his legs over the side and leaned toward me. "I have an opinion you may not like."

When he put it like that, I reconsidered how smart it had been to ask Tristan for guidance. "Maybe keep it to yourself then."

He chuckled. "That doesn't sound like something I'd do. Hear me out, okay?"

"Fine. Let's have it." I sighed in resignation.

"Well, it's safer with him, right." It wasn't a question. "I mean he does have a point."

"Okay, I'm starting to regret agreeing to listen to you."

"I'm just saying that if you don't have real feelings for him and are just attracted to him, that's okay. There wouldn't be anything wrong with it as long as you're both on the same page."

I didn't know how I felt about Nash. Sure, he got under my skin and made me forget that I hated how cocky he could be. But that was in the heat of the moment.

While I lay there with my thoughts drowning out the party around me, I questioned if that was true. As often as I thought about him, how could it be? Maybe he was always under my skin. Like an itch that needed scratched, I didn't know how much longer I could resist.

A few minutes passed as I basked in the sun, my mind playing over what had happened between Nash and me.

"So, are you considering it?" Tristan asked.

If I said no, it would be a flat out lie. "Maybe."

TEN

NASH

IT HAD BEEN three days since the pool party and I hadn't heard from Rendon. Hadn't spotted him on campus either. As the days ticked by with no word from him, I was having trouble focusing on football.

The familiar drills Coach assigned the team only went so far to keep my thoughts at bay. And I sat through my academic classes without hearing a word the professors said. Patience wasn't my strong suit and I'd never waited on a response before for any guy, or girl for that matter. But I was trying for Rendon.

"Heads up!"

The warning came just in time for me to shake the thought of Rendon away and catch the ball drilling through the air into my arms.

"Get your head in the damn game, Sterling!" Coach yelled. "What's gotten into you, boy?" He was getting more and more irritated as practice went on.

"Sorry, Coach. I had something on my mind, but I'm in it now." I glanced at the team. "My bad, guys."

Memphis shot me a concerned glance and Shaw had

ignored me for days. I gathered he knew something was going on but could *guarantee* he didn't know about my proposal to Rendon. He'd have already had my nuts cut off. He wanted to witness my downfall with his brother and things hadn't panned out that way. I couldn't get inside his head to see those wheels spinning but he seemed troubled. And, while I knew Shaw well enough to know he wasn't being malicious and was only worried about his brother, he shouldn't be. Rendon was a consenting adult and this was between him and me.

The rest of the team seemed frustrated with my lack of focus, and they'd only let me slack off so far before they'd start raising hell. I was pushing the limit.

Time to leave my personal issues off the field. Having foregone gloves, I wiped the sweat off my hands with the white cloth hanging from my practice pants.

Tossing the ball back to Memphis, I lined up with the o-line again, facing our defense. On opposite ends of the line Shaw and I readied with one foot placed in front of the other, hands on one knee. Coach was testing our defense, and offense had been giving them hell for over thirty minutes.

"Down. Set." Memphis grunted as our center hiked him the ball. He retreated to the pocket as Shaw and I skirted the line of scrimmage and then raced downfield.

Defense was practicing man on man coverage and my guy was solid, practically glued to my side. But Shaw got free and Memphis let loose the ball. Shaw plucked it out of the air easily and we all trotted back to the line.

We were soaked from the heat and had spent the last two days on the indoor practice field. But because today was the coolest day in the forecast, Coach had marched us outside. He was pushing us hard for the few errors we'd made in the last game—a couple dropped balls, unnecessary penalties and the two touchdowns our defense had allowed due to miscommunication on the field.

Though we'd ripped the other team apart and drops were inevitable, there was no excuse when you were wide open. I'd claimed one of those drops but had also been responsible for two touchdowns. We were only allowed twenty-four hours to celebrate wins before he dropped the hammer on mistakes we made. I was used to the routine but some of the new guys had been having a rough few days.

Next week's game was against a higher ranked opponent and he made adjustments for the whole team to learn in a short time. In other words, I needed to focus on football and get my mind off Rendon. It was messing with my game.

"Again," Coach yelled as he and the defense coordinator studied our movements.

After a few more rounds, Coach seemed satisfied when Shaw and I couldn't get a clean grab which meant the guys shadowing us were doing their damn jobs. His words.

He had us split off with our specialty coaches and went over more drills, new plays and then we were made to execute them as well. Needless to say, after a full day of workout, classes, film and practice we were all wrung out.

Once we were dismissed, I practically collapsed against the tiled wall beneath the shower spray in the locker room.

"That was brutal," Shaw said from the opposite end.

Bishop always took the spot next to him, blocking him off. In the past I thought it was ridiculous but with Rendon in the picture, I'd do the same damn thing if he were mine. The stray thought caught me off guard, but I didn't have the mental energy to examine it. I'd worry about it later.

"No worse than usual," one of the guys yelled, his voice

echoing off the tiles. His statement was followed with exhausted agreements.

Memphis followed me out of the shower and as we dressed, he lowered his voice. "So, you and Rendon work things out yet?"

Though I hadn't let Memphis in on the conversation I'd had with Rendon, I had told him I confronted him about the profile—which he already knew based on the way I'd acted like a jealous asshole at the party and we'd disappeared into Bishop and Shaw's house. Not my finest moment, but I *had* been a jealous asshole.

And I'd let slip that I asked him a question he'd yet to answer. He probably thought I'd asked him out or something equally innocent, but nope. I'd suggested a hook-up arrangement for Rendon to use me as he saw fit and to ditch that fucking app. Whatever. I was gaining something in return. Like my sanity once I worked him out of my system —which I wasn't so sure was possible—or figured out what was going on between us. Something had to give because he had me more confused than I'd been in my entire life. Rendon was clearly affected too, whether he admitted it or not.

"I wish," I admitted. "He needs to put me out of my misery and give me an answer."

Rendon had to know it was driving me crazy and he may have even done it on purpose, though that didn't sound like him. Hell, it was possible he'd already thought about it and decided to cut me off and wouldn't that make me feel like a fool.

Memphis chuckled. "You two didn't seem miserable when you came downstairs Sunday."

My lips twitched as I slipped my green t-shirt on and

yanked a pair of shorts up. "Yeah, definitely *not* miserable then."

"Maybe you should ask him again," Memphis suggested as I sat on the bench. The thing about Memphis was that he didn't pry too deep and at the moment I was grateful.

As I laced my shoes, I glanced at Memphis with a frown. "Shouldn't I give him more time? I mean, is three days enough? I don't want to come off clingy."

I cringed the moment the word left my mouth. Clingy. I wasn't clingy. I was...fucking frustrated. And a tad anxious but there was no way I was admitting that.

"I think if you keep screwing up during practice, you're going to regret not taking the leap of finding out." He glanced over his shoulder at the guys. "I think some of the guys are over it."

"No shit." No one wanted to work with a slacker and that's what I'd been the last few days. Maybe he was right.

Bishop and Shaw dressed next to us and I hadn't noticed them, so when Shaw stepped forward, I groaned under my breath.

"Listen, I've been trying to stay out of your business." Bishop scoffed but went back to tending to his routine. Shaw poked his massive shoulder. "What? I have. But Nash is playing like shit."

I couldn't argue with him. I stood, grabbed my gear bag and gave Shaw a derisive laugh. "Thanks, Wakefield."

Shaw turned back to me with an arched brow. "It's true." He hesitated and then rubbed his temple before shooting me with a half-ass glare. "This is killing me, but he's working tonight."

When I stood there waiting for more, he ignored me, opting to ask Bishop what was for dinner. That was it? What was he trying to say?

"Dude, you look so lost." Memphis patted my back as if I was dense. "You look like you need some coffee."

"What? I should ambush him at work?" I frowned. Rendon wouldn't appreciate that.

Shaw turned. "Damn it, Nash. Go get some fucking coffee."

The room exploded in laughter and I tensed. Shaw couldn't possibly know what he was attempting to help me with. Should I feel guilty? Maybe. But I was too wrapped up in questioning if showing up unannounced at Rendon's work was a good idea.

Bishop mocked Shaw. "And you're trying to stay out of it."

"This is disturbing. I want it over with," Shaw defended himself. "Rendon will make the right call"—Shaw glared at me—"and we can go back to playing some ball." Shaw's expression had shifted, unease turning his lips down at the corners and his forehead creased. Suddenly he didn't appear convinced Rendon would tell me to fuck off.

Now we were on even ground because neither was I. It could go either way and that was what ate at me.

I hated coffee but looked like I was off to buy some anyway. And now the entire damn team knew I was hung up on a guy. On Shaw's brother. I'd never hear the end of it. I groaned under my breath as I made my way out to the parking lot.

Who drank caffeine this late in the day? Apparently, a lot of people. The coffee house was jam-packed as I joined the line and waited to order. Rendon stood behind the counter, running the register. In a black collared shirt, red apron, and matching hat, he looked so damn cute, even if a little exhausted.

Maybe it was a mistake just showing up. How was I supposed to talk to him when he was busy with a never-ending stream of caffeine junkies? Still I waited patiently and had to admit that the smell of muffins and scones wasn't unpleasant. Though I could take or leave the bitter scent wafting out of steaming cups.

As I waited, I surveyed the room painted in black and red. The place had a modern feel with eclectic black and white photography adorning the walls. The red-top tables with iron legs dotted the seating area and oddly placed partitions almost gave it a maze-like appearance.

When I made it to the front of the line, Rendon glanced up with a wide smile. "What can I get... Nash?" His smile faltered. "What are you doing here?"

Placing my hands on the counter, I leaned forward. "If I said I came for coffee and a bagel, would you believe me?"

He rolled his eyes but a reluctant grin played across his face. "No."

"I'll take a small coffee, black." I winked. "And a bagel."

He shook his head and rang me up. After I paid, he showed me where to wait at the end of the granite counter for my order beneath a hanging sign that said "Pick Up".

As I waited, I watched him work as I waited. From where I stood, I had an excellent view of his tight little ass covered with black chinos.

"Nash?" a smiling brunette I didn't recognize asked, tearing my attention away as she held my order.

"Yup, that's me."

She grinned and handed me my cup and bag. "Enjoy."

After giving her a polite smile, I weaved my way around the packed coffee house. Almost every table was taken by students with their laptops and tablets, some with books and then there was me, empty-handed except for my order. I squeezed my body between customers to the back where I found a lone vacant two-stool table that afforded enough privacy for the conversation I intended to have with Rendon. But as I sat, I wondered if he'd come talk to me at all and how stupid I'd look if he didn't. If he'd even be able to.

Fucking Shaw and Memphis and their bad advice.

I took a cautious sip from the cup and grimaced.

Rendon's laugh followed as he pulled the chair out across from me. "Regretting it already?"

"No." I took another swallow and coughed. "It's great."

"Liar." His lips tilted to one side. "What are you doing here for real?"

"Aren't you going to get in trouble for being over here?" I cocked a brow. "Not that I'm complaining."

"I took an early break, but I can leave if you want." He gave a casual shrug but humor glinted in his eyes.

"Don't even think about it," I warned but my lips twitched.

He rested his elbows on the table. "So, tell me why you're here."

"You know exactly why I'm here." I rolled the styrofoam cup between my hands, the heat almost too hot to touch. "Have you thought about what I said at the party?"

Rendon dropped his gaze to the tabletop, hesitated and then lowered his voice. "Of course I have, and I wanted to answer you."

I bolted upright, spine straight, continuing the hushed conversation. "Then why didn't you?"

He shook his head and then glanced up. "Because I didn't know what to say."

"Yes or no are usually appropriate answers." I smirked and any nervousness fled from his expression and he kicked me under the table. I reached down to rub my shin. "Ouch."

"Sorry, I didn't mean to do that. Reflex to jerk comments." There wasn't an ounce of an apologetic tone in his voice.

My fingers itched to reach out and grab him, swing him around onto my lap and bust his cute little ass. "I'll have to remember that then."

He worried his lip in-between his teeth before he sighed, still whispering. "You were right about a random hookup. I don't know if I can do that anyway. Not with a stranger."

While I was glad he didn't want to hook up with a stranger, the idea of Rendon with anyone else sent a spike of jealousy through my chest and made me want to pound the table like a fucking caveman and scream *Mine!* The notion should have bothered me. It didn't. And I hadn't lied when I voiced my worry about him being easy pickings for the wrong type of man, and the thought... I blinked hard, refusing to think about it.

"Ren, all you have to do is tell me what you want," I implored him while leaning toward him with my elbows on the table.

He covered his eyes. "This sounds so stupid."

Reaching across the table, I pulled Rendon's hands from his face. I wanted him to look me in the eye. "Tell me anyway."

His entire face flushed and he closed his eyes. "I'd be a lot more comfortable with you and I'm so tired of not experiencing the things I want."

"Stop doing that. Look at me," I coaxed as I clung to his hand. Once he did, I continued. "There's nothing wrong with wanting sex, but you don't need to hit fast forward."

Rendon jerked his hand back and I missed the warmth of his palm immediately. Even while whispering, his tone was sharp. "See? That's the kind of thing I expect people to say, but I'm ready. I want those things now. And I don't want to be judged for wanting them."

"Hey, I'm not judging you." I was the last damn person who would criticize anyone for that. We sat in silence staring at each other as he nibbled on his pink lower lip. "What do you want from me, Ren? I can give you those things or you can say no and walk away. Just tell me." *So I can stop obsessing over it.*

He ducked his head before meeting my gaze again. "The uh, the thing we did before. I want to do that again."

"You want me to jack you off?" My cock ached and my voice sounded like someone had taken sandpaper to my throat. Fuck me, but that shy expression was going to get us both in trouble.

"Jeez, Nash." His color deepened and he glanced around to see who might be listening, though it wasn't possible for anyone to hear us while separated and whispering.

"That's a yes." I growled as my cock hardened. "Done. What else?"

"I want to do other stuff too." His cast me a cautious gaze as if I might turn him down. Not fucking likely.

My cock was fully on board with this conversation and pulsed in my shorts. "You aren't going to get an argument from me."

Rendon pursed his lips. "This is weird."

"Who says it's weird?" I leaned across the table, and my tone dripped with hunger. "I think it's hot."

"But we aren't like dating, so I don't know whether to call it a hookup or..." Confusion twisted his features.

My chest tightened at his words though I didn't know why, other than it sounded so fleeting. Like this thing between us had an expiration date only Rendon knew. But what could I say when I had no idea what to call what we were doing? A fling? Friends with benefits? Or was I simply just a guy he could use to experiment? I was down for whatever. The sudden unwelcome surge of uncertainty that caused me to hesitate, disagreed. But I shook it off. "Calm down, Ren. It's whatever you want to call it."

His breathing picked up and his gaze dropped to my lips. He licked his before shaking himself out of whatever thoughts were racing around that smart brain of his.

Instead, he pulled out his phone, glanced at the screen and stood. "I have to get back but...I'll text you when I get home."

My gaze traveled over his uniform, wishing I could remove every stitch, leaving him bare for me. "I'll be waiting."

When I didn't stand, Rendon tilted his head and his brows drew together. "Planning on staying for my whole shift?"

"Ah, no. I just can't walk around like this." I glanced down at the bulge in my shorts.

He swallowed audibly and cleared his throat. "Good luck with...that."

"I'm hoping for a lot of good luck with that." When his gaze jerked back to me, I made a show of running my hand down my chest, stomach and beneath the table.

His mouth popped open before he took a step back and nearly knocked into a customer. Rendon apologized and then turned to me and bit his lip before spinning around and hurrying back through the employee door.

I waited for my raging hard on to calm down before I made my way out of the shop, dropping the still full cup in the trash can by the door where I paused and took one last look at the cutest barista I'd ever seen. His gaze shifted to mine and I winked before I walked outside, smiling ear-to-ear.

Turned out my boys gave good advice after all.

ELEVEN
RENDON

AFTER MY SHIFT ENDED, I'd emptied and organized the small bag of cheap groceries Tristan had brought home but failed to put away, found the receipt and paid him my half. Then I spent a rather long time arranging the few drinks in the mini fridge into perfect rows, taken a shower and tidied up my side of the dorm.

Tristan kept giving me the side-eye from where he sat at his desk. When I started wiping invisible dust from the bookshelf with a disposable wet wipe, he huffed. "You going to tell me why you're acting like a spaz?"

After tossing the useless cloth in the trash, I fell back on the mattress and left my legs to dangle over the side. I'd never noticed the ceiling had so many cracks. I tilted my head as I followed one of the deeper grooves.

Tristan grabbed my attention by smacking me in the face with a well-aimed rubber eraser. "Hey, you're being weird and that job is claimed by me. What's up with you?"

I turned my head to face him as he twisted back around to continue applying his eyeliner. He squinted at the lighted pedestal mirror he'd bought for his desk, pulling the skin taut as he drew a thin black line around his eye.

"Nash came to see me at work today." *And I told Nash I wanted him to jack me off.* My dick twitched as I remembered the way his eyes had smoldered.

Tristan swiveled around on his desk chair, stopping in the middle of applying the makeup so only one eye was done. "What are you not saying?"

I rubbed my palms on my blue and white checkered pajama pants. "He asked me if I'd made a decision."

Tristan rolled his wrist as if to say *go on*. "Am I going to have to drag out every word? What did you tell him?"

"I said I'd text him when I got home." Over two hours ago.

His brows rose, but didn't look surprised. "Well, I saw that coming. So that's what all the cleaning and annoying, restless pacing was about."

"What do you mean?" I adopted a confused expression and toyed with a loose thread sticking up from my bedspread.

"You're not fooling me." With a pointed look, Tristan leaned forward, hands on knees. "You're stalling. Why?"

Tristan was right. I was stalling while I tried to get over the apprehension clouding my thoughts and build the courage to text Nash.

I'd already done the hard part and confessed to Nash that I wanted to experiment with him. So why was the idea of talking to him more difficult than ever? "I don't know. He's intense. You know?"

"Um, yes, I noticed." He shot me a wry grin. "If you already told him you're up for it, what's the big deal?"

"You don't think it's a horrible idea?" I asked, doubt still weighing heavily on my shoulders. Maybe I wanted Tristan to talk me out of it. Why? Because I was chickening out. What if I was a total failure? What if Nash was disappointed in my lack of skill?

"Not really." Tristan offered a half-shrug. "Like I told you before. You're into him, he's into you. You're both down to get dirty with no expectations." He tilted his head. "Seems simple enough."

"I'm overthinking it, right? I mean it's not a big deal. This is what I wanted. And I know he'll make it g—" I smashed my lips closed.

Tristan shot me an evil smile. "Good? Oh, I bet he will. I can only imagine how long and thick—"

"Stop talking about him like that. You have no filter," I snapped. Tristan had been right. A thread of possessiveness wove around my tongue causing me to lash out. I didn't want anyone else thinking about Nash's dick. Especially my friend. Though I couldn't fault him. But I also knew Tristan was only trying to rile me up.

He rolled his eyes. "You're making this too hard. What's the real problem?"

I shook my head. "I'm nervous, I guess. I mean it was only the one time. What if I suck at *stuff*?"

He grinned again.

Before he could pounce on my choice of words, I pointed at him. "Don't."

Tristan snorted and turned back to his mirror, working the black liner around his other eye. "You're right. It's a horrible idea." He placed the cap on his makeup pencil with a click, stood and strode over to his closet.

"You just said I should..." I was wasting my breath. Trying to figure out my roommate was a lost cause. Besides, I changed my mind. I didn't want Tristan to talk me out of it. I needed a pep talk.

"What? Horrible ideas are the best ideas," he explained as if I should know this already. He rummaged through his closet, holding up a shirt and then returning it to the rack. "And Nash is smoking hot."

"*Stop* talking about how hot he is." With a hard yank, the thread I'd been messing on my comforter came loose.

Tristan glanced over his shoulder and smirked. "Sorry. But it doesn't mean I'm not thinking it."

"You're annoying." And unfortunately, brutally honest.

Tristan clicked his tongue. "And you're boring."

"I'm not boring," I argued, though I wasn't sure I could back up that statement with hard proof.

"Boring," he sing-songed as he nodded at the blood-red shirt he'd pulled out next and slipped it off the hanger. "Get out of your head about it, okay? You know what you want and you know what he wants. I say just go with the flow."

Chewing on my lip, I thought it over. "So, I just message him."

"So, you just message him," he agreed.

"But now I don't know what to say."

"Say *Nash, I'm horny. Think you can help me?*" He winked. "I guarantee he'll respond like that." He snapped his fingers.

I reached across my body, grabbed my pillow and hid my heated face beneath it. "You are literally no help." My words were muffled by the thick cotton.

The pillow was ripped away a second later. "Get. Out. Of. Your. Head. If you don't want to do it then say so. You're allowed to change your mind. You're not married to the idea."

"But I do want to." Decision made, I sat up straight and grabbed my phone before I could change my mind. "I'm just going to do it. Rip off the Band-Aid."

"Go get him, tiger." Tristan pawed at the air.

I squinted. "When you say things like that, it makes me seriously wonder why we are friends."

He chuckled and pulled his shirt over his head and wiggled his way into a pair of skinny jeans. "Does this look okay?"

"It's not black," I stated the obvious.

He nodded while examining his butt in the full-length mirror on the closet door. "Thought I'd try to switch it up. My ass look okay?"

Pinching the bridge of my nose, I sighed in exasperation. "It looks fine."

"Good. Well, I'll leave you to it then." He sat and laced up his army boots. "I have a date."

"A date?" I lowered my phone to my lap. "Like an actual date?"

"Okay, yeah, *date* is a strong word." He waggled his brows as he stood and then grabbed his keys. "I'll be home later. Don't do anything I wouldn't." He gestured toward my phone with a smirk. "Don't wait up."

When the door shut behind him, I rose to lock it. With a deep exhale, I sat on the edge of my bed and held my phone.

What was I doing taking on someone like Nash? Someone with more confidence and experience is his pinky than I had total. Oh, right, he turned me into one giant raging hormone. I pulled up his contact info and my fingers hung over the keyboard as I debated on how to start the conversation.

"Hey." One word. Groaning at my lack of game, I could only hope Nash would take the lead.

Heart thudding, I drummed my fingers on my thighs as I waited for the reply. The dots started bouncing seconds later. *"What are you doing?"*

"Hanging out in my dorm." I hesitated, took deep even breaths, and then continued to type. *"I was thinking about what we talked about earlier."* I studied the words I'd tacked on and hit send before I could back out.

"Which part?" His response was so fast that I wondered if he'd been waiting for me to message him.

To answer his question, my mind went straight to the memory of me on his lap as he jerked me off. A wave of anxiety-ridden excitement rolled through my already overworked nervous system as I tapped on the screen and then held my breath as I hit send. *"What we did before."*

"Okay? You gotta give me more than that. We've done a few things now. Is it when you dry fucked me? When you came all over me? Or was it when I pinned you to the wall, spread you and was close to finger fucking you?"

Holy... My dick swelled as I read over his dirty words. Throbbed at the images playing through my mind. *"All of it."*

The response took longer this time and I wondered if it was purposeful.

"Ren, are you alone?"

My already racing heart pounded. *"Yes."*

"Good." Another message followed. *"Do you have any idea what I'm going to do to you? Hint: Anything and everything. I'm going to kiss, suck, and lick every inch of you."*

My blood heated as a full-body shudder quaked through me. Reaching down, I squeezed my dick through the thin cotton of my pajama pants. His messages came in rapid-fire.

"If you were here, I'd kiss you and you'd let me taste that sweet mouth of yours. Then I'd strip off your shirt, lick down your neck to your nipples and tease them, driving you crazy."

"I'd press you against the wall, drop to my knees, jerk your pants to your ankles and mouth your cock through your

boxers until you leaked all over them. Until I could taste you on my tongue."

Air. I needed air. My lungs constricted—my breaths choppy. The picture he painted was so vivid. Closing my eyes, I saw it all. Nash on his knees as I stared down, wanting him to uncover the last barrier between my dick and his mouth. He'd set me on fire and watch as I burned.

On a gasp, I came back to the present. I was so in over my head.

Shoving my hand beneath the bunched elastic and into my briefs, I fisted my shaft. Imagined it was his hand, larger and a dark contrast to my pale flesh, working me with confident, slow strokes. A zap raced down my spine and I gripped the base of my dick hard so I wouldn't come yet.

My phone buzzed again. *"Okay so far?"*

More than okay. With my free hand I typed back a response. *"Keep going."*

Was Nash getting off too? I could almost feel how thick his dick was as he rubbed against me and I wanted him as crazy as he was driving me. Seconds later, I got my answer.

"I don't know how much more I can take, I'm about to shoot, imagining my lips closing over the tip of your cock, playing with the slit and running my tongue around every hard inch. Fuck, all I can think about is when I saw you come. I want more. I want to swallow every drop next time."

My dick erupted. Come streaked my stomach and chest. Leaked over my fingers. And still I moved my hand fast and tight while my body spasmed and my hips bucked.

Sagging into the mattress, I pulled my hand free and didn't hesitate for once. Didn't overthink it as I typed back. *"You caused a big mess. I'm covered in come."*

"Holy hell, that's hot. I'm so close."

My phone went silent and I could only imagine his

expression as he lost control. My spent dick perked up. I wanted to see Nash in that moment. I was ready.

Finally, he messaged again. *"Damn, I'm wrecked."*

I bit my lip. *"Can we do it again?"*

"Hell yes. Give me a minute to recover."

TWELVE

NASH

MY COCK WAS rock hard at the worst time.

The cool spray from the locker room shower did nothing to ease the pulsing ache. It wouldn't be the first hard-on in the locker room—far from it. Still, I faced away from the guys. If taunted, I'd blame it on adrenaline from our early morning workout when really, I couldn't stop thinking about Rendon and our texts the night before. It wasn't enough. My fingers flexed with the need to touch him. To be the one getting him off.

After I managed to convince my cock that it wasn't the time or place, I quickly dressed, hurried to my truck to trade my gear bag for my backpack and headed out for my single morning class. I'd just ripped open a cherry sucker and stuffed it in my mouth when I spotted Rendon and his roommate crossing the courtyard. My stare honed in on the blond.

Speaking of my morning obsession.

Crossing paths with him on campus was rare, and I wasn't one to waste an opportunity. Tossing the sucker in a nearby trash can, I jogged across the green grounds and fell into step beside him.

His hair hung down over his glasses, and he was cute as hell wearing a pale blue short-sleeved button up shirt over gray shorts and white tennis shoes.

"Hey, Nash," Tristan said with a big smile.

"Hey, emo."

Tristan rolled his eyes and Rendon glanced over at me, cheeks adorably pink. "Oh, hi."

Last night I'd pictured that flush all over his body and I had to bite the inside of my cheek to hold back a groan.

"Hi, yourself." My voice pitched low as I struggled to overcome the mental image tattooed in my mind.

"We have class," he said and turned to stare straight ahead.

I chuckled and stuffed my hands in my pockets. "Yeah, that tends to happen in college."

He cut his gaze toward me again. "Don't make fun of me. What are you doing?"

"Walking you to class." I shrugged. "That okay?"

"I guess so." He swiped his hair from his forehead. I didn't know why he bothered when it always fell right back into place. "I didn't realize this was part of...you know."

Tristan cleared his throat. "I'm going to go ahead. I'll save you a seat, Ren."

Rendon nodded and waited for Tristan to hurry ahead of us. He faced me and whispered, "You don't have to..."

Bumping my shoulder into his, I flashed a grin. "I know I don't have to. Can't I just do it because I want to?"

"Well, yeah. I just didn't expect you to."

Neither did I, but I was doing a lot of things I never expected to. "What are you doing tonight?"

"Nothing. Homework, I guess." He met my eyes and he raised a brow. "I didn't get any done last night."

"Boring." I leaned down toward his ear and lowered my voice. "Come to my place."

"Why does everyone keep calling me boring all of a sudden?" He stopped at the entrance to the History building. His lips twitched as he attempted to keep a straight face. "And why exactly do you want me to come over?"

"Why do you think, Ren?" When I bit my lip, his gaze dropped to my mouth and his tongue darted out to wet his bottom lip.

"I don't know," he said, continuing his little game.

Well, if he needed a demonstration, I was up to the task. Grabbing him by the hand, I dragged him into the building and opened the door to the first classroom a sliver. The lights were off and the room was empty. "Come here."

"What are we doing?" Rendon whispered as I pushed the door open and tugged him inside. "I don't think we are supposed to be in here."

"So?" I shut the door behind us and pinned him against the wall, shoving my knee between his legs, prying them apart.

"Here?" he asked.

"Here," I confirmed and bent my head down, hovering my mouth over his lips. "Now."

He gasped when I slowly lifted my knee, grazing his sensitive sac, and I swallowed the sound as I took his mouth in a deep kiss. Leaving one hand on the wall to brace myself, I placed the other against the side of his neck, slipped my thumb beneath his jaw and my fingertips massaged the base of his neck.

Rendon moaned as I directed the kiss and his pulse raced beneath my palm. He began rocking against my thigh, his hips moving restlessly as I continued to devour his mouth.

Fingers dug into the cotton of my shirt, pulling me closer and tugging the fabric until I heard a rip. Rendon was lost in the kiss and I let myself fall into it. His movements became frenzied and, surprising the shit out of me, he tore my hand from his neck and slipped it down between us. Oh, fuck yes.

The metal button of his shorts pinged onto the floor as I plunged my hand into his shorts and briefs. I'd buy him a new pair. I wrapped my hand around his shaft and his needy moan vibrated against my tongue. He panted as he thrust through the tight ring of my hand.

"Nash, please," he pleaded against my lips.

Groaning, I snapped my wrist up and down trying to keep up with his frantic thrusts and looked down. My cock ached at the sight. There was enough space created by my forearm to see his dick, hard and leaking, in my hand. I adjusted my grip around his shaft and rubbed my thumb in circles along the tip, smearing the wet bead from his slit.

He cried out. "I'm so close." Pulling my hand from the wall, I covered his mouth.

"Shh... I don't have anything to clean you up with." I removed my hand, dropped to my knees and jerked his shorts and briefs down just enough to free his cock. "My mouth will have to do."

"Nash." Rendon's voice shook as I circled one hand around the base.

A growl clawed its way up my throat when Rendon's hands found my hair. "Fuck, Ren. I've wanted to suck you off for so long." I swiped my tongue over his tip, lapping the new salty drop that quickly replaced the first. "So damn long."

He wobbled on his legs and tugged at my hair. "I don't know if I can handle this."

"Want me to stop?"

"God, no." He tilted hips forward.

Thank fuck. My already hard cock throbbed behind the barrier of my shorts, begging to be set free.

I jerked his shaft with one hand and snaked the other through the leg of his shorts, bunching the fabric as I tunneled under the elastic band of his briefs snug on his thigh and cupped his bare sac. I rolled, tugged, and massaged while he fucked my hand.

Rendon let loose a long moan and I winced. Sexiest sound ever but if we wanted to finish what we started, we couldn't get caught. "Ren, we gotta stay quiet. Can you do that?"

He gave me a distracted nod and quieted. Knowing he was close, I quickly wrapped my lips around him and sucked him hard and deep. A muffled cry came from above my head and I glanced up. He'd released my hair with one hand and was covering his own mouth. With my gaze glued to his shadowed face, I silently cursed the dark room for obscuring my view. Fortunately, I still had the soundtrack. The wet sucking and muffled moans were enough to damn near come in my shorts without a single touch.

Keeping a steady pace with my mouth, I ran a finger behind his sac, rubbing over the sensitive patch of skin. Rendon's hand tightened in my hair as his back snapped off the wall with a sharp arch, sending his cock to the back of my throat until I was deep-throating him. And when I swallowed around him, his jaw dropped and sac drew tight in my hand.

"Oh." His breathy moan barely made it past his lips

before I greedily welcomed the burst of his salt-tinged come on my tongue.

I drank it all and asked for more with my tongue as I continued to tease him. His body spasmed with aftershocks. Over and over, he shook and jerked as I eased him back down to earth.

When he sagged against the wall, I copped one last feel of his balls and removed my hand. After I fixed his shorts and zipped him up, I rose from my knees. My arms went around him, drawing him against my chest. I hummed in contentment and he glanced up with a dopey smile.

"I accidentally tore your button off," I told him with a smirk.

With glazed eyes behind crooked glasses, he shook his head. "I don't even care."

"You don't, huh?" I cracked a grin before dipping down and brushing his lips with mine. "How was your first blow job?"

"Best thing that's ever happened to me." As soon as the words left his mouth, he covered his face.

I barked a laugh before I pulled his hands away and straightened his glasses. "One of the best things for me too." He bit his lip and eyed me skeptically. I kissed him again, soft and quick. "You really have no idea how much I want you, do you? Even now."

His eyes softened but then he jerked away from the wall, making me take a step back and drop my arms. "Oh, no, I have class."

Tilting my head, I winked. "I think you might be late."

Hell, I was too. But now I was tempted to skip. My shorts were tented to the point they tugged tight on my ass so I wasn't going anywhere anytime soon anyway.

He dug into his pocket, retrieved his phone and checked

the time. With wide eyes, he glanced up at me and muttered something under his breath while he smoothed a hand over his shirt then through his hair. "I gotta go. I'll...see you later? Tonight?"

"Counting on it."

He flashed me a shy smile and I dropped a quick kiss on his lips before he scurried out of the room. As his footsteps echoed down the hallway, I stood in place, once again trying to talk my cock down for the second time that morning. Licking my lips still fresh with the taste of him, I groaned. It wasn't going to happen this time. I'd never craved anyone as badly as I did Rendon.

Peeking into the hall, I found it blissfully empty and found the closest bathroom. Five minutes later, the immediate issue was taken care of and I was relatively under control.

Now I just had to manage until the end of the day before I talked to him again and convince him to stay the night with me. We'd need all night. I had too much pent-up sexual energy and my cock wanted in on the action. The next time I came it would be with Rendon and I didn't want to stop until we were both unable to move.

I left the building smiling around another cherry sucker as I took the path to my class. I was going to be late, but I doubted I'd be able to pay attention anyway.

THIRTEEN
RENDON

THE LINE from the counter reached all the way to the door with people looking for a late afternoon caffeine fix. The bold aroma of coffee beans and sweet pastries drew them in all day long. I'd finally gotten comfortable with the position and moved swiftly through customers, but I was distracted with thoughts about what had happened in that empty classroom with Nash hours ago.

Though I knew I hadn't imagined what had taken place, I still had a hard time wrapping my head around it. And I'd be lying if I said I wasn't flooded with nervous anticipation about seeing him again tonight.

"...and a large Americano."

The blonde woman across the counter stared at me expectantly and I realized I'd dazed out. "I'm sorry can you repeat that?"

The woman frowned. "A blueberry scone and an Americano."

"Size?"

She huffed. "Large."

I shot her a tired smile. "I apologize. It's been a long day."

Her features softened. "Well, I can understand that." Under further inspection she wore a sharp business suit. But under the pristine makeup, dark circles shadowed her eyes.

After cashing her out, I directed her where to wait for her order and moved on to the next customer. I was tapped on the shoulder and glanced behind me, meeting my manager's gaze.

"Take your fifteen-minute break. Lauren has you covered."

Nodding, I stepped aside as my blonde coworker took over and made my way into the break room. I untied my apron and hung it on the wall hook before digging in my locker, retrieving my phone and my bag of off-label chips I bought by the case to snack on at work. Grabbing a bottle of water from the refrigerator, I sat down at the four-chair plastic table, glad to get off my feet, and checked my phone.

A message waited from Nash and my stomach flipped. Anxious about what it might say, I was hesitant to open the message. If he was going to cancel for tonight, I'd be disappointed.

Twisting the cap off my water, I sipped from it as I unlocked my phone and clicked over the preview.

"Still coming over tonight?"

A relieved sigh filled the otherwise quiet room. Not able to resist, I decided to mess with him though I'd already made up my mind to go. *"I have homework, remember?"*

The reply was instant and I laughed. *"Lame."*

"I'm tired." Another excuse that wouldn't change my mind.

"You can sleep here."

Of course, he had an answer for everything. But sleeping there? Was that crossing the line of our agreement? I didn't know, but if he was offering then I had to assume it didn't change anything between us. Still... *"Why would I do that?"*

"So, I can wear you out properly and not worry about you falling asleep at the wheel."

Well, that made sense. I had no idea what he had in store for me. Would we have sex? My internal muscles clenched, imagining him stretching me wide. Yes, I'd experimented with my fingers and even a toy here and there, but knowing how large Nash was...I had to admit I was a little intimidated.

But now there was another problem. My blood traveled south and I had less than ten minutes to get myself under control before I had to return to my post.

"Always so cocky."

"Persistent."

Understatement. He was the most persistent person I'd ever met. And although I'd call him cocky, I was starting to think there was more to Nash than the light-hearted playboy he portrayed to most people. He was more like the guy I met at the party when we'd talked outside on the porch. His self-assured attitude didn't ring of vanity. Only confidence. And in that I envied him.

His one-night standard had been shelved it seemed, based on the way he relentlessly pursued me. Something I found extremely flattering. He was also possessive, if the pool party taught me anything. It made me feel a little justified in the way I wanted Nash to myself. Only mine. He made me feel as if he wanted me as bad as I wanted him. Even if it was slight, I was struck with a new sense of self-confidence I'd never had before. Because of Nash.

But I also had to wonder what was at the end of this path we were on. Yes, I wanted to experience sex. But I also only wanted to do that with Nash.

Shaking my head, I scolded myself for overthinking things once again. I was getting way ahead of myself and decided to stay in the moment. To stick to our agreement.

Thinking of our earlier encounter helped me as I responded. *"No one's arguing with you there."*

"It'll be worth it."

And I didn't doubt him.

Checking the time on my phone, I quickly typed out a last message. *"My break is over. I'm gonna run by my place after work and then head over."*

I locked my phone, put away my things and returned to work.

Nash opened the door wearing the same sleeveless black shirt and gray basketball shorts from the first night I met him. My gaze travelled over his body. If possible, he'd filled out even more since then. With muscular arms and toned legs, he had the build of an athlete who'd put in serious time to define his physique.

Then I met his gaze and warmth blossomed in my stomach. There wasn't a single part of Nash I didn't react to and knowing I'd soon see his bare body sent warmth blooming in my stomach and chills skating over my skin. Mouth dry and eyes wide, I could only stare up at him.

"You can look all you want, but would you like to come inside?" He flashed a cocky grin.

I rolled my eyes as he let me by. No need to add my drool to his already inflated ego.

"Thirsty?" he asked as he closed the door behind us.

I needed something to ease my parched mouth. "Water would be great."

He left me in the living room before returning with two bottles of water. He held one out to me.

"Thanks." I accepted it, screwed off the cap and took a long sip. I wrapped my arm around my middle, lost as to what to do next. "So how does this work? Do we just meet up and hook up? Or..."

He took my water from me, setting it on the coffee table before backing me against the wall. His voice held a slight edge and his eyes narrowed just enough to question whether I'd hit a nerve. "Is that how you want this to work? Text, fuck around and then leave again?"

I wasn't sure I liked the sound of that. My brows furrowed.

"Or"—he offered an alternate option—"we hang out *as friends*. And we hook up when you want and try what you like. This is about you and I'm just along for the ride. A very amazing ride."

Ducking my head, I hid a smile. Did friends have this kind of sexual tension? When I glanced back up, and nodded. "I think I like that idea better."

"Good, me too." His tone lightened and he dropped quick kiss on my lips before taking a step back. His teeth sunk into his lower lip. "So, you want to watch a movie?"

Sitting through a movie while knowing where it was going to lead and being nervous about it the whole time? It would be better to skip the movie and head straight to his bedroom, wouldn't it?

"Can we just have sex?" The words rushed from my lips before I lost my nerve. I winced. The question hadn't sounded so bad in my head, but hearing it out loud made me realize I should have thought it through. For a moment I considered turning and hightailing it back to my car.

"Jump right into it then?" Nash's brows shot high and I could tell that wasn't the response he'd expected.

That made two of us and my voice shook. "I think that's what I want to do."

"You think?" He arched a brow. "I can't work with that."

"No. I definitely want to, but I'm just too nervous so I want to get it over with," I admitted.

Nash folded one arm over his chest while he rubbed the slight scruff on his chin with the other hand. His expression was hard to read so I had no idea what he was thinking.

"You want to get it over with," he repeated and then after a beat, chuckled.

I nodded. But he shook his head and then grabbed my hand. "I'm going to take my time with you. Come here."

Nash led me down the short hall to his bedroom and flipped on the light. The black iron bedframe was draped with a black bedspread, brightened with pops of gold on the pillows, and a Saints throw blanket was folded at the foot of the bed. The rest of the furniture was black wood with matching industrial accents. What surprised me was how tidy everything was.

"Is your room always this clean?" I wondered aloud. Or had he done it just because I was coming over. The one time I'd been in his room, there had been no light so I took in the details now.

"Habit from back home." Nash sat on the raised bed with parted legs and then drew me between his thighs and gripped my chin. Standing in front of him, we were nearly at eye level. His hands went to each side of my waist and slipped beneath my shirt. "Now, the last thing I want to do is *get it over with*. I want to make this good for you."

"I don't know what I'm doing," I mumbled.

"Let me do the work and then do what feels natural." He pulled me against him and kissed me soft and slow as his hands rose to the buttons of my light blue shirt. "You on board?"

Relieved, I nodded as he leaned back and his gaze heated as he unfastened the last button. A wicked grin spread across his face and I broke out in shivers. "You have no idea how much I want this with you. I'm going to touch you, suck you and everything else I've imagined for months now."

I sucked in a deep breath as he slid my shirt off my shoulders and down my arms, dropping it to the floor. He skimmed his rough fingertips down my smooth chest and teased the skin of my belly with the warm pads of his thumbs in slow circles. I bit my bottom lip hard as my dick swelled from his touch.

When he popped open the button of my shorts and then unzipped them, I grew self-conscious again and reached down, stilling his hand.

"What's wrong?" His brow furrowed. "We can stop, just say the word."

"It's not...it's not that," I stuttered. "You're built like this." My hand loosed from his and I reached out to trace the contours of his stomach through his shirt, my gaze following the path. "I'm just worried."

He'd already seen me without a shirt at the pool party, and even the tip of my dick months ago. And when he'd gone down on me, the classroom had been darkened. He'd never seen me fully naked in the light. No one had.

He released my shorts completely and grabbed my jaw, forcing me to look back into his hooded eyes.

"You are going to be perfect. I want to see that pale, slim body spread out on my bed, and I want to lick and kiss every inch of it." He bit his bottom lip. "Ren, I've craved you since the moment I saw you and have never wanted someone this much."

"Really?" Though he'd made no secret what he was after, I guessed I hadn't realized how much. Or maybe I hadn't believed him. With the way he looked at me, hunger in his gaze, I did now.

"You are a walking wet dream. I want to slide inside you and stretch you wide. I want you to know exactly how hard you make me. You are the sexiest little thing I've ever seen."

The hesitation melted away and my arms lowered at my sides.

"Keep going?" he asked.

"Yes," I whispered.

He hummed a sound of approval, and I held my breath when his hand dipped beneath the elastic of my underwear.

Nash watched my face with such intensity, I couldn't help but stare back as I waited for him to touch me. When his finger grazed my tip, I hissed as a prickle of need shot straight to my balls. With molten eyes, full of promise, he gripped the sides of my shorts and underwear and yanked them down until they pooled around my ankles. His gaze dropped to my bobbing erection and a breath rushed from his lungs, gliding over my sensitive tip.

"You drive me fucking crazy," Nash ground out and then gripped the base of my dick. He ran his closed fist to the tip and back down my shaft with lazy strokes that made my balls tingle.

"Oh." I sucked in a sharp breath and squeezed my eyes closed.

"Open your eyes," he demanded as he kept the steady pace and brought his other hand to cup my sac. "Can you come like this?"

"I was close this morning before you—" I gasped when Nash tugged on my sac.

"Before I what?" His grin was devious.

Not allowing my inexperience to cloud my thoughts, I leaned forward and nipped his bottom lip. Nash's cocky expression melted and I parted my lips. He took the invitation, slipping his tongue into my mouth and tangled it with mine. The taste of cherries filled my mouth and I gripped his shoulders to steady myself. Without thought, my hips snapped forward, thrusting into his hand and a moan ripped from my throat when his grip tightened.

He growled into my mouth. Stroked me faster. Kissed me harder.

Then he released me and my feet left the ground as he lifted me and tossed me onto his bed as if I weighed nothing. The bed didn't even squeak as I landed on the cloud-like mattress. Nash stood and tugged off my socks and shoes, throwing them blindly behind him. Impatient, he untangled my shorts and underwear from around my ankles before tossing them aside. His gaze ran over my naked body and mine focused on the large tent in his shorts.

My heart hammered a relentless beat as his gaze lingered over my hard length.

"I knew it. I fucking knew you'd be perfect." He reached over his head, grabbed the back of his shirt and pulled it over his head, revealing miles of light brown skin ripped with defined abs. His nipples were dark disks that contrasted to my light pink ones that almost blended in with my skin tone. I wanted to wrap my lips around them, suck and tease them with my teeth, the way I'd only ever imagined.

As Nash prowled forward, placing his knee on the bed, I instinctively bent my legs and spread them apart. He let loose a growl of approval, crawled between them and propped his elbows on either side of my head. Slowly he lowered his hips against mine. Long, thick and covered by his silky shorts, he rubbed against my bare dick. The slip and slide of our shafts meeting over and over again and those intoxicating eyes peering into mine drove me to madness. With urgency, I lifted my hips, grinding back.

A tortured groan crawled up his throat before he lowered his head and attacked my lips savagely. Caught up in the frenzy, I grabbed the back of his head and kissed him back. The sounds coming from deep in his chest vibrated against my lips and throat. Needing more, I reached over and tugged on one of his hands, directing it between us.

"Is this what you want?" Nash rolled to my side, took me in his hand and stroked.

"Yes," I hissed as he swiped his thumb over my tip with each pass. Reaching blindly at my side for him, I gripped him through his shorts.

"Fuck," Nash shouted. He pressed his lips to my jaw, then my neck, placing open-mouthed kisses then traced a line with his tongue down to the hollow of my throat.

He was so thick, my hand barely circled his girth. I could only image how it would fit inside me. Could it? The question broke through the charged moment and I faltered, loosening my hold on him. "Are you sure it will work?"

He pulled back with swollen lips. "What?"

"Will it..." I glanced away. "Will it fit?" It was a valid

concern. I was so much smaller than him and wasn't sure I could accommodate his size.

He shuddered and his voice sounded like it had been dragged through broken glass when he spoke. "I heard what you said earlier, and I know what I said...but I didn't think you actually... You want to go that far tonight?"

My ears burned hot but I wasn't too proud to beg. "Please."

"I knew you'd flush everywhere." His gaze caressed my skin, dropping from my cheeks to my neck and down to my chest. I hated how easily my skin pinkened, but his dick jerked against my thigh.

He buried his face into my neck. "Give me a minute. I think I'm going to come thinking about sliding inside your virgin ass. You can't surprise me with shit like that."

A smile spread across my face. "Well, I *did* tell you."

I rubbed his back while he collected himself.

Once he'd gained control, he sucked gently on my neck and whispered in my ear, "I'll prep you first and we'll go slow."

"Okay." My pulse raced as he rose over me.

His finger roamed the flat planes of my chest and then circled my nipples until they tightened into firm buds.

"Sensitive," he murmured to himself and dipped down to draw one into his mouth.

My nipples *were* sensitive and straining toward that twisting tongue that was driving me crazy. He spent minutes worshipping them before drifting down my sternum. His slight stubble scraped against my skin as he paused to suck the pinkened areas, leaving bruised patches behind. When he reached my soft stomach, he nipped me there. The slight pinch of pain bloomed into pleasure as he followed with kisses from his plush lips. I held myself still, prepared for him to take my dick in his mouth, but he ignored it. He angled his head, purposely working around it while teasing me with his lips, tongue and teeth.

"Nash," I panted out when I couldn't take anymore.

"What do you need?" He lowered his stomach onto the mattress between my legs and hovered his lips over my tip. When he glanced up, his gaze flashed with the challenge.

"Your mouth," I answered.

"What do you want me to do with my mouth?" With torturous, slow movements he gripped my base with one hand, arched over my tip and licked a ring around the head. "This what you had in mind?"

Before I could answer, he sucked me deep, taking me to the back of his throat, engulfing my entire length into the warm wet cavern of his mouth. My nails dug into the comforter as my back arched. With on hand on my stomach, he firmly pressed my back to the bed as he bobbed his head

It felt amazing. Too amazing. A zap raced down my spine. "I'm not going to last."

"That's okay," he said as he mouthed my shaft. "I want it. Give it to me."

Attempting to shift away from him, I wiggled around. "I want to last. Stop being so good."

He released me with a pop and dropped his head to the crook of my thigh as laughter shook his shoulders. "When you're not making me second-guess myself, you're great for my ego, you know that?" He turned his head and sucked gently on my sac.

"Not helping," I ground out through clenched teeth as he continued his ministrations.

"Then this is really not going to help." He sat back on his calves, pressing his hands into the back of my thighs until the most intimate part of myself was fully exposed. A wave of embarrassment mixed with excitement swept through me and I held my breath as I waited for his next move.

Nash stopped moving. His eyes were cast down and his chest rapidly rose and fell. His tongue darted out to wet his lips. "Ren...I want to taste you everywhere."

I froze. "You mean...?"

"I mean fucking *everywhere*." His gaze flicked to mine. "Trust me, Ren. I'm going to take care of you. Flip over, onto your knees."

As I rolled to my stomach, I had a moment of uncertainty. I hadn't mentally prepared for this. I'd seen it plenty of times in porn and had been plenty curious. Intrigued even. But—

My thoughts were interrupted when Nash's hand tapped the inside of my thighs. "Spread them wider."

I swallowed hard as I followed instructions. "Okay."

Nash's calloused palm ran up my back, his lips up my spine. He stopped at my ear as he draped his heavy body over mine. "We don't have to do this. Just say the word. We don't do anything you don't want to."

"I want to," I said as I looked back over my shoulder. Nash wore a skeptical expression. "I do. Just you know, nervous."

And it was the truth. A mixture of nervousness and anticipation buzzed in my veins. Not having a single clue what I was doing, I rested everything completely in Nash's hands. I trusted him.

A soft kiss landed on my shoulder before his body heat pulled away. The mattress shifted behind me and then warm palms settled over my cheeks, pulling them apart. And then nothing.

Needing to see what was going on, I glanced back. Nash

had his eyes closed as he took deep inhales and slow exhales. "Nash," I whispered as doubt set in again.

His lids cracked open. "Sorry, almost came in my shorts."

He quirked a grin and my body relaxed. When he lowered his head, I whipped around to face the headboard. It was too much. I couldn't watch, and then it happened. One long exhale was all the warning I got before his tongue stroked straight over my hole. My mind went blank, and my chest fell to the mattress, leaving my butt in the air and completely exposed as a moan dripped from my lips.

Hands tightened around my hips to keep them in place and I cried out at the next exquisite swipe of his tongue. "Oh, god."

Nash answered with a series of toe-curling, languid passes from my taint up to my entrance over and over again. My dick throbbed, balls drew tight and cheeks clenched. "Nash!"

"Oh, hell yes. Say my name," he demanded and began licking me like I was the last meal he'd ever have.

His name tumbled from my lips as I tightly clenched the comforter between my fingers.

"You are fucking perfect. I could do this to you for hours." He reached between my thighs, under my stomach and jerked my dick. With his tongue he lashed out, setting my nerve endings on fire. When he stiffened his tongue and prodded my entrance, my dick pulsed and precome leaked onto his bed—a sticky mess that I was too far gone to care about.

"It's too much. I'm too close," I warned him and he pulled back, guiding me around to lie on my back again.

"What do you want? Tell me and I'll do it." His eyes

were wide and feverish. A powerful rush swept through me. I did that to him.

"I want to feel...you." I spread my legs wide and reached down to palm myself.

His jaw ticced and hands on my thighs squeezed. "Are you sure?"

Zero hesitation. I'd never wanted anything more in my life than to feel him inside me. "Yes, I'm ready."

Nash studied me more a moment before releasing his grip on my thighs. He reached over me and slid open the top drawer, retrieving a bottle of lube and a condom. The latter he tossed next to us on the bed. Just seeing it made my hole clench tight. *Okay, this is happening.*

He settled on his knees, those muscular thighs bulged between my slim legs. The sound of the cap being flicked open filled the quiet room and I squirmed. He slicked his fingers and brought them to my entrance.

"Breathe," he instructed as he circled the puckered flesh until I softened and then slid one fingertip inside me.

The uncomfortable sting was instant and my body stiffened as a hiss slid through my teeth.

"Relax," he coaxed and when I was ready, he slipped in cautiously until I'd taken it all. My muscles tightened around his finger and he took my dick in his other hand, stroking me, distracting me.

With his finger buried deep, he gave me time to adjust to the new sensation. His finger was so much larger than mine. I rolled my hips and gasped as the discomfort melted away. I needed more...something.

"I want..." I didn't know how to finish the thought and looked to Nash for answers.

He nodded, crooked his finger, and massaged a spot so

sensitive a string of unintelligible words flowed from my mouth.

In. Massage. Out. He repeated the motion until I couldn't hold still. The pressure increased as he added another finger alongside the first, gently stretching me. When a third finger joined, the burn was intense. His gaze flicked from my face down to where his fingers were buried in me. Fire blazed in his eyes and a wet spot formed on his shorts where his tip pressed against the fabric.

My mouth watered and the bite of pain ebbed, replaced with pure need. "I'm ready."

He looked conflicted, but when I began rocking my hips, riding his hand, Nash cursed and removed his fingers. I whimpered at the loss and his wild eyes roamed my face as he yanked at his shorts, cursing them when he struggled to kick them off. He reached for the condom and tore the wrapper with his teeth. He quickly rolled the rubber over his tip and down his shaft.

My eyes widened, locked onto his sheer size as he coated himself with lube. My view was stolen when he settled between my legs, propped one forearm beside my head and lined his tip to my entrance. I glanced up and met Nash's scalding gaze.

"Ready?" His legs and arms trembled as he held himself back.

"Yes." I tried to pull him to me but he resisted.

"It will probably hurt at first."

"I know, but I want it," I assured him and this time he didn't resist when I urged him forward, placing the slightest amount of pressure against my hole. My lungs froze up and he stared into my eyes.

"Breathe," he reminded me. And then he pushed.

My muscles clamped around him and Nash hung his

head as he shuddered. "Ren, relax, or I'm going to come and this will be over before it starts."

He wasn't even halfway in yet and I didn't know if I could take it. As if reading my thoughts, he dipped down and kissed me until I relaxed. Inch by inch he eased in farther into me, taking care to pause and let me adjust. He cursed into my mouth and I hissed and begged, caught between pleasure and pain.

When he was fully seated, I breathed a sigh of relief. I was full. So full...and restless. I tentatively shifted my hips, testing the new sensation.

Nash's eyes rolled back and he stilled my hips. "Don't. Move."

We lay quiet together, both breathing hard. He calmed and ran one hand over my cheek. "Still okay?"

"Yes, please move," I begged as I hooked one ankle behind his thigh.

He brought his other arm down, elbows on the bed on either side of my head, caging me in. And then he slid back before snapping his hips forward.

A full-body tremor traveled through me and my blunt nails dug into his biceps. I hadn't even come and it felt better than any orgasm I'd ever had. With Nash filling me so completely, eyes locked on mine, my body burned for him.

"Kiss me," I whispered and Nash's lips collided with mine.

FOURTEEN
NASH

RENDON WAS tight as hell as I continued to thrust into him, tangling my tongue around his. I'd never get enough of the way he tasted. Sweet and untouched—in that moment Rendon was mine.

I broke free from the kiss and rose to my knees. With both hands under his ass, I lifted his hips to change the angle. His eyes slammed closed as he raised his arms over his head, fingers curling tight around the black iron bars of my headboard.

The walls echoed with the sounds of unleashed cravings each time I hit the sensitive spot inside from the new position. His moans mixed with whispered chants of my name and the sound of skin slapping skin were driving me crazy. I wanted to make this good for him, but hell, my impending climax was teetering at the edge of a sharp cliff.

Rendon was perfect—everything I imagined and more. His hard cock jerked and bounced, leaking everywhere as pleas for more fell from his lips.

"Tell me what you want." I lifted one of his legs onto my shoulder and turned my head to nip at his soft skin.

"Touch me." Releasing one hand from the bar, he reached down and curled his fingers around his shaft.

I knocked his hand out of the way, replacing it with mine. Fist tight, smooth twists of my wrist on the upstroke and rubbing my thumb on the underside of his shaft beneath the head, I synced with the rhythm of my thrusts.

He grew restless and his hips jerked all over the damn place. He was losing control, which was making my orgasm harder to hold back. I pumped into him hard and redoubled my efforts on his cock.

I wanted to make him beg. Deny him until he was mindless. But being his first time, I also wanted him to be completely comfortable with me and I was too close to finding my release to play games. My balls drew tight and I ground my molars as I focused on him. He *would* come before me.

"Nash!" My name burst from his lips, splintered over a broken cry at the same time his cock erupted. I stroked him through his release, but every time I thought he was spent and I was free to empty my balls into him, another wave hit him and more streamed from his tip. *Holy shit.*

My fingers flexed around the grip I had on his ass while I took in the mess covering his chest, cock and my hand. And then I was falling right over that edge with a gravelly groan.

"So. Damn. Good." I punctuated each word with a thrust of my hips and slammed in one last time, stopping as deep as I could go and held still while my orgasm wrecked me. Wrecked. Me. Pulse after pulse, his grip on my cock was like a greedy vice, clenching as it dragged out every last drop come it could. Still, after I had nothing left, I was reluctant to separate from him. I pulled back only to ease back into him once more.

When my legs and arms were close to giving out, I lowered him back down to the mattress and hovered over him on arms that shook. My breaths were heaving in and out of my lungs as I gazed down at a blissed-out Ren.

"Wow," he whispered, giving me a lopsided smile. Rendon's bright green eyes were dazed behind his askew glasses.

Chuckling, I eased out of him. He winced and I rolled to my side, pulling him against me. "Okay?"

He nodded and curled in tighter. "Yeah, I think I just need to get used to your size. You're so big."

I hid a smile against the side of his face because he was killing me and probably didn't know that his words were dirty as fuck without meaning to be.

"You will," I assured him as I lifted his chin and kissed his lips, short and soft.

He latched on to the back of my head and kissed me back until we were both dizzy. When we parted, we were both panting.

"You are going to be the death of me." I grinned and reached around to knead his ass. "Let's go get cleaned up."

After helping him off the bed, I led us to the shower and washed us both beneath the hot spray. He tensed when I washed around his entrance, but relaxed as I kissed him. I loved that he let me take care of him and was surprised at how badly I wanted to make sure he was comfortable with me. I'd never been concerned about or attempted something so personal with anyone before.

Once clean, I turned off the shower and wrapped us each in oversized, navy towels. "Let's go crash."

Nearly dead on his feet, Rendon swayed as he followed me to my room. I flipped off the light and we dropped our towels on the floor before climbing into bed naked. His skin was chilled from the air conditioner so he wasted no time draping himself over me to warm up.

Skin against skin, I breathed a contented sigh followed by an exhausted yawn.

Despite waking up early to find that Rendon had snuck out sometime in the early hours, I was on fire and fully focused at practice. The ball sailing downfield was up for grabs between me and one of my teammates. With a longer reach and higher jump, I went up and got it, plucking another ball in a contested catch situation from the air and tucked it in close to my chest. The third of the day.

My teammate knocked his shoulder into mine and his lips curled into a half-grin. "Show-off."

"So, nothing new?" I raised a brow and mirrored his grin. He laughed and shoved me as we trotted to the back of the line of receivers.

Coach stood beside Memphis as he launched another long ball to the next pair of guys. He patted me on the back as I passed him before turning back to Memphis.

"Good." Coach nodded in approval to Memphis. "Now, do it again."

The rhythm of the familiar drills dragged me from wayward thoughts of the night before. And when we lined up against the defense to test our skills, I played better than I had in months. The burn in my muscles, smell of the turf and sweat, texture and weight of the football as I held on tight—it was what I lived for and hoped to be lucky enough to do for the rest of my life.

Only one thing in recent memory compared to the

exhilaration that came from a good practice or game. Rendon.

By the end of practice, Coach appeared pleased with his staff's adjustments and how we executed them.

Happy coach, happy life. That wasn't the exact saying, but for football players it was damn well true.

"Nice job, boys! Partner up and hit the weights. Upper body. Don't strain," Coach stressed. "And be ready for tomorrow." With that parting instruction, he walked off to the side of the field where his coaching staff stood in a huddle, and crossed his arms as they discussed strategies and areas that needed improvement.

Dismissed, we made our way back inside the practice facility. Once I stepped inside the air-conditioned building, I waved my practice jersey back and forth, attempting to cool off.

Shaw jogged beside me and slapped my shoulder as we crossed the indoor field. "On it today, huh?"

"You too." After ignoring me for days and then all but shoving me in the direction of Rendon's work, I wasn't sure what to expect from him anymore. He hadn't said much to me during yesterday's practice but hadn't gone out of his way to snub me either. "So, are you officially talking to me now?"

Shaw pursed his lips and his steps slowed. "I don't know what to do. You really like Rendon? Not like the others?"

"Nothing like the others." I matched his stride until we both came to a stop.

Shaw put his hands on his hips, gaze on the turf. "That's what I thought. You leave an older brother not knowing what to do, you know? If I hadn't seen you two together... The way you both act around each other—hell, especially you with your puppy dog eyes following him around and pouting when he doesn't give you enough attention—I don't think I would be handling this as well." He lifted his gaze back to mine, tight lines around his eyes. "So, I guess I was wrong and things went well the other night at Rendon's work... You know what, never mind."

Puppy dog eyes? My nose scrunched. I did not follow Rendon around with puppy dog eyes. Did I? No, he was nice to look at and I just wanted to be around him a lot. What was wrong with that?

"That's what big brothers do. We worry and I get it. My poor sisters are in for it." I hesitated. "But can you just let us be? Think you can do that?"

He shot me a wry grin. "Do I have a choice?"

"You do...but it won't change anything."

He groaned. "Why did you pick Rendon?"

"I didn't *pick* Rendon. Ever had a pull to someone that you couldn't ignore? No matter how bad you wanted to?" I looked over Shaw's shoulder and a hulking dark shadow appeared.

"That's not fair," he replied as Bishop silently took up the space on his other side.

"Life's not fair." I jogged off, calling over my shoulder, "But it turned out okay for you."

Comparing my relationship with Rendon to theirs might have been off base, considering they were completely different. But my comment on not being able to resist him stood. I couldn't.

When I entered the weight room, I sought out Memphis since we regularly partnered together. I approached the bench where he was lying down with his arms braced on the bar. Circling around the back, standing behind his head, I hovered my fingers beneath the bar to spot him. "Someone's impatient."

He glanced up and rolled his blue eyes. "This is me waiting. I've got plans tonight so I need to get through our sets."

"Plans?" I asked.

He gripped the bar tight. "Mom and Dad need me to run out to one of their vacancies. Newlyweds moving to town are interested."

Memphis's parents were real estate moguls. They flipped properties to rent and sell. To say Memphis came from money would be an understatement, though you'd never know based on his casual image with basketball shorts, worn t-shirts and general laid-back attitude. I'd never seen him once wear something fancy, and his truck was several years old and had more than a few scratches and dings.

"Backroading in high school," he'd explained offhandedly while giving a careless half-shrug. *"Why do I need a fancy new one?"*

Drove his parents crazy. That and the fact that he'd left a prestigious school to come back to Sugar Land where he'd grown up and had always wanted to go to college.

"Better you than me." I smirked as he huffed and raised the weights from the bracket and brought them down to his chest before pushing back up.

As he continued to lift, I forced myself to stay focused, counting his reps. My teammate needed my attention but thoughts of Rendon crept in anyway after talking with Shaw. Why was I always thinking about him? I thought for sure once I'd had him, the obsessive part would take a hike. But instead, I wanted more. More time to explore his body and I'd even enjoyed falling asleep with him tucked in beside me.

The bracket rattled as Memphis finished his set. He

sat up and stretched his back before running his hand through his damp brown hair. He paused as he studied my face.

"What? Do I have something on my face or do you just like what you see?" I taunted as we switched places.

"Hell no, you ugly fucker." He scowled before amusement twisted his lips as he took the stance behind my head to spot me. "Just noticed you're in a good mood."

"Why do you say that?" I reached up and grabbed the bar.

He hummed. "Stellar practice and you've been smiling like an idiot."

"I don't know what you're talking about." As I adjusted my hands on the bar, I fought a smile, but it crept across my face.

"You totally hooked up with Rendon," he accused with a devilish smile that caused his dimple to pop.

"Jesus, keep your voice down," I whisper-yelled and surveyed the room to see who may have overhead him.

He winced and lowered his voice. "Sorry, but you're not denying it?"

"It's none of your business and Shaw is like right there." I nodded my chin to a bench a few rows away. I'd told Shaw I was going after Rendon, and he'd likely come to his own conclusions after our conversation. But that didn't mean I wanted him to hear that I was sleeping with his brother for fuck's sake.

He followed my gaze and sighed. "Oh, right. So much for locker-room talk."

"We're not in the locker room. And whatever, I wouldn't tell you anyway."

Both brows rose as he scanned my face. "Then it must be serious."

Serious? I frowned as I considered his words, but... "No, it's not."

"Whatever you need to tell yourself." He scoffed, but a playful gleam lit in his blue eyes. "Now, let's get lifting. I have to get out of here as soon as possible."

He could rag on me about it all he wanted. Just because I didn't want everyone to know about what me and Rendon got up to in private, didn't make it *serious*. I just liked him. A lot.

Lifting the bar, I puffed my cheeks as the weight bore down on my arms and started my set.

FIFTEEN
RENDON

"DON'T THINK I didn't catch you sneaking in this morning." Tristan swept aside the long hair that covered one side of his head. His blue eyes glowed in the low-lit lecture room.

The white screen up front was lowered and a projector displayed a map of America showing the thirteen colonies before they broke away from Britain.

When I didn't respond, Tristan pinched my thigh. "So how was it?"

We were in the fifth row up so I elbowed him before the professor called us out for interrupting class. Thinking of my night with Nash made me squirm in my seat. In an effort to appear nonchalant and hide my fidgeting, I straightened the collar of my forest green shirt and smoothed a hand over my shorts.

"Oh, it's like that." He chuckled.

"Be quiet," I whispered back and shifted away in my seat to discourage him from probing at the topic I was still trying to process. It *was* like that.

It had been the best night of my life. Sex with Nash was

so much more than I could have ever imagined. I was glad I hadn't given up my virginity to some random guy I'd known for all of five minutes. But I found myself wanting to protect the details of what happened between us.

After I'd woken up to Nash's soft snores well before the sun was up, and baking beneath the covers trapped with Nash's body heat, I'd gotten up for water. All I'd wanted to do was go back and curl up against him. Everything felt right. Too right. It had been a little overwhelming, so I'd dressed and left, only realizing once I'd gotten back to the dorm that I'd likely overthought the situation.

"So, you did do something," Tristan stated with a thoughtful hum.

My cheeks heated. I hated that my emotions were so transparent thanks to the horrible blush that so easily spread across my skin.

"I knew it!" He bumped my shoulder. "Welcome to the club, my friend."

"I'm not talking about it with you."

"Oh, come on." He lowered his voice further. "It was amazing, right?"

Though I had no intention of telling him anything, I couldn't stop the small grin that tugged at my lips.

Tristan laughed and leaned back in his seat.

"Shut up," I mumbled with a sharp glance.

He lifted his hands in surrender but a satisfied smile stretched his cheeks.

I concentrated on the Professor as he spoke on about Virginia while selecting the colony with a laser-pointer aimed at the screen.

"You know who I think is superhot?" Tristan tapped his pen on the desk. "The quarterback, Memphis Hale. I've always had a thing for dark hair. Those blue eyes and that tall, lean body." He gave an exaggerated moan. "He even has fucking dimples, which I'm a sucker for. I would devour that."

He couldn't shut his mouth for more than a minute, but my curiosity was piqued. So I shifted to face him again. "One, you sound like an obsessed fan. Two, how do you know Memphis?"

"Well, I don't *know* him. But I saw him at the pool party, caught his name and I *might* have looked him up on social media."

"Stalker," I whispered as if shocked.

"Whatever. The guy didn't even look my way." He gave a half-shrug and spun the pen around on his desk. "Must be straight."

I had no idea whether Memphis had noticed him or not, but I didn't tell him that Memphis was into guys. How else would he have found me on that app? His role in Nash discovering my profile had been left out when I'd told him about Nash's proposition.

"Maybe," I agreed. A stab of guilt hit my stomach for the omission, but I didn't know Memphis well enough to share that information. For all I knew, he wasn't out and I didn't want to get Tristan's hopes up if Memphis wasn't interested.

"Too bad. That's okay though. He probably couldn't handle me anyway." Though his eyes lit up, his tone was all wrong. Defeated maybe.

Before I could ask what was bothering him, a chuckle replaced the hint of doubt that trickled through his voice. Maybe I had only imagined it. "So tomorrow we get to watch your boyfriend play. You ready to root him on?"

He switched topics so fast sometimes. It was hard to keep up.

"He's not my boyfriend, and you know it. Also, my parents are going to be there so you better be on your best behavior."

Tristan's hands flew to his chest and his voice rose an octave. "Moi? I'm always on my best behavior."

"Gentlemen." The professor's voice boomed, shifting our full attention to the front of the room. His eyes were narrowed right at me and Tristan. "I'm sorry my lecture is getting in the way of your important meeting. However, you can hold it until later or take it elsewhere." He indicated the door.

We both slumped low in our seats as he gave us one more pointed look and then turned back to the screen. I shot Tristan a dirty look and he winked, but thankfully kept quiet for the rest of class.

That night while Tristan went out on another *date*, I holed up in the dorm catching up on homework and studying. For once, I was thankful for the distraction. I had several chapters to read for US History and research to do for a paper I'd need to write soon for English. But Tristan's comment was messing with my ability to focus. *Boyfriend.* I shook my head and got back to work.

An hour later, as I was finishing a final passage in my History book, my phone buzzed with a text from Nash. *"Wear my number tomorrow."*

"Not happening. My parents will be there." And about a million other people.

"So if they weren't, you'd wear it?" He added a wink emoji and my lips curled up on one side.

"Night, Nash."

"Night, Ren."

The final quarter wound down as I sat in the stands with Tristan on one side of me and my parents on the other. We were decked out in Saints shirts, along with most of the fans sitting in our section. Even Tristan had opted to show some team spirit. Of course our t-shirts were mostly black so he gave them a big thumbs up.

Among the sea of black and gold attire, small sections were peppered with bright red and white, the Hawks colors.

With almost no breeze on the hot and humid day, we were roasting in the sun with no relief. But, for the most part, the gathered crowd was so caught up in the game that they didn't seem to mind.

The smells of hot dogs and nachos hung heavy in the air making my stomach growl. With plans to go out to eat after the game, I checked the scoreboard. The two-minute warning had been announced what felt like ages ago, but since both teams still possessed all three timeouts for the half, two minutes of playing time stretched much longer.

Our offense was on the field and I spotted my brother's and Nash's numbers lined up together on the same side of the field. They each faced opponents who rivaled their size and build.

Though I wasn't a major fan of the game, having a high school and college hot-shot football player as a brother, I knew more than I honestly cared to.

The details from seeing the game live on TV were missing from so far away, but there was something special about being there in the crowd as the Saints took over the game, leading by fourteen points.

The atmosphere was electric. Spectators screamed out for just about every call on any play, but my focus was on Nash. Throughout the game, I'd traced every one of his movements—his toned, long legs that carried him down the field, the way the muscles in his arms and calves flexed, and the formidable way he broke through tackles and stiff-armed the guys trying to take him down.

Nash had already claimed two touchdowns, my brother one, and the stout running back had barreled his way into the end zone twice.

I had to admit I was more into this game than any I'd previously attended.

"Am I the only one getting hot and bothered?" Tristan waved his hand over his face when I glanced at him. He must have completely reversed his position on jocks because he couldn't seem to get enough of them.

"The only thing I'm getting is possible heatstroke." There was no way I was admitting that I was seeing the sport in a new light now that I was intimately familiar with what lay beneath the jersey and pads of number thirty-four.

"Told ya you were boring."

"Sweating my butt off because of the crazy heat is boring?" I shielded my eyes from the sun with my hand when Memphis called for the ball and stepped back into the pocket, surrounded by players shielding him to the best of their ability. "Wait until the end of the season. We'll be freezing."

"I should have brought some sunglasses or, god forbid, worn a hat," Tristan complained.

"Truth," I agreed. The pass Memphis made was a throwaway since none of our guys were able to get open and one of the pass rushers was close to sacking him. "Do you even know what you're watching?"

I glanced over at him and he rolled his eyes.

"Football, duh." He followed the vague answer with a wink. He hadn't the slightest clue what was going on and had spent the first ten minutes of the game asking questions and gave up, claiming it was too complicated.

"Run, Shaw!" my mother screamed, and jumped to her feet as the arena broke out in chaos.

Having missed the beginning of the next play, I darted a look to the field and sprang up along with Tristan.

My dad cupped his hand around his mouth. "Show 'em how it's done, Wakefield!"

Shaw had the ball and was sprinting down the sideline with the ball tucked tight to his chest but was chased out of bounds at the five-yard line. The play was met with excitement and disappointment at being so close to a touchdown.

Taking my seat back, I watched as players ran off and onto the field, trading exhausted players for fresh ones.

"First and Goal." The announcer's voice echoed from the speakers.

Playing fast, they skipped the huddle, quickly lined up at the new line of scrimmage and Memphis gave the signal. The center hiked the ball and the Saints' and Hawks' front lines collided into each other in a clash of big bodies, fighting for dominance. Receivers ran in different directions. I didn't know where to look but easily singled out Nash. He angled for the corner of the end zone and stopped short, twisted around the defensive player covering him.

Memphis threw the ball and it was in Nash's hands before the other team could make a play for it.

Nash spun the ball on the ground and held up three fingers to show how many touchdowns he'd scored, and photographers ate up the pose.

Idiot. I rolled my eyes, but a small smile snuck up onto my face.

The rest of the offense joined him in the end zone and

postured for group pictures that would be all over the internet within hours.

"Yay, your boyfriend scored," Tristan said with all the enthusiasm of a joyless troll. "Now when do we get to go talk to the guys? It's over, right?"

"Shut up," I whisper-hissed. "My parents are right there. And for the last time, he's *not* my boyfriend."

Thankfully, my parents were caught up in the excitement as everyone watched the Saints' kicker drill one, dead center of the goal posts for the extra point. The final seconds of the game were purely a formality and the Saints fans were already celebrating. Nash's touchdown had shut down the possibility of a rare successful onside kick and even more rare perfect Hail Mary. The Hawks couldn't win.

Tristan's lowered voice was nearly drowned out when the clock ran out and the two teams met in the middle of the field. "Keep telling yourself that."

"Whatever. My butt hurts." Standing up, I stretched. The unforgiving seats were brutal and I'd left my seat cushion behind at home. I'd have to ask my parents to bring it next time. "And yes, all that noise means the game's over."

"Sounds the same as it has the whole time. So, we won! Go Saints!" When Tristan stood, he winced. "Seriously, my boney ass was not up for that."

"Tristan," my mom scolded with a raised brow, and Tristan's eyes widened.

"My boney *butt*, ma'am."

She wrinkled her nose, eyes sparkling. "Only teasing."

Tristan pretended to wipe sweat from his forehead as if relieved and grimaced, eyeing his hand with disgust, when he realized he'd actually succeeded.

"Are we hanging out to wait on Shaw, or is he meeting

us at the restaurant?" I asked my parents as I glanced around. Reporters, players and staff flooded the field and I had no idea how long it would take Shaw to finish up. The crowd had already started leaving the stands, filing out in long lines, but we hung back.

"Waiting," Mom answered, distracted as she dug around in her purse, retrieved her phone and tapped out a message. "I'm letting Shaw know now."

"Where are we eating?" I asked and wrapped my arm around my stomach as a sharp hunger pang reminded me how long it had been since breakfast. I should have taken the hit to my wallet and ordered nachos.

"Thought we'd visit the steakhouse up the road. Sound good?" Mom beamed.

The urge to ask if they could afford it sat at the tip of my tongue, but I swallowed the question. "Sounds great."

"Tristan, would you like to join us?" she asked.

Tristan grinned and rubbed his flat stomach. "Yes, please. Thanks, Mrs. W."

My parents and Tristan had hit it off immediately when we'd joined the line to claim our complimentary tickets hours ago. Especially because he and I had forgone the student section so I could sit with them.

My mom shot him a pleased smile.

When the rush of people leaving the stands slowed, we stood at the end of the aisle until an opening in the line allowed us to merge into it. Dad led the way out of the stadium, and when we finally made it to the parking lot, we loitered, along with several other groups of people, by the door the players would eventually exit.

Shaw strolled through the door first, followed by Bishop. Their hair was still damp from the shower and they had changed into comfortable shorts, t-shirts and tennis shoes.

My brother jogged over and scooped up Mom into a hug.

"I bet it feels good to get out of those pads and cleaned up. You two played so well." She pecked Shaw on the cheek.

"Thanks, Mom. I'm glad you both made it." Shaw released her, gave Dad a hug and then ruffled my hair.

"Stop doing that," I griped, trying to finger comb it back into place. Tristan helped.

"Don't mess with your brother," Mom scolded Shaw with a traitorous twinkle in her eyes. "Your dad and I wanted to take you boys to dinner. Up for steak?"

Shaw's lips parted and then closed. The same question I'd pondered seemed to hover over them as he shot me a confused look. Rather than kill the mood, he smiled. "That sounds amazing."

Just then Nash stepped through the door and like a magnet, we locked eyes. His gaze roamed in lazy sweeps over my body and he bit his lip.

As the familiar heat rose to my skin, I balled my fist and attempted to ignore the way my body reacted to him.

Tristan whistled low and whispered, "You are so on that menu tonight."

"Don't start," I whispered back.

Nash brushed his arm against mine as he stopped next to my family, or rather next to me. Tingles rushed over the spot he rubbed and I took a deep inhale. He smelled of clean soap and the citrus cologne he wore.

"Nash!" my mom squealed. "You were incredible out there."

My dad patted him on the back. "You and my boy looked like stars today. Nice job."

"Thank you both." He bowed his head, a humble gesture that almost made me snort.

With my gaze glued to Nash, I didn't notice Memphis when he came through the door until Tristan grabbed my elbow. "O.M.G. Quick, how's my eyeliner?"

My gaze flicked to the quarterback and with a heavy sigh, I reached out and rubbed away a smudge under Tristan's eye.

When Memphis simply waved at our group as he strolled by, Tristan jutted out his bottom lip. "Definitely straight."

"We're heading to the steakhouse up the road. Feel like tagging along?" My dad's voice drew my attention. The question was pointed at Nash and I groaned under my breath. How was I supposed to keep secret what I had going on with Nash when being around him turned me into a blushing idiot?

As if sensing my thoughts, Nash hesitated, darted a glance at me and then back to my parents. "Sure, I mean, if it's not a problem."

"Of course it's not." My mom stuck her finger in the air, twirling it like a lasso. "Let's get this show on the road, but we can't all fit in my car."

"Rendon can ride with me. Tristan too," Nash blurted at the same time Shaw replied with, "I'll ride with Bishop."

Thanks to the too-quick suggestion by Nash, my parents paused and levelled a confused look my way, and then Nash's. My mom's brow furrowed as she tilted her head, an assessing look in his eyes as she studied the two of us. "Are you two—"

"Have you tried their ribeye, Ren? Almost the best meat

around," Tristan interrupted with a wink. Not only had he saved me the need to lie to everyone, he of course had to throw an innuendo in there.

"Seriously?" I mouthed silently. But out loud I said, "I haven't actually, but maybe today."

"Good call." He smirked.

Though my mom eyed me carefully, my dad seemed to let it go as he checked his phone before announcing we'd better head out due to their long drive home.

I chanced a glance at my brother and his boyfriend. Neither appeared fazed by Nash's over-the-top offer to drive me and Tristan which surprised me. Both were aware Nash and I had history, and after the party at their place, Bishop had to at least suspect something was going on between Nash and me and had likely told Shaw. If he had, Shaw hadn't mentioned it to me. But my parents were completely in the dark.

Promising myself to get back at Nash for putting me in a tough spot, on purpose or not, I took a step back, and then another. "Okay, well I guess we'll see everyone there."

Mom pursed her lips and finally nodded before she and my dad walked away, whispering to each other.

"Well, that wasn't weird." Tristan snorted as we crossed the parking lot to Nash's truck.

"Thanks for the save, but was the innuendo necessary?" I asked as Nash opened the passenger side doors.

"Innuendo is always appropriate," Tristan said then climbed in the back, leaving me staring at the back of his head.

"He's *your* roommate," Nash said with humor dancing in his eyes.

"He's impossible," I grumbled and stepped onto the running board to take my seat up front. Nash swatted my butt and I glared through the windshield as he rounded the hood and hopped behind the wheel.

He met my narrowed eyes with a lopsided grin. "What? You have a nice ass."

Tristan's laughter filled the cab and I fought the urge to cover my flaming cheeks.

SIXTEEN
NASH

EACH TIME the door to the restaurant opened, the scent of grilled steaks and spices tickled my nose and my mouth watered. After I'd told Shaw to pick something for me off the menu, the rest of our group had gone inside. But I hung back on the sidewalk under the shade of a large oak tree that provided some relief from the blazing mid-afternoon sun with my phone pressed to my ear.

"Hell of a game." My dad's scratchy voice came through the receiver.

"The Hawks made us work for the win for sure. How you feelin'?"

Even though I visited as often as I could, it wasn't enough. Thankfully, my mother worked as a computer programmer for a large corporation that allowed her to work from home. She had moved her high-rise office to the house years ago so she could tend to my dad on the frequent bad days when his joints refused to cooperate and help him through the never-ending battles with Rheumatoid Arthritis, an autoimmune illness that caused his own immune system to attack his joints, internal organs, eyes, heart and blood vessels. With varying degrees of the disease possible, he'd been diagnosed with the worst.

Once an active, lively man he'd grown tired and was in constant pain. The drugs used to battle the progression only slowed the damage and weren't a cure. When he'd lost the ability to do manual labor, he began running admin for his landscaping business from home.

Behind my parents' back, I'd applied to a local community college without a football program after high school so I could be of more help. But after my acceptance letter came in from Sugar Land, Dad had told me in no uncertain terms that I was going. Mom had pulled me aside, telling me the guilt would eat Dad alive if I stayed. That didn't mean I didn't question my decision from time to time.

"Not a bad day," he assured me as the familiar sound of a wooden rocking chair on the back deck creaked in the background. He spent a great deal of his time outside watching boaters speeding across the large lake behind our home.

"What are you boys doing to celebrate?"

A group of women filed down the walkway and I stepped out of their path, raising my hand to shadow my eyes against the harsh rays. "I'm out to eat now with the Wakefields, but no clue what's going on after."

"Well, stay out of trouble." He chuckled then paused. "Nash, I'm super proud of you."

My chest tightened. "Thanks, Pops."

"All right, here's your mother."

"You always were a showoff." The first words out of her mouth made me chuckle as I reclaimed my space beneath the protective canopy of leaves. Though she'd spent her entire life in Texas, growing up living next door to my great-grandparents who spoke in heavily-accented Jamaican

Patois had rubbed off on her and a trace of that same accent slipped through.

"Who me?"

She scoffed. "Don't try to fool me, boy. You've always known you were talented." Her voice lowered to a whisper and pride saturated her tone. "You're going to go so far."

Though my parents rarely made it to games due to my dad's health, they were my absolute biggest supporters. Had been since I was in pee-wee ball and my dad had been my coach.

"You're feeding my ego," I warned.

"Boy, your ego doesn't know how to take a hit."

My shoulders shook as I held back a laugh. "That's not very nice."

"I raised you to be honest. What kind of example would I be setting if I wasn't?" she said and my dad laughed in the background, a gravelly booming sound that I missed.

Shaking my head at the two of them even though they couldn't see me, my lips curled up on one side. "I love you, Mom."

"I know you do, baby. I love you too and can't wait to see you at Thanksgiving. It seems like such a long time away."

We could agree on that. "I can't wait either. Tell Dad and the girls I love them."

"I will. Talk soon." She smacked a kiss into the phone and I hit end on the call before making my way to the entrance of the steakhouse and through the heavy door.

The hostess looked to be around my age, probably a student. She greeted me with a smile and raked an appreciative gaze over my body that made me uncomfortable. I'd never shied away from a little flirtation before, but lately it wasn't the same. When I cleared my throat, she tore her gaze away. "Do you have a reservation?"

"No, I'm looking for my group."

She nodded and flipped a page on top of the hostess stand she stood behind. "Name?"

Not a Saints fan then at least.

"Nash." My gaze swung around the restaurant but because of all the partitions, I couldn't find them.

After a moment, the girl glanced up. "They left a note. Follow me."

I trailed behind her as she led me through the packed restaurant, between the tables and booths brimming with people wearing Saints and Hawks fan gear—typical for game day. The deeper we worked our way into the crowd, the higher the noise level rose.

Because of my size and likely recognition from televised games, several sets of eyes stared at me as we snaked through the crammed room. Hearing my name along with Shaw's and Bishop's among the conversations, confirmed we'd been recognized. I could only hope no one approached us while we spent time with Rendon and Shaw's family.

When we made it to the table where the rest of my party sat, everyone glanced up and I shared a look with Bishop then Shaw. There was a reason we rarely went out to public venues on game days.

Without thought, I sought out Rendon, and he bit his bottom lip. My gaze latched on to the movement and everything around me faded away. And though the timing was awful, my cock stirred. I wanted him again. Now. In my bed, stripped bare, ass in the air as I buried my tongue deep in his hole.

If it weren't rude, I'd blow off this dinner, carry him back to my truck, drive straight to my place and make him come so hard he—

"Nash," Shaw barked. "Dude, sit down."

Grinning at Rendon, I shook free of the dirty thoughts. Wrong place, wrong time, I reminded myself.

Pulling back the chair, I took the empty seat next to Shaw and across from Rendon. Before I had time to utter a single word, a waiter unfolded a stand next to our table and placed a large tray on top. Behind him another man with a white apron over black attire parked a second tray. Dishes were passed around and my stomach rumbled as a plate loaded with a steak and sides of mashed potatoes and grilled asparagus was pushed in front of me.

"I'm starving," Shaw echoed my thoughts.

After the waiters left us, we all wasted no time digging in. I watched Rendon as he ate and he seemed to be having the same struggle as he kept glancing up at me. Inching my foot across the wood flooring, I hoped like hell it was his and not Tristan's ankle I hooked my foot around. Rendon's fork stopped halfway to his mouth as he let me draw his leg toward me until we sat with them resting together. I don't know why I'd done it, only that I wanted to touch him in some way.

Shaw shoved his phone in front of my face, forcing me to read a post on social media about a celebratory party for the Saints hosted at one of the frat houses on campus. I considered whether I wanted to go and finally nodded in silent agreement. I didn't have to stay long, but all the players needed to show appreciation for our supporters. And the guys needed to cut loose once in a while. But I was hoping Rendon would be up for staying over again and spending tomorrow together since I was free from all football obligations.

Mrs. Wakefield was talking to Shaw about finishing up his degree in journalism this year. And Rendon's dad and Bishop were busy talking about cars. Thanks to the loud chatter around us, only tidbits of conversation broke through, but I discovered he was a mechanic and thought Bishop's car was a dream.

I was glad they were all involved in their own discussions because my attention was elsewhere. I pulled my phone from my pocket and texted Rendon.

"We are going to a party after."

He stopped eating and pulled his phone from his pocket, frowning when he read it. He only tapped his screen a few times and rested his phone on the tabletop.

My phone buzzed. *"Have fun."*

"You're going too."

He didn't glance at me when he picked up his phone. *"Says who?"*

After I read the message, I jerked my head up and met Rendon's challenging stare. He arched a brow.

Under the table I roughly tugged his leg closer to me. *"Says me."*

Shaw shifted next to me and I glanced over at him. His eyes were narrowed and swung from me to Rendon. He sighed and went back to eating. I fired off another message. *"I think Shaw's onto us."*

Though I'd been referring to Shaw suspecting we were texting each other, it brought the conversation I'd had with him at practice to mind. I needed to tell Rendon about it. I didn't know how Rendon would feel about Shaw assuming we were dating. Though Shaw hadn't used that specific word, he definitely didn't know what was really going on between Rendon and me.

Hell, I wasn't sure *I* knew what was going on between us anymore.

My phone vibrated against my palm again. *"Ya think?*

We are sitting across from each other texting. It's actually kind of weird."

A laugh burst from between my lips, drawing quizzical looks. Thinking fast, I gave a half-shrug. "Sorry, thought of something that happened today."

"What happened?" Shaw asked with a smirk, knowing damn well it had been an excuse. Ass.

I glanced at Bishop for help.

He rubbed his temples, his normal unflappable expression appearing uncomfortable. Bishop gave Shaw a meaningful look and forced an awkward smile. "You know, the thing that happened at practice."

Well, he wouldn't be winning any acting awards anytime soon.

"Oh, lord," Tristan muttered before shoving a massive piece of bread in his mouth, filling his cheeks like a chipmunk.

Rendon's parents simply accepted Bishop's flimsy explanation. His mom went back to keeping conversation flowing and his dad began sawing at his medium-rare steak again.

After shooting me a wink, Shaw shoveled food into his big, annoying mouth. Good, it should keep him quiet.

Ignoring the chatter around us, I dipped my head again, focusing on convincing Rendon to go with me. *"Say you'll come. And then I'll make you come after."*

Rendon choked and I glanced at him in concern as Tristan patted his back, never pausing as he tore into another roll.

Tristan dropped his hand when Rendon cleared his throat. *"My curiosity is satisfied. I think I'm good."*

"You're a liar." We peeked up at the same time and

shared a secret smile before I went back to our messages.
"Want me to pick you up?"

"I don't know if I'm going. I'll think about it."

"You want me to beg?" I snuck a look at him to catch his reaction.

Rendon's pink tongue darted out to wet his lips before he turned off his phone and pushed his plate away. "I'm stuffed."

He'd barely knocked out half of the food on his plate.

Everyone mumbled agreements and after the bill was paid, Mrs. Wakefield cleared her throat and waited until she had our undivided attention.

"We have some exciting news. Boys, we wanted to take you all out today to celebrate because... Well, I don't know if you're aware, but we haven't had a lavish lifestyle. My sons had to work hard to get to where they are now and we couldn't be prouder." Her voice cracked. "But we are celebrating two things today! Obviously, your win. But also your dad"—she looked at Shaw and Rendon—"after working twenty years at the shop, finally got a promotion!"

"What?" Shaw sat up straight and faced his dad. "Really? I thought Old Man Watson said he'd never open a manager spot, so what did you get promoted to?"

Mr. Wakefield beamed, creases around his eyes and mouth. "Apparently the old codger changed his mind. You're looking at the new manager right now, kiddo."

"That's awesome, Dad!" Rendon got up from his chair and circled the table, leaning in to give him a hug.

Feeling like I was watching something private as Rendon and his dad wrapped their arms around each other, I turned my head and met Bishop's eyes. There was an uncomfortable gleam in his eye as Shaw huddled into his side.

"It's crazy." Shaw's voice lowered, but seated right next to him it was impossible not to eavesdrop, not that I was trying to avoid it. "We were just talking about this over the weekend. My dad would *not* leave that job even though he was underappreciated and his boss took advantage of his loyalty. He deserved this after..." he trailed off before shooting a sharp glance at Bishop. His words were barely a whisper. "Did you do this?"

Curious I watched the exchange. When Bishop only stared at Shaw, shoulders tensed as if waiting for the blow, it became obvious the rich fucker *had* made this happen. My lips curled up on one side.

Instead of whatever Bishop had expected, Shaw buried his face against his chest and his words came out muffled. "You are everything. You know that?"

Well shit. Now, I was uncomfortable and couldn't watch anymore. Thankfully Rendon chose that moment to reclaim his seat and picked up his phone.

"Congrats, Mr. Wakefield," I offered and a proud grin crossed his face. His mom had fucking tears in her eyes. I knew Rendon and Shaw were scholarship students and even knew they had little money, but shit, I didn't know they were struggling that hard. Even I had a lump in my damn throat. Though I wouldn't admit it if asked.

My phone buzzed on the table. *"Pretty sure my dad didn't see, but Bishop did this, didn't he?"*

I glanced up and hesitated, wondering if I should admit what I heard. In the end, I nodded.

Rendon darted a quick look in Bishop's direction with a glint of gratitude in his eyes before turning back to me. *"He's like a giant teddy bear."*

A laugh tried to burst from my chest but I buried it with a cough. *"Sure, a giant grizzly one."*

Tristan who had been silent spoke up. "Mr. W., does this mean I get free car work now?"

Mr. Wakefield laughed. "Unless I want to lose the position, I'm thinking I better hold off on that."

While they bantered back and forth, I tapped another message to Rendon. *"Don't think all this gets you out of going to the party."*

"Mood killer," he accused.

My grin was devilish when I looked up. *"I know how to get you in the mood."*

He rolled his eyes when I looked up but a slight pink stain colored his cheeks.

"Um, guys?" Tristan stood at the side of the table with a hand on each of our shoulders and squeezed. "Everyone else is standing up ready to leave. Feel free to join us."

We both jerked back and stood quickly. Not suspicious at all. No one called us out on it and we followed in a line out to the parking lot.

After their family passed around hugs, we all parted ways, Rendon and Tristan back in my truck.

Tristan spoke up once we pulled out onto the service road. "I've never eaten with two people sexting so close to me. That was kind of hot. Except for the part when you almost killed my roommate. I can see the headlines now." He held his hands up as if framing the article title. "Nash Sterling, Sugar Land Saints Wide Receiver Causes Death by Baked Potato and Sexting".

From the passenger seat, Rendon groaned. "We were not *sexting*."

My brow rose and from the corner of my eye I noticed Rendon stiffen. Though I had a pretty good idea Tristan was aware of what we were getting up to, Rendon had never confirmed it and I'd never asked. It hadn't even crossed my mind to be concerned. "Why would he think we were *sexting?*"

He fiddled with the hem of his shirt. "Did I not mention I might have told him...everything?"

"You didn't." Reaching over, I loosened his fingers from his shirt before he destroyed it.

"Are you mad?" he whispered. "I wasn't trying to hide it. I just hadn't thought about it and...needed advice."

Lacing my fingers through his, I squeezed. "Not mad. In fact, maybe I should thank him."

"Good lord," Tristan mumbled. "Even if he hadn't, I'd have figured it out. I mean if you two were dating, everyone would know. You two wouldn't be playing secret footsie under the table and"—he leaned forward and flicked my ear—"you did brush against my foot, you know. I could have gotten the wrong idea."

"Tristan," Rendon hissed and Tristan fell back against his seat.

Lips pressed together, I bit back a laugh. "My bad."

"And you guys are terrible at keeping shit secret," Tristan continued. "I'm guessing everyone thinks you two are dating."

Shit, that reminded me to tell Rendon about the run-in with his brother. "Shaw approached me at practice. He thinks we *are* dating. Or at least headed in that direction."

"What?" Rendon's voice was shrill and grating.

"Hey, calm down. What was I supposed to say?" I asked as we rolled up to a red light then turned faced him. "I mean he didn't say *dating*, but obviously my nuts are intact...so..."

"I bet they are and totally..." Tristan groaned. Rendon freed his hand from mine and reached behind the seat.

There was a thud and Tristan grunted. "Fuck, I was only kidding. Jeez."

Rendon spun back around with a huff. "Well, that explains why Shaw didn't seem surprised that you informed everyone I was riding with you. Could you have been more obvious? *Rendon's riding with me.*" He deepened his voice and attempted to mock me.

"That's not what I said," I argued.

He rolled his eyes. "I'll deal with Shaw if it comes to it, and that means Bishop thinks that too." Rendon groaned. "This is getting ridiculous. Does Memphis know?"

"He thinks the same thing as your brother and Bishop, I guess. I haven't really told him anything, but he guessed *something* was going on."

"What?" His brow scrunched in confusion. "How?"

I wasn't about to tell him that apparently my actions had given me away. Puppy dog eyes and smiling like an idiot, they'd said. I scowled. Fuckers.

Instead I said, "Would that bother you if he knew the truth?"

All this talk about how Rendon and I were only hooking up soured my stomach and my lips fell flat. But it was the truth, wasn't it?

When I looked at Rendon, the words rang false. My gaze traced the contours of his face—the lips I couldn't get enough of, the bright eyes that drew me in and his skin I always wanted to touch. It was more than that to me. Maybe always had been. Struck hard by the realization, my fingers tightened around the steering wheel.

"I don't know. I guess not. As long as Memphis doesn't tell Shaw," Rendon said as he brushed the hair away from his forehead.

His words bounced around my mind until they settled, reminding me that while I was a mass of uncertainty, Rendon had a grasp on what he wanted and it didn't involve anything more from me than what I could give him between the sheets. I spoke around the tightening in my throat. "He wouldn't".

Memphis wouldn't breathe a word, but I wasn't sure how he'd react when he'd already made clear that going after Rendon was already a risky move.

Pushing through the unease tightening my chest, I glanced at Tristan in the back seat. "There's a party tonight. Make sure Rendon's there."

"What am I? Your personal assistant?" Tristan scoffed.

Shrugging, I feigned nonchalance and returned my attention back to the road. "Or don't. I know lots of guys will be there. Even Memphis."

"Wait a minute," Tristan rushed on. "I've reconsidered."

Grateful for the reprieve from the downward turn of spiraling thoughts, I pressed my lips together, humming while I pretended to think it over.

Tristan was hot for Memphis. It was obvious to me since Tristan couldn't take his eyes off him at the pool party. And when Memphis left the stadium earlier, I'd overheard his squeal to Rendon and a panicked possible crisis about his eyeliner.

Because Memphis seemed attuned to everyone else's life, it always surprised me how oblivious he was of his own. He was likely unaware of Tristan's attention—or at least he hadn't mentioned it to me—and was still in the closet which meant I couldn't tell Tristan anything. Memphis might not even know what to do with a guy like Tristan. The thought made me chuckle under my breath and I squinted at him in the rearview mirror. "So, you'll convince him?"

Tristan saluted me and adopted a serious tone. "I will have him there."

Rendon grumbled to himself. "I love how you both talk about me as if I'm not sitting right here."

"If you'd just agree, I wouldn't have to ask your roommate to persuade you." The light turned green and I took a left to head back to campus.

From the corner of my eye, I noticed Rendon crossing his arms and slumping in his seat. "Fine, I'll go."

"You won't be disappointed."

"Can I bring a friend?" Tristan asked. "You know, for when Rendon ditches me for you."

"I wouldn't do that." Rendon sat up and looked over the seat.

Tristan let out an exaggerated sigh. "That's the problem. You really wouldn't, but you should. If a certain someone wanted to drag me to a darkened corner and have his way with me, your ass would be flying solo."

"Liar," Rendon accused and Tristan laughed.

"You can bring whoever you want," I cut in.

Pulling up to the curb near the entrance of their building, we said our goodbyes and I waited for them to climb out, watching until they were safely inside.

While I drove back to my place, I was already wondering how long I'd have to stay at the party. I popped open my center console and stuck a sucker in my mouth. Rendon had no idea what the night held in store and I needed to reset. My earlier thoughts had left me shaken but it didn't change what was between Rendon and me. And I planned to enjoy every inch of that body for as long as I could.

Sigma Chi was famous around campus for throwing the biggest, wildest parties. The house was dim, lit only with strings of clear Christmas lights draped along the wall that highlighted the streamers of black and gold littering the room. Any and all surfaces were Saints themed, probably decorated by the president's girlfriend and her sorority sisters.

The lower floor was packed with students dancing to the loud, thumping music. Body shots and open make out sessions were typical, and this party was no exception.

Memphis and I hung back in the dining room, leaning against the wall where I had a clear shot of the front door. Normally I'd have been crushed in the center of writhing bodies, but that didn't sound appealing. If anything, I'd rather go home than get involved with that.

I'd chosen to wear a new navy v-neck t-shirt and a pair of stone-washed jeans that hugged my body tight, and regretted it. When I'd picked the outfit, I'd had Rendon in mind. I knew my ass looked great in denim, but my dick and balls were uncomfortably cramped. The minute I escaped this place I was exchanging them for my usual attire that gave my boys room to breathe.

Of course, the other option was to strip naked, which I intended to do once I got Rendon alone anyway.

Memphis leaned close enough to be heard. "Did you see any scouts today?"

"No, I figured since we didn't see them in practice last week, they'll be around sometime soon. Maybe this week."

"Nervous?"

"I try not to think about it. If I do, I'm liable to screw up." Thinking about scouts was the last thing I wanted on my mind. There was only a small window they were permitted to study us like lab rats during practice and even smaller when they were allowed to actually check out the games. The added pressure of being aware of them scrutinizing my every mood was intense.

"You got this." He held his beer out and I clinked my bottle to his.

Deflection was my go-to any time scouts were brought up so I switched topics. "Whatever doubts anyone had of you as a QB were squashed today."

He grinned, blue eyes shining. "Thanks, man."

"You earned it."

I once against focused on the front door, waiting for Rendon. He hadn't returned my text when I asked what time he'd be at the party. I'd only arrived fifteen minutes ago, and already worried he'd blow me off. I swore he did that shit on purpose to fluster me and second-guess if he'd even show. It was working. Maybe he'd figured out how much power he held over me, not that I cared. I hadn't tried to hide it but hadn't voiced it either.

Memphis snapped his fingers in front of my face. "Who are you waiting for?"

Giving him a quick glance, I lifted one shoulder. "Expecting a friend."

"Ah," he said. "Shaw's little bro?"

"He has a name." Rendon hated being saddled with that title. Hell, I would too. Intending to intercept him the moment he stepped inside, I faced the door again.

"I don't even know why I asked." Memphis chuckled. "You're screwed, aren't you? Completely wrapped around his little finger."

My interest in him wasn't a secret, but admitting out loud how much I craved him was hard and caused me to hesitate. Was it still an obsession? An addiction? I didn't know anymore. But I did know I wanted him around all the time. If my hands were all over him each time he was within reach, it didn't take away that simply lying together in bed had felt right, and I wouldn't mind falling asleep like that more often.

Since I couldn't tell Rendon or anyone else, maybe confessing to Memphis would help. I sighed and scrubbed my free hand over my face before meeting his eyes. "You know I am. Quit pretending you don't."

"I can't say anything about wanting someone even when it's a dumb idea." Memphis took a long pull from his beer.

Memphis had crushed on Shaw over the summer but easily moved on once he realized he was off the market. He had no trouble finding interested guys and girls, though he kept that info locked down tight. As far as I knew, I was the only one who was aware he swung both ways. He'd entrusted me with that secret and I had no intention of sharing it.

"Yeah," I agreed. "It sucks that he's a teammate's brother. But if he wasn't, it's possible I wouldn't have even met him."

"Are you two officially a thing now?" he asked.

Though Rendon had said it would be okay to tell Memphis the truth, I waffled on whether to come clean. With a cautious glance in his direction, I hedged, "Not exactly."

He paused with his beer pressed to his lips and shot me a confused look. Understanding appeared to dawn on him as he lowered the bottle and he grimaced. "Aw, man don't tell me you're just fucking around with him."

"Fine, I won't." Wasn't even sure I could say that and mean it.

"Fuck." He rubbed his temples. "And if Shaw finds out?"

"Shaw thinks we're dating or talking...whatever," I muttered. "He didn't say those exact words but... He caught up to me at practice and I think he sort of gave me his blessing for us to date. Not that he was thrilled." Which not only shocked me, but left a stab of guilt behind.

Memphis tipped his head back against the wall. "Don't know why I didn't see this coming or I wouldn't have encouraged your dumb ass." He lifted his head and held my gaze. "I'll say it again...just be careful. This season means a lot to both you and Shaw. Hell, the whole team. Other guys are NFL prospects. You know?"

I nodded. "We will be. But this is going to be harder than I thought."

"How so?" He eyed me quizzically. "You actually worried Shaw will find out you two are just fucking?"

"Well, it's more complicated than that." The forceful words took us both by surprised. His eyes widened and I imagined my looked the same. "But yeah, he'd see it the same way."

"You sure that's all there is between you two?" Memphis squinted.

I studied my bottle and peeled at the label. "Honestly? I don't know. I'm confused, I guess. I mean..." What was I supposed to say? Rendon was a virgin and had been basically looking online for some stranger to remedy the situation, although honestly, I wasn't sure he would have gone through with it. So I volunteered to be his sex slave and helped him get rid of that pesky V-card. But that backfired and Rendon was now calling the shots because there wasn't much I wouldn't do for him?

His next words were almost drowned out by the blaring music. "You like him. You really want to be with him."

Why did Memphis have to be so damn perceptive? "I've

always really liked him, but you know me. What business did I have trying to date the guy?"

"Past tense." He tapped his fingers against his beer. "Interesting."

"Well, whatever. Even if I wanted to take things a step further, he's not into me like that and I'm fine with the way things are."

"We'll see about that." He pointed his bottle toward the front door. "You're about to miss his grand entrance."

He laughed when my gaze jerked toward the door. Rendon took slow steps across the foyer, followed by Tristan and then a guy with a head of spiked blond hair and decked out in black clothes brought up the end of their group.

Cute as hell, Rendon wore a black, short-sleeved button up shirt paired with gray shorts. His hair was windblown and his glasses perched on his scrunched nose as he scoped out his surroundings. I couldn't take my eyes off him as a lightness filled my chest. Did he even own a single t-shirt?

Rendon continued to survey the room and I knew he was looking for me. Change of plans. He should have answered my texts. I stepped back into the shadowed corner that still allowed me to watch him.

Memphis tilted his head and his forehead creased. "What are you doing?"

Instead of answering him, I waggled my brows.

Memphis's lips twitched and he waved me away. But he shouted, "Catch you later, Nash."

Scowling, I refocused on Rendon. He hadn't seemed to hear Memphis—the jerk—and dug in his pocket, pulling out his phone. He tapped at the screen and my phone buzzed against my thigh. With a laugh on my lips, I retrieved it and brought up the message.

"I'm here. Did you make it already?"

"Yes."

His brows drew together and he glanced up again, scanning the room before refocusing back on the screen.

"Where?"

"Can you ditch your friends?" Tristan had given his blessing but I had no way of knowing what they'd talked about once they'd gotten home.

Rendon faced Tristan and the new guy so I could no longer see his face. Tristan rolled his eyes but smirked before physically pushing Rendon away. Both short, Tristan and his guest, whoever he was, disappeared in the crowd.

Leaning against the wall, I crossed my ankles in front of me. *"Turn left and follow along the wall."*

"Nash!" A high-pitched squeal pricked my ears just before a body slammed into my side, nearly knocking us both on our asses. I uncrossed my legs to catch myself and glanced down at a brunette with too much shiny lip gloss and brown eyes surrounded by false lashes—I knew because one was peeling off. She wobbled on spiked heels and her hands slipped onto my torso as she used me to steady herself. In the process she got handsy, walking her fingers up my chest as she gave me a flirty smile that came off sloppy. Her top barely contained her large tits, short skirt barely covered her ass and she smelled like she'd had five too many drinks. Alcohol practically seeped from her pores.

"Sorry. Do I know you?" I gripped her arms, pressing her back several steps.

She batted her long black eyelashes. "You could. I've heard things about you." She pursed her lips and my body shuddered. Not in a good way.

"Listen, I'm expecting someone."

"I could be that someone." She leaned in closer and her

perfume that smelled like flowers mixed with alcohol suffocated me. Whose idea was it to come to this damn party?

"Actually, unless you have a dick and lose a few inches, dye your hair blond, gained some glasses and green eyes, you aren't him."

Someone cleared their throat and I glanced up. Rendon stood there with a furrowed brow as he glanced at the two of us.

"*No.* Rendon, it's not what it looks like." Holding my hands up as if guilty, I took a step away from the girl, creating more distance.

"I know. I heard you and I'm not stupid. You wouldn't ask me to come over just to see a girl pawing at you." He tilted his head and my chest swelled with the trust that showed in his eyes.

The girl straightened. "Him?" She eyed Rendon with thinly veiled jealousy. "You'd rather have him? Everyone knows you go both ways but I assumed it would be with someone like you. Like other hot guys."

"Only person I'm interested in right now is him, and he's hot as fuck. If you'll please excuse us." Reaching out, I grabbed Rendon's wrist and tugged him against me.

She gaped for a moment longer before teetering off, catching herself on a wall.

"Someone needs to give that girl a ride home. Give me a minute."

Rendon leaned into my side as I tapped out a message to Memphis since I trusted him to get her home safely instead of relying a bunch of drunk frat boys to take care of it. Despite being a pain sometimes, Memphis was the kind of guy that looked out for others. It wouldn't be the first time either of us handled similar situations and it wouldn't be the last.

"Done." I glanced down at Rendon and met his cautious stare. "What's wrong?"

"Is it always like that. Girls throwing themselves at you?"

I didn't want to lie to him, but I also didn't want it to be a thing between us that caused issues. "Sometimes. Girls like that are always going after guys on the team. I'm not special."

He rolled his lips together. "If I hadn't shown up, would you have blown her off?"

Wrapping my arms around him, I peered down at him. "Yes, I would have given her the boot." I bent down and pressed my lips to his. "I told you it was *only you* while we did this. I meant it."

He stared up at me with wide green eyes. "I believe you."

"Kiss on it?" I suggested with a wink.

"You just kissed—"

My lips crashed into his. He opened to me and I dipped my tongue into his mouth. My jeans grew tighter and once again I regretted my choice to wear them. At this point, I regretted the party completely and was ready to whisk Rendon away, back to my place. When I released him, he rested his forehead on my chest.

"This party sucks," I said against the top of his head. "Would you be horribly disappointed if we left?"

His shoulders shook as he laughed and pulled back. "Can't say that I would be."

"What about your friends?"

"Tristan won't care." Rendon ran a hand through his hair. "He brought a guy with him. I haven't met him before, but he gave me a quick rundown before we picked him up. Apparently, they didn't work well in...you know.

In bed. But kept in touch and he brought him as a wingman."

I couldn't see the color in his cheeks because of the dim lighting, but knew they were flushed. I grinned. "A wingman, huh?"

"He, ah, might be trying to see if anyone on the team is interested."

Of course he was. "Oh yeah? Anyone in particular?"

"You know who. I gathered from the bribery about Memphis that you'd figured out he had a thing for him. But he thinks Memphis is straight." He pulled away and fished his phone back out of his pocket. "Let me text him real quick before we leave."

My mouth dropped. "How do you know about Memphis?"

He tapped the side of his head. "The app and your hissy fit. Remember? You told me Memphis found it. Unless he trolls gay dating apps..."

I'd been so mad at the time I hadn't even thought about it. "You didn't tell Tristan?"

"I don't really know Memphis, so I didn't know if he was out," he said distractedly as he typed on his phone.

"He's not, so...you know..."

"Lips are sealed. Promise."

I nodded though he couldn't see since he was still texting. Rendon shoved his phone in his pocket so hard his elbow caught my side and my gaze flicked down to him. "What did he say?"

His expression screwed up in embarrassment. "You don't want to know."

Because it was Tristan, I had a good guess about what he'd written back. "Actually, I might."

"He went into detail about how to..." He covered his face with his hands. "Let's just go."

Chuckling, I grabbed his hand and tugged him toward the front door. More than a few people watched as I dragged him through the house and down the steps to the lawn. Let them look. Rendon was mine.

I urged him to move faster as we hurried to my truck, and Rendon laughed as I pinned him against the passenger door. Ducking my head next to his ear, I bit the lobe. "You drive me crazy. You know that, right?"

"It's only fair, because I feel the same." His hips shifted, sliding his hard cock against mine, grinding against me.

"All that just from me kissing you?" I pressed my hips tighter to his.

"All that because of how you feel inside me and I can't wait to get back to your place."

"*If* we make it back to my place," I growled and gripped his ass. I went back in for a kiss but he shoved me back.

"Nope." He turned, opened the door and climbed up into the seat. "You coming?"

SEVENTEEN
RENDON

NASH SLOWLY STALKED me backward across the front porch until I was pressed against the door. Staring at me intently, he reached around me and the door swung open. With his arm around my waist he backed me inside and kicked the door closed behind him and locked it. Unconcealed need clouded his gaze before he crashed his lips into mine, prying open my mouth and tangling our tongues together. Then his hands were between us, deftly unfastening the buttons on my shirt as he continued moving us across the room. As the third button came undone, I tripped over my own feet, almost taking us both to the floor.

Nash caught me just before my butt collided with the carpet and yanked me to his chest. Chuckling, his ran his nose over the side of my neck. "Only thing smashing that ass tonight is me."

Balling the soft fabric of his shirt in my grip, I groaned. "You did not just say that."

"What? Not smooth?" He drew back with a raised brow.

"Not at all." I matched his expression.

With a slow grin but quicker hands, Nash spun me around. "That wasn't very nice. I think you're going to have to pay for that."

My body went on high alert as he held me still just before he brought his hand down on my butt, a slight pop.

"You are *not* spanking me." I wrestled from his grip and took off toward the dining room, half laughing, half seeking safety.

"You bruised my ego, so time to bruise your ass," he threatened, a twist of amusement playing on his lips as he took measured strides in my direction.

"No way. I'm not into that kink." Circling the dining table, I created as much distance as I could with him on the opposite side.

"This isn't kink. It's punishment," Nash corrected with a smirk. He moved fast. Too fast and caught me around the waist as I tried to dart away. Caught between laughing and trying to wiggle free, I received another swat. "Those are warning shots."

"Let me go," I squeaked as he hauled me back to the couch. Before I could plead my case, I was tossed over his lap, butt up in the air.

"Say you're sorry." His hand kneaded my cheeks through my shorts and I held back a moan.

"No way." Glancing over my shoulder, I narrowed my eyes and wiggled around in a fruitless attempt to escape. "It was totally lame. Possibly the worst line I've ever heard."

"Last chance," Nash warned as he raised his hand. "Say you're sorry."

"Never," I swore and squealed when he smacked me several times with the most pathetic spanking ever. Shifting my hips, I attempted to dodge the mock blows, much to his amusement if the snort he let out was any indicator. "Let me up, you weirdo."

His hands were back to massaging as he hummed as if considering whether to release me. "Nope. I can't because you haven't learned your lesson."

"And what's that?" A muffled moan slipped free when he dug his thumb in to work the muscles.

Nash flipped me over in his lap, maneuvering my body until I was straddling his thighs. His finger tipped my chin until I was staring into those hypnotic eyes that glinted with humor. "That I'm a sensitive man with a fragile ego that should be handled with care."

"Liar." I huffed.

Nash smiled and my heart flip-flopped.

Slipping beneath my shirt, he skimmed his fingers over my back, leaving a trail of shivers behind. His dick hardened between us and...my stomach rumbled embarrassingly loud.

We froze.

I dropped my forehead to his shoulder. "Can you pretend you didn't hear that?"

Rich laughter echoed in the room and his whole body shook.

Climbing from his lap, I crossed my arms over my chest. "Don't make fun of me. We ate hours ago."

"I'm not making fun of you. Just the timing..." Flashing me an amused grin, Nash rose and stepped toward me, stealing a quick kiss. "Let's put this on hold. I'm hungry too, but I don't have much food stocked. You like spaghetti? It's about the only thing I know how to make and I'm pretty sure it's all I have. Or we can just call something in. Your choice."

"Spaghetti sounds good." Without access to a full

kitchen to cook anything, Tristan and I were limited to what we kept in our dorm. When I wasn't living off cheap microwavable noodles or peanut butter and jelly sandwiches to save money, my budget limited me to dollar-menu fast food and the occasional splurge at the sandwich shop. The steakhouse had been a one-off, so homemade food sounded amazing.

Nash stepped around me and I followed him into the kitchen. He pulled out a matching copper pot and pan from the cabinet, set them on the stove and then patted the countertop beside it. "Hop up."

Planting my hands on the counter, I didn't have time to jump. Nash's massive hands gripped my hips and turned me around to face him before lifting me onto the surface.

"Impatient much?" I pursed my lips to keep from smiling.

"I think you'll find I'm being very patient at the moment." He winked before crossing the room to the pantry, retrieving a box of noodles and a can of red sauce. When he carried them back, he placed them on the opposite side of the range.

My keys bit into my thigh so I wrestled my wallet, keys and phone from my pocket and tossed them next to me. Hooking my ankles together, I settled in to watch him work around the kitchen. As he filled the pot with water, placed it on the stove, and gathered bowls and cooking utensils, his gaze flicked to me several times as if he was afraid I'd disappear. And each time we traded grins.

"I don't know how I'm supposed to focus with you sitting up there looking like that." Nash threw a dishcloth on the counter as he bit his bottom lip. His gaze dipped to my chest and I glanced down to my partially unbuttoned shirt. With unhurried steps, he moved in front of me, jerked my legs apart, stepped between them and gripped my hips as he slid me forward until we were pressed flush together. "The water will take a minute to boil. Any idea what we might do to pass the time?"

Nash's gaze dropped to my lips. My fingertips itched with the need to touch him, and my lips tingled with the reminder of his mouth felt on mine.

"I have a few ideas," I murmured.

A wicked smile spread across his face. "Why don't you tell me about them?"

I cocked my head and pretended to considered my options. "You could kiss me."

His mouth kicked up on one side as he leaned in and brushed his lips against mine, a fleeting caress. When he leaned back, I made a sound of protest and he growled as he dove back in and kissed me harder. He swallowed my moan, groaning deep in his throat when my hips rolled, seeking friction against the bulge in his pants. I clung to the back of his neck as he drew his head back.

"Fuck, I never should have worn jeans," he complained while his fingers dug into my flesh, guiding me, rocking me against him. There was a hiss and sizzle next to us, and Nash jerked away, causing me to nearly topple off the counter.

He steadied me as I let go of his neck. "You stay put. I need to put the noodles in."

Having been forgotten, the boiling water spit over the sides, landing on the burner. Nash adjusted the heat and ripped open the box of noodles before dumping them in. He moved on to searching for the can opener and then heated the sauce. I watched on in silence as he stirred in simple spices of onion and garlic, his brow furrowed in concentration.

When Nash heated frozen meatballs in the microwave, it reminded me of how meals were cooked back home and I snorted. If I was witnessing the extent of his culinary skills, Nash and I did have something in common.

"What? You don't approve?" Nash asked as he shook the still half-full bag of meatballs on the way back to the freezer.

"Actually, I was just thinking that's exactly how I'd make spaghetti."

He arched a brow. "Yeah?"

"Yup, if I can't microwave it, then it's a lost cause."

The microwave timer went off and Nash grabbed the paper plate and dumped them straight into the sauce. He flicked his gaze toward me with a playful glimmer in his eyes. "And here I was hoping you'd whip up a decent dinner sometime."

"Only if I can call it in and have it delivered."

"Your mom didn't teach you?"

"Oh, no, she tried. But she's not any better."

"I'm going to tell her you said that," Nash threatened while pointing a wooden spoon covered in sauce in my direction.

"Go for it." I gave him a half-shrug. "She'll tell you the same thing."

He stirred the sauce and the smells from the spices permeating the air made my stomach growl again.

"You look like her." He poured the noodles into a strainer. "I didn't notice it until today. I always thought you were like a miniature, hotter Shaw."

"Because that's not weird or gross." I reached for the paper towels, ripped one off, wadded it and threw it at him.

"What? I said hotter." He chuckled. "Now, get your cute ass down and let's go eat."

After grabbing forks and napkins, Nash filled the bowls and carried them into the dining room. I hopped down and followed him. As I took my seat, he disappeared into the kitchen again and returned with a glass of water and was that... "You have tea?"

"It is." He slid it in front of me and sank onto the chair beside me. "Sweet."

"I love sweet tea. How did you know?" Taking a greedy sip, I closed my eyes as sugar exploded on my tongue.

Nash cleared his throat. "You ordered it that day at the sandwich shop and earlier when we went out to eat, so I took a guess and grabbed some on the way home from dropping y'all off. Figured I should have some here." His smile was *almost* sheepish. "It's just the kind in a jug."

It surprised me he'd paid that close attention and my heart warmed at the thoughtful gesture. "It's good. Thank you."

He looked relieved but then eyed my plate. "Now we just have to hope the food will be edible."

If Nash had put a bowl full of dry oatmeal in front of me I'd have happily eaten it at this point, so I took a bite. The noodles were overcooked, but I was so hungry I barely noticed. A small sigh of contentment escaped my lips as I chewed.

"Any good?" he asked. When I nodded with enthusiasm and twirled my fork around to gather more, he chuckled. "I only make the basics. My mom is a damn good cook and my dad is a beast on a grill when he's up to it, but I'd rather eat than cook." Nash stuffed a large forkful in his mouth, wrinkled his nose and cast me a suspicious glare as he swallowed. "I thought you said this was good."

"What? I like it." I speared a meatball and shoved it in my mouth.

The mention of Nash's dad, brought back a memory of what he'd revealed about his health months ago. Not sure what was allowed in the fine print of our agreement, I cautiously broached the topic. "How is your dad?"

Nash wiped a napkin over his mouth and his gaze roamed over my face. A small grin tugged at his lips as he seemed to consider me and his gaze softened. "I talked to him outside the restaurant earlier. He sounded good."

Not wanting to assume I could probe deeper, I simply returned the smile. "I'm glad."

While he still regarded me with a thoughtful expression, I wondered if I shouldn't have asked. Dropping my gaze from his searching stare to my bowl, I finished off the rest of my meal and pushed back the empty dish.

Nash had already polished off his food and when I glanced up, his lips twitched. Leaning toward me, he rubbed his thumb over my chin. "You left some on your face."

"It's a good thing I have you around." My skin tingled from his touch and my heart thudded in my chest from the soft way he still looked at me. I was likely misreading the situation, but it felt intimate. Glancing away before my expression could betray the odd butterflies in my stomach, I lifted my glass and swallowed a drink down my tightened throat.

Under the table, Nash settled his hand high on my thigh and squeezed. Startled, I dropped the glass and leapt up as the cold liquid drenched my lap.

"Oh my god, I'm so sorry. I'll...I'll clean it up," I stuttered as embarrassment lit my cheeks on fire and I plucked the unbroken glass from the floor.

Nash rose to his feet and took the glass from me. "You're soaked. Calm down, Ren. This isn't a big deal, okay? I'll clean it up and you go hop in the shower before it starts to get sticky."

Sweet tea dripped from the hem of my shirt and shorts, dripping onto the linoleum floor. "I am so sor...sorry." I continued to stumble over words and ran a hand through my hair, realizing too late that the mess hadn't spared my hands.

"Ren, it's not your fault. That one's on me." He gripped me by the shoulders, angled me toward the bathroom and gave me a subtle shove. "Now, go wash off."

I hurried off down the hall to the bathroom, closed the door and stripped down. Glancing around, I decided the sink was the best place to leave my clothes and caught a glimpse of myself in the mirror. I cringed at my disheveled appearance—blotchy red skin that extended from my face down my neck to my chest and hair that stuck up at odd angles.

Despite Nash taking the blame, I felt like a clumsy idiot. It wasn't his fault and we both knew it. My thoughts had been on whatever connection we'd experienced and had been caught off guard.

I removed my glasses and had just stepped in the shower and closed the curtain when Nash tapped on the door and let himself in. "I'm going to toss your clothes in the washer."

Tugging the curtain aside, I created a small gap and peered at his blurry figure. "Okay, thanks." My voice steadied instead of sounding like a stuttering fool for once.

Nash gathered my clothes. "I'll be back."

After the door closed behind him, I slumped against the tiled wall as the hot water rained down on me. *So stupid.* But there wasn't anything I could do about it. I'd already made the mess.

Grabbing Nash's body wash from the built-in corner shelf, I uncapped the bottle and the calming scent of citrus and spice that always clung to Nash's skin filled the steamy room.

As I inhaled deep, the shower curtain whipped back and the bottle slipped from my hands. With a small yelp, I hopped to the side to avoid it hitting my toes and it landed with a thud against the bottom of the tub.

Nash stepped over the lip of the bath, into the shower with me. "You're a jumpy little thing tonight."

My brain short-circuited. Nash's naked body was something I'd never get used to. Complete perfection. Swallowing hard, my gaze drifted over his muscled form down to his soft dick that hung low and thick. How had I fit that inside me? Even in this state his size was intimidating. As I stared, his dick stiffened and my mouth went dry.

"See something you like?" he teased and my gaze swung up to meet his.

My humiliation from the mess I'd made slipped away as I caught the challenge in his eyes. "Maybe I do."

"Well, I definitely like what I'm seeing." Nash made a show of running his gaze over my body and I forced my hands to stay at my sides instead of covering myself from his molten stare.

He bent and picked up the body wash, squirting some onto his hand and set it back on the shelf. Rubbing his palms together, he worked up a lather, and then washed my arms and shoulders. He dug his thumbs in my knotted muscles, loosening the tense kinks.

"You really worked yourself up, didn't you?" He made a *tsk*ing sound before encouraging me to face the wall and continued down my back and legs.

"I should make more messes," I mumbled when Nash

hit a sweet spot on the back of my thigh. He continued to work the area and my body went slack, but my dick didn't get the message, swelling as he expertly manipulated my body.

"If it gets you naked in my shower, I'm okay with it." He reached around my front, touching every inch of my chest, teasing my nipples.

With a moan, I pressed back against him and he groaned in approval as he ground his hard length along my crease. He slid his soapy hands lower, wrapping a warm, wet palm around my shaft and the other dipped to cup my sac. He stroked and fondled until I was a gasping mess, desperately seeking purchase with my hands against the slippery tiles to stay balanced as my knees wobbled.

"I think we need to make sure you are thoroughly clean." Nash released me and took a step back, much to my disappointment. But then he gripped both cheeks and spread me wide. His heavy breaths filled the small room and I tensed as he paused while I was exposed. "Fuck," he whispered. "You have got to have the hottest ass I've ever seen."

He freed one hand and with a deliberately slow skim of his fingers across my skin, he brought them to my entrance and ran the rough pad of his thumb over my hole.

Boneless, I melted as Nash rubbed circles and my breath hitched when he added pressure, slipping a single digit inside.

"Nash, I want you." My hips rolled to the steady rhythm he set and I clung to sanity by a thread as waves of pleasure rippled throughout my body.

Instead of answering, he slipped his finger free, and I whimpered at the loss.

"Turn around." His words were no more than a strained

rasp and I forced my legs to cooperate, using the wall to help me roll around to face him.

His lids were heavy as he washed himself, making sure to give me an eyeful as he stroked his dick. My gaze followed his fist as he jerked himself and shivers raced over my skin. My lips parted as thoughts of dropping to my knees for him became more and more difficult to resist. This was his show and I was trying hard to be patient, but it didn't last.

I lowered myself and he growled, shut off the shower and yanked me to my feet. "Out now."

He stepped out first and grabbed two towels from a metal rack, tossing one to me as I scrambled after him. The sense of urgency pulsing in the air was potent as we scrubbed ourselves dry. When I wrapped the towel around my waist, he scowled and ripped it off.

"What are you do—" My words were cut off when he roughly lifted me in his arms. Instinctively, I wrapped my legs around him, trapping our hard shafts together.

When I rocked against his length, he cursed, whipped his hand out to grab my glasses from the countertop and slid them on my face. "I want you wearing these."

There was no way I was arguing with the heat in his gaze as he carried me to his bedroom and tossed me on the soft mattress. The swish and slam of the side table drawer sliding open and closed hit my ears before he climbed between my legs, settling on his stomach.

Without warning, he swallowed my dick to the back of his throat. My back arched and I cried out a string of words that had no meaning other than *Oh. My. God.*

He groaned around me as he bobbed his head, taking my length deep. My eyes slammed closed and I fought hard to keep my orgasm at bay. I didn't want it to ever end. But when he snaked a hand between us and went right back to my hole, gliding inside with a slick finger, I nearly rocketed over the edge. I hadn't heard him open the bottle of lube, but the surprise was short-lived. All I cared about the smooth thrusts that matched the fast, hot suction around my dick.

My legs shook and blood whooshed in my ears. I was close. Too close. And then just as suddenly as he'd started, everything stopped and I was left empty and aching.

"I need inside you. Now." Nash sprang to his knees, dick bouncing off his abs. He leaned back as he picked up a condom from the bedspread and ripped it open.

"Wait." Reaching out, I stilled his hand. Even wrapped up in the heat of the moment, I hadn't forgotten what I'd wanted to try with him in the shower. "Can I..." My lips clamped shut. Why was saying it so hard?

"Can you what, babe? You only have to ask." His gaze blazed with barely-repressed fire and genuine sincerity.

I rolled my lips together. "I...I want to try it on you."

"What do you want to try?" Nash cocked his head as he set the condom back on the bed.

"What"—my voice cracked—"you just did to me."

He leaned over me and gazed into my eyes. "Rendon, you can say it. There's no embarrassment in this bed. Understood?"

"Okay," I whispered as I gave a slow nod.

He grinned before dropping a quick kiss to my lips. When Nash pulled back, he quirked a brow. "Are you asking to blow me or finger fuck me?"

"Do you have to say it like that?" I frowned.

Nash laughed and rolled to his back beside me. "My body is your playground. Do whatever you want." He placed his hands behind his head, bent his knees and spread his legs, putting himself on display without an ounce of modesty.

Puffing out a nervous breath, I climbed on all fours and crawled in front of him, stopping from closing the distance to examine his sculpted form. My gaze jumped to each part of his body, unsure where to start. I wanted to taste and tease everything, but... I paused over his dick, hard against his belly, and then took in his heavy sac. My mouth watered at the idea of wrapping my lips around him, weighing his balls in my palm. But I also wanted to see...

As if he knew what I'd been thinking, Nash shifted his legs back and I got my first glimpse of his hole. My dick throbbed and I swallowed hard.

"Baby, you're killing me," he ground out. "Keep staring at me like that and I won't be responsible for what happens next. Fingers. Mouth. Fucking pinky nail. I don't care—just touch me."

I wanted to drive him as crazy as he did me with his expert hands. But an overwhelming sense of insecurity held me still. I didn't know what I was doing or where to start.

"Hey, look at me." He waited until I met his unguarded gaze. "Just go for it. Whatever you want. I'm serious, Ren. I trust you."

A breath rushed from my lungs. "What if I do it wrong?"

"You aren't going to get a complaint from me, but I'll guide you if you want me to. Just say the word."

With his reassuring gaze and words, I moved closer and reached out to trace my finger over his skin, warm and soft beneath my touch. Starting at his chest, I followed along the indent that ran between his solid pecs and down rows of abs, stopping short of where his tip rested just under his bellybutton. My heart might as well have been a battering ram the way it knocked around in my chest, so I took a deep, steadying breath.

The short nails of my free hand dug into my thigh as I deliberated whether I'd be able to fit my mouth around him. But I was determined to try so I bent over him. With surer hands, I moved my fingers from his stomach down to curl around his base and position his tip to my lips.

I licked the wet bead from his tip. Salt. Tang. Man.

Saliva flooded my mouth and my dick responded with pulsing need. Moving my hand to my shaft, I squeezed to alleviate the building ache.

Nash sucked in a sharp breath and I looked up, watching him as I stretched my mouth around his tip.

"Fuck me, that's hot." He reached for me, paused and clenched his fist as he forced his hands behind his head again.

Curiously, I probed my tongue at the slit and tasted more precome.

His legs jerked and he ground out through his gritted teeth, "If I die from this torture, make sure you tell the team they better win next week's game."

When I hummed a laugh, my mouth vibrated and he groaned, stuffing his fist between his teeth. Stretching my mouth wider, I fit more of his length between my lips.

A slew of expletives ripped from his throat and he flung an arm over his face. As I continued to inch down his shaft, he audibly ground his teeth. He was so thick my jaw began to hurt. After a deep breath through my nose, I took as much of him as I could manage. And gagged.

"Fucking shit," Nash cursed as his stomach muscles contracted and his chest rose and fell at a rapid pace.

I released his dick with a pop and gasped for air. He'd taken me down his throat and it had been amazing, so I was determined to figure it out. Giving it another try, I relaxed my throat, but gagged again. He cursed and squirmed. I considered his reaction and realized he was getting off on it, so the next time I purposely gagged.

Nash sat up with a violent jerk and pushed my shoulders back to release his dick. "Ren, you have no idea how bad I'm struggling not to thrust down your pretty little throat so stop tempting me."

He grabbed the back of my neck and kissed me hard, punishing me with his lips and tongue. When he drew back, we both panted as we stared at each other.

I managed to rasp out, "I wasn't done."

His nostrils flared and hands clenched as he nodded and lay back down before muttering, "You really are trying to kill me."

Lowering my head, I went to work, this time avoiding taking him too deep and focusing on sucking him faster. I closed my eyes as his groans and filthy words filled the room. Disbelief that I had Nash's dick in my mouth and he was the one groaning and chanting my name swept over me as more precome hit my tongue.

"Here," Nash gritted between his teeth.

I glanced up and saw he held the lube out to me. Reluctantly, I pulled my mouth off him and sat up. Grabbing the bottle, I frowned. "What's this for?"

He cocked a brow in answer.

My lips parted as I searched his eyes. "You want me to..."

"You're not the only one who enjoys it," he said unapologetically. "I want your fingers in me."

After a brief hesitation, I bit my lip and uncapped the bottle, coating my fingers as he had. Slowly, I lowered my hand, bringing a single finger to his hole. My gaze lingered on his entrance as I rubbed in circles, trying to mimic what he'd done to me.

He thrust his hips in the air and his dick jerked. "I'm all for teasing, but you gagging on my cock has me on edge. Fuck me with your fingers the way you would yourself, babe."

My cheeks tingled hot. Though I'd definitely practiced on myself, it was weird hearing it out loud. I slowly applied pressure and my finger sank inside him. And then I began a steady rhythm, sure to curl my finger the way he had.

"Yes," he hissed and drew his legs back further, giving me a perfect view as I slid a second finger along the first.

When he tensed and clenched around them, I leaned over and took his dick back in my mouth. Once he released a needy groan, I picked back up the same pattern. Thrust. Massage. Curl. Withdraw. He began rocking his hips and I peered up at him, wanting to capture his expressions.

His penetrating gaze latched on mine as a drop of sweat rolled down his temple. I could only imagine how much restraint it was taking to hold himself back.

Sitting back, I switched from sucking his dick to stroking him with my free hand while continuing to stretch him. Trying to keep in mind he'd said I could ask for anything in bed and not be embarrassed, I fought through the nerves trying to force my words back.

"Nash? Would it be okay if I..." I'd been a blusher my whole life but my cheeks had never burned hotter. "Would it be okay if maybe I topped y-you?"

He spasmed around my fingers. "You can do whatever you want, babe. I'm game. If you want to fuck me, then do it."

A relieved breath rushed from my lungs when he didn't

make me feel stupid for asking. "It's just I always saw you, ya know...on top. But I'm curious."

"Stop, I'm totally in." He paused and then adopted a casual tone. "Do you have condoms?"

I glanced at the condom on the bed, realizing it was useless to me unless I doubled in size, and the tips of my ears tingled hot. Closing my eyes, I eased my fingers from him. When I'd prepared to move from home, I'd bought a box and tucked one into my wallet. Wishful thinking at the time, but it was happening. Now. With Nash. "I have one in my wallet in the kitchen."

"Want me to get it?" he offered and I backed off the bed while shaking my head.

"Be right back." Was I really going to do this? He was easily twice my size and it seemed odd, but my dick twitched and my balls drew tight at the idea of sliding inside Nash. I'd be lucky if I made it that far before I came.

Gathering my things, I hurried back and removed the foil wrapper from my wallet before tossing everything else on the nightstand.

As I resumed my place between his legs, I questioned whether I was about to make a fool of myself and what was I thinking asking to top him. The doubts swirling in my mind must have been transparent because Nash tugged me over him and yanked me down, chest to chest.

"As much as I love fucking your tight ass, I don't mind you topping when you want. I told you, anything you want to do is fine. But you better believe I'll have your sweet ass again. Soon." And then he kissed me until we were both breathless.

Wondering if he'd prefer a different position, I asked, "Do you want it like this or..."

"How about like this the first time," he suggested and again I nodded, thankful he'd made the decision.

Once I'd regained my bearings, I rested back on my calves, tore the condom wrapper open and rolled it on before coating my length in a generous amount of lube.

A muffled groan whispered through Nash's lips.

"Okay, I'm ready." I said it more to myself than Nash, but peeked at him. "Are...are you ready?"

With hooded eyes, Nash sank his teeth into his bottom lip. "You have no idea."

"Okay," I said again and moved to brace myself over him.

Placing one hand on the bed beside him, I wrapped the other around my shaft as I guided myself to his entrance. With the first brush of my tip over his hole, we both shuddered and then I pressed in. His body easily gave way as I breached the ring of muscle and inched further inside him. Heat surrounded me and he tightened like a fist around my dick. The feeling was indescribable. Better than I'd imagined. But halfway in, he stiffened and I held still. "Did I hurt you?"

"No, it's just been a while. Keep going. I want to feel you. All of you."

Biting my lip in concentration, I waited until I felt him relax and then pushed again. In one smooth glide, I was completely surrounded by his clenching walls. We both groaned and my balls threatened to explode if I moved an inch. My arms trembled as I struggled to hold myself up. "This feels..."

"Try moving," he rasped out, and I shook my head and closed my eyes.

"If I do, I'll come."

Nash coughed, and I snapped my eyes open to find his

shoulders shaking and his lips pressed together so tight the color blanched from them.

"It's my first time," I defended myself. "And stop laughing, you keep squeezing my dick."

"Don't worry, I'm riding the edge already." As if to prove his point he reached down and trailed his finger through the precome dripping onto his stomach.

My gaze jerked back to his. "That's not helping."

His lids grew heavy as he leveled me with a heated gaze. "Fuck me."

Crossing my fingers that I didn't completely embarrass myself, I eased back and thrust back in. Fireworks shot off behind my closed lids and I bucked into him hard, a burning need to get deeper, go faster. Worries forgotten, I moaned and broken words fell from my lips. "I... This... Nash... No idea..."

"Open your eyes," Nash ordered and I hadn't even realized I'd closed them. "Look down."

I did. My shaft disappeared into his body over and over as he stretched around me. "That's the hottest thing I've ever seen."

He groaned and lifted his hips to meet my thrusts. "Agreed."

But he couldn't see me entering him. When I glanced up, his eyes were scanning over my features as his hand wrapped around his dick, stroking in time to the rhythm I set.

Between the fire in his eyes, watching him jerk off and the way his body squeezed my shaft, I was lost. My hips snapped forward and he hissed, "Yes. Fuck, yes."

His hands latched onto my butt, forcing me to ride him harder, making my eyes roll back. I tried to hold off, but my orgasm was a lit fuse ready to blow and when it hit, my arms gave out beneath the force. My jaw dropped into a soundless *Oh*—the sensation so intense it stole my voice.

Trembling as aftershocks wreaked havoc on my spent body, I managed to lift myself on arms that shook while remaining buried deep inside him. I could only watch between our bodies in silence as Nash jerked his dick hard, and when he came on a deep drawn-out groan, he clamped around me like a vice, sending a fresh wave of tremors rocketing down my spine as he shot ropes of come onto his stomach.

Seeing what I did to him made me feel powerful. I wasn't familiar with this side of myself and I reveled in the moment.

When Nash went slack beneath me, I carefully slid out of his body and disposed of the condom before collapsing beside him. On my back, I lay there, staring at the ceiling in a state of disbelief. Okay, that had really just happened.

"Be right back." Nash climbed from the bed and walked out of the room, returning minutes later cleaned up and flipped the light off. He pulled back the comforter and slid beneath it, lying on his back before he flipped the switch on the bedside lamp. He patted the space beside him. "Come here."

I lifted enough for him to wrestle the blanket from beneath me and then scooted next to him, resting my head on his shoulder as he tugged the blanket back over us.

Nash wrapped his arm around me. "So, what did you think?"

"It was hot and I loved it," I admitted. "But I think I prefer you on top."

"It was definitely hot," he agreed. "And I have no problem either way, but I do love watching you beneath me."

We lay there quietly for a few minutes and my thoughts raced through the eventful day. The big football player who had played so roughly on the field and masterfully handled my body had trusted me enough to let me do something he hadn't done in a while. He'd given guidance and been patient—two things I wouldn't have expected from him only weeks ago—while I fumbled my way through my first time.

To my surprise it wasn't hard to fit the newfound facets of his personality with everything else I knew about Nash. The more I learned about him, the more I realized I'd made assumptions that couldn't be further from the truth.

Nash wasn't someone who could be labeled and tucked neatly into a single box. There were so many sides of him, each of which I was coming to appreciate. Knowing how close I'd been to walking away from him made me ill, and I realized in that moment what a huge mistake that would have been.

My mind circled around what he'd said about not bottoming for a long time and I wondered why he'd let me. Was it because he was simply allowing me to explore or was it...more?

"So you don't bottom?" The words flew from my mouth and I backpedaled as I tilted my head up to peek at him. "Sorry, I was just thinking out loud. You don't have to answer that."

"Ren, it's fine. You can ask me questions," he assured me with a kiss to my forehead. "No, I don't normally. I have before, but not often and it's been years."

"Years?" I took a moment to absorb that information and drew circles with my fingertip on his chest. "So why with me?"

He appeared thoughtful and then gave a half-shrug. "I

wanted you to experience it and I wanted your first time to be with me."

His honesty surprised me. "I'm glad my first everything has been with you. You've made everything easy. Comfortable."

"Are you calling me easy?" he teased as he tickled my side.

Wiggling away from his fingers, I brushed his hand away. "Stop, I hate that."

"Noted." Nash smirked, and I had no doubt he would remember and use it against me one day.

"Anyway, that's not what I was saying. That could have been terrible or embarrassing...and it was the opposite."

A smile stretched his cheeks with a hint of arrogance. "Mind-blowing, right?"

"Cocky," I accused without a trace of annoyance.

"Confident." He grinned and tightened his hold on me.

Sighing, I gave in and matched his grin. "Fine, you're right. It was amazing and more than I could have asked for."

He studied my face with a softness in his features. "*You're* more than I could have asked for."

Stunned mute, I glanced away and slipped my arm around Nash and held him just as tight. Other than the sound of breathing and my heart beating like crazy, the silence was thick and overwhelming. What was happening? What did that mean? Those questions raced around in dizzying circles.

Forcing myself to stay in the here and now, I cleared my throat. "I was just thinking about watching you on the field today. You're so different than when we're just lying here in bed."

"I'm not just football, Ren. I mean I love it and it's been my dream since I was old enough to have dreams, but it's not everything." He moved a hand to my jaw, running a finger along the fine edge as he coaxed me to meet his eyes again. "This is just another part of me. And to be honest it wasn't a part I realized I had before..."

My chest squeezed. I wanted him to finish that sentence but after a stretch of silence passed it became clear he wouldn't, so I latched on to what else he said. "I'm jealous that you know what you want to do with your life."

"Because you don't?" He placed his arm back around me.

"Not at all," I admitted. "It seems like the moment I make a decision, my path will be set in stone. Like marrying a particular degree and an expected job. I know I'd still have options, but I want to focus on one thing. I just don't know what yet."

"Well, what are you interested in? There's so much about you I don't know." His brows dipped as if that bothered him.

"Honestly? I'm kind of smitten with the college environment. The rush of classes and people. I never thought I'd enjoy that. I was a loner back home."

"Why were you a loner?" He began rubbing my back and his easy demeanor called to something inside me that wanted to be open and honest with him.

"Shaw was out, you know?" I whispered. "Everyone knew he was bisexual, but he was the reason our school had so many football trophies, so no one said anything. At least, that's the only reason I've ever come up with." I bit the inside of my cheek as I gathered the courage to tell him how different high school had been for me. "When I came out, I expected it to be the same I guess. But it wasn't. People avoided me or spread rumors. I didn't have friends because no one wanted to make themselves an outcast just by being seen with me, so I stuck to myself."

"That couldn't have been easy and I wish I'd known you back then. I'd have made sure it didn't happen. But why did you keep it from your brother? He could have helped."

"He'd have tried to fix it, you're right. But without him there all the time it would have only made it worse." Tugging myself out of his embrace, I sat up. "And I didn't need his help. I managed just fine."

"Stop getting riled up. I understand why you think that, but it hurt you. Don't lie to me. Ever. Please." Nash waited while I peered down at him. Seeing the vulnerability in his eyes, I finally nodded. "Letting someone have your back doesn't make you weak, Ren. Now, lie back down."

The tension bled from my shoulders and I sank back down beside him. "Okay, fine. It hurt but what could I do? I'm just glad it's over and I really do like it here." By here I'd meant Sugar Land, but as soon as I said it, I realized I liked it here in Nash's bed, talking about real things. Though I knew it was dangerous, I admitted to myself there was nowhere else I'd rather be.

He turned on his side to face me. "It's their loss. Those people have no idea what they were missing out on by not getting to know you."

My heart warmed as I scooted closer and tried to force my leg between his massive thighs, wanting to being completely surrounded by him.

His eyes sparkled with mirth as he accommodated the space, slightly parting them. "I'm going to crush your little chicken leg."

He was right. My leg may as well have been caught between two boulders, but I refused to move. Instead, I refocused on what we'd been talking about before my trip down memory lane. "Well, anyway, my thoughts have been circling around possibly becoming a teacher, maybe even a professor one day. What do you think?"

Nash shot me a lopsided grin. "I think you'd be the teacher the whole school crushed on."

I rolled my eyes. "Whatever. I'm so not that guy people crush on."

He slipped a hand down to my butt and squeezed. "I would have totally crushed on you."

Swatting his back, I scowled. "Be serious."

"The fact that you don't know how sexy you are is crazy to me. Like how you ended up being mine is weird."

My heart stopped and I froze. "Yours?"

His body went rigid and he paused for a beat. "You know what I mean."

We watched each other, and maybe because the moment was too intense, or maybe because I worried he'd see the effect those words had on me, I had the sudden urge to shift topics. Because belonging to Nash and having him belong to me made a swarm of butterflies take off in my belly. "What made you dream about playing football?"

Nash's muscles loosened and he seemed grateful for the change in conversation. "My dad played in high school and college. He didn't want to go pro, but when I came along, he still had a love for it and got me into the game. He was even my coach when I was in elementary school." His laugh was hushed and his gaze unfocused.

"It made me feel good to win, especially because it was something we'd bonded over. And it taught me how to lose and better myself. I didn't have siblings then and a lot of our time revolved around my games. It was a family thing and I loved that as much as the games." His fingers skimmed up the back of my neck as his gaze sharpened on mine again.

"So, I gave it my all and found that I loved pushing myself, especially once I got older and played against tougher teams. I'm competitive and it just...fits. It's all I've ever wanted. But..."

Curling against him, I soaked up his body heat against my naked skin and yawned. Breathing in his soothing scent, my lids drooped as I fought the sudden wave of exhaustion from the long day, but I was determined to listen. "But what?"

He rolled his lips together and then sighed. "This week, maybe the next, scouts should start coming around practice to scope out the goods. There is only a short window they are allowed in, and it's a lot of pressure to be perfect. No do-overs, you know? I thought I was ready but I'm...nervous, I guess."

"You guess?" I quirked a brow and mirrored his words. "Don't lie to me. Ever. Please."

His smile was laced with amusement. "Okay, fine. I'm definitely nervous."

"You can always talk to me about it, but for what it's worth, I think you're going to set the NFL on fire," I murmured and fought to keep my eyes open.

"Thanks, Ren," he whispered and leaned forward, kissing me softly. "Now go to sleep."

"No, we're talking." My words slurred and I closed my eyes. "I'm listening. My eyes just won't cooperate."

He chuckled. "For some reason, I'm feeling better about it this week. Maybe because a certain someone believes in me."

The brush of his fingers over my temples as he slipped my glasses from my face was followed by the tap of them hitting the nightstand and the light from the lamp was cut off.

"Always," I mumbled.

His arms squeezed around me. "Back atcha."

I drifted off for a moment, but when he gently untangled himself from my limbs, I cracked one eye open just enough to watch his naked body slide from beneath the covers as he climbed out of bed. "Where are you going?"

"Be right back. I need to toss your clothes in the dryer."

A sullen huff escaped my lips as he left the room.

There was so much I didn't know about Nash, but I had grown to believe that he was a good man with a good heart.

Guilt settled in the pit of my stomach about the terrible misconceptions I'd had of him. Everyone thought he was just another playboy on the football team, but he wasn't. Nash was so much more. And I wasn't falling for him. I'd dove straight off the cliff and all I could do was hope there wasn't a bed of razor-edged rocks waiting to shred my heart into a thousand pieces at the bottom.

The bed dipped and strong arms wrapped around me before the scent and warmth of his skin against mine tore me from thoughts of an uncertain future and lulled me to sleep.

EIGHTEEN
RENDON

THE ROOM WAS dark when I woke and a thin sheen of sweat covered my overheated skin thanks to the massive body enveloping me. Lying face to face, my leg was trapped between Nash's large thighs again and his arm was draped over my side. Blindly, I reached behind me to the nightstand for my glasses and came up empty. Frowning, I searched the entire surface before remembering Nash had taken them off.

When I shifted to pull away, he grunted and I stilled. Once his breathing steadied to a slow, even pace again, I freed my leg with careful movements and sat up. My foot tingled and I cringed as the blood began to circulate. After the agonizing minutes of my foot waking up passed, I vowed to never sleep that way again.

My thoughts drifted to the night before and a rush of emotions too heavy for me to process this early in the morning swept through me.

Sometime after I'd fallen asleep, I'd shifted to my side with Nash wrapped around my back. I was woken by a half-asleep Nash rocking his hard length against me. Minutes later he'd suited up and slid into me from behind. With Nash moving slowly inside me, the realization I'd had hours before only deepened. With each soft caress of his hands on my skin, featherlight kisses he'd placed on the back of my neck and shoulders, deep breaths that matched my own, and the sensual way he moved his body against mine, he'd shattered my mind and body.

It had been the most powerful moment in my life and I swallowed the lump in my throat. Being with Nash had been more than an experiment and I was forced to acknowledge the truth in my heart.

I loved Nash and it was terrifying.

Rubbing my eyes, I tried to alleviate the pressure building behind them. This was bad and put me in a difficult situation. Because if last night meant nothing to him, I'd end up hurt. But I also didn't want to end things between us and walk away.

It was a lot to take in while I was still groggy from sleep, so I climbed off the mattress and was blasted with cold air blowing from the vent. Still in search of my glasses, I tiptoed around the bed with cautious steps so I didn't smash into anything and patted around Nash's night stand, sighing quietly as my hand wrapped around the wire frames. Slipping them on, I left the room to hunt down my clothes and something to drink.

The kitchen was lit by the slightest gray haze of dawn breaking through the blinds and I found the stackable washer/dryer tucked into an alcove next to the pantry. When I pulled the dryer door open, I winced at the clang that echoed off the walls but the house remained quiet. Since Sunday was his only day free from football, I wanted to let Nash get as much rest as possible.

After I dressed in my clean clothes, I found the cold jug

of tea Nash had bought for me and poured a glass before carrying it out to the back porch. The forecast was predicted to be in upper nineties around noon so I wanted to take advantage of the cooler morning breeze while I had the chance.

The moment I set foot outside, the unmistakable scent of cigarette smoke assaulted my nose and I glanced next door.

Jesse perched on his top step wearing rumpled clothes, and a gust of wind carried the strong scent of stale liquor. Taking a drag of the cigarette, he narrowed his blood-shot brown eyes, running his dull gaze over the length of my body. His lips curled down and I got the impression I'd been judged and been found wanting.

Brushing the hair from my forehead, I offered him an awkward wave. "Hey, you're up early."

In truth it didn't appear he'd even gone to sleep yet.

He only blinked and exhaled another cloud of smoke. Growing uncomfortable, I decided maybe I should head back inside. But then he smiled though it appeared forced. "You stayed the night again."

It hadn't been a question, but when he continued to stare at me, I wondered if he was waiting for confirmation. Shuffling on my feet, I gripped the glass of tea tight. "I...I did. Yes."

His lips flattened. "Did you enjoy the party last night?"

"What?" How did he know I'd gone to a party and why did he look so mad to find me at Nash's?

Jesse chuckled—the sound almost cruel. "I saw you and Nash there, though it didn't look like you stayed long."

He kept his eyes trained on me as he continued smoking, and the edge in his tone bothered me. My brother had said Jesse was cool and Nash never mentioned an issue with him. But Jesse seemed to have a problem with me.

"Oh, yeah, I guess it was fine," I lied. Though I hadn't stayed long enough to enjoy it, I doubted I would have. "I didn't see you there."

His glare made my skin crawl. "I guess you wouldn't have since you beelined for Nash and then you two rushed off."

My brows furrowed in confusion. The awkward conversation was made worse because of the hostile vibes he radiated. The fresh air I'd sought was no longer appealing, so I stepped back and placed one hand on the doorknob. "I need to get going."

"You know you're just a passing amusement, right?" His lip curled on one side. "Though I'm surprised you're still around. Not his normal MO, I admit. I just hope you don't think that makes you different."

Something in his tone made me still. My spine went rigid and every cell in my body screamed to dart back inside the safety of Nash's unit, yet my feet wouldn't move. "Different how?"

He smirked as if he'd won, clearly pleased I'd took the bait. "Don't think he'll keep you around. He doesn't keep any of us for more than a night."

I reared back as his meaning became clear. "You and Nash?"

He gave a half-shrug. "Nash and *a lot* of people. He's stellar in the sack, am I right?"

My stomach sank and my hand tightened around the doorknob. "I don't know if we should be talking about this."

"Relax. He doesn't mind." His tone lightened and he winked, though his jaw ticced. "And anyway, it was just one time last year."

The mental image of Nash with Jesse sent nausea spiraling in my gut and my eyes stung with tears. Of course I knew he'd been with other people. Many in fact. And I'd known what I was getting into. What I hadn't counted on was being found out and having to face anyone throwing Nash's past in my face. It hadn't even crossed my mind as he'd taken my hand and rushed me out of the frat house.

I had no response to give Jesse. What could I say that wouldn't come off as pathetic and give him more ammunition to hurt me?

What happened between Nash and me last night and then again hours later had been something I'd never forget. Something that meant more to me that I could have ever expected. The revelation had already been terrifying, but I realized there was a part of me that hoped he'd experienced the same connection. But now the most meaningful night of my life was tainted with cruel words. I'd already known I was in over my head, but now I was drowning in self-doubt.

While I stared at him in silence, he grunted as he stood and immediately stumbled, catching himself against the wood railing. The gray sky had brightened as we were talking, revealing dark shadows that loomed beneath Jesse's eyes.

"I'm still drunk as shit. You two missed a wild party. All-nighter as you can probably tell." He swayed as he let go of the rail. "Of course, you likely had yourself an all-nighter too, huh?"

My lips finally loosened. "I don't understand why you're telling me all this."

He ignored my comment but his eyes narrowed.

"You must have a killer dick." He glared. "Or maybe a tight little ass."

"Maybe...maybe you should sober up," I suggested. Not

only had he been completely crude and out of line, he'd robbed me of the morning I'd hoped to spend with Nash. All I wanted was to leave and hole up in my dorm.

"Huh, *maybe* you're right." He tossed his cigarette that had burned down to the filter in the ceramic pot. "But you don't look like my mother."

"I don't know what I've done to you, but I'm going inside." I twisted the knob.

"Run and tell your boyfriend that the neighbor was being mean." He gave a low laugh and then frowned as he rubbed his eyes. "Fuck, I didn't mean to say all that. You're right, I need to go lie down and sleep this off."

Jesse staggered to the door and tipped forward when the door swung open. Without thinking, I ran over and helped him, trying to keep him upright with my hands around his arm though touching him sent waves of nausea roiling in my gut.

"I got this." He knocked my hands away and I jerked back.

"I'll just lock the door," I told him, though I shouldn't have cared.

"Do whatever you want." He waved me off and kicked off his motorcycle boots.

I didn't stick around for more. After I twisted the inner bottom lock and closed the door, I hurried back to Nash's.

The churning in my stomach continued as I set my glass in the sink. Hunching over the countertop, I dragged a hand through my hair. An overwhelming need to escape and get my thoughts in order set my feet in motion.

Nash didn't deserve to deal with my emotional meltdown. We weren't in a relationship, and I had no right questioning him about Jesse or asking for reassurances. He didn't owe me that and hadn't made me any promises. We could talk once I calmed down and could think objectively.

Quietly, I crept down the hall and entered his bedroom, gathering my things. I glanced at Nash one last time. The dark room made it hard to distinguish more than a large form resting in his bed where less than an hour ago I'd been wrapped in his arms, safe and secure. I wanted to rewind time and climb in beside him. Instead, I backed away and stepped lightly through the house.

After I locked the front door and took one step on the porch, I slumped as I remembered my car was still parked at the dorm. Not only had I caught a ride with Tristan and his friend to the party, I'd then rode with Nash to his house. Crap.

Staring down at the phone in my hand, I debated over calling Tristan. It was early and I had no idea how late he'd stayed out. And I wasn't sure I could handle the questions he'd undoubtedly have. Not until I had time to think it over and figure out my next step.

Deciding the money was worth it, I looked up a driver on my phone. With a promise of only a ten-minute wait, I crossed the driveway, sat on the curb and hung my head. I wondered if Jesse saw me sitting outside. Was he satisfied, giving himself a high-five for being such a jerk? What would Nash think when he woke up? And was I stupid for falling for Nash? Jesse had pretty much said I wasn't good enough for Nash. Though I was aware I shouldn't listen to him, I couldn't help but wonder if he was right.

Wrapping my arms around my knees, I made myself as small as possible.

The questions ate at the little confidence I'd gained since moving away from home. This was on Jesse, not Nash. But attempting to reason with myself that I was making a big deal from nothing wasn't working. Without any experience in this situation under my belt, I was relying solely on the instinct to get away. I didn't want to be on the verge of tears when I talked to Nash.

I let out a sigh of relief as a red SUV stopped in front of me and the window rolled down, revealing a man with dark red hair and a smattering of freckles over his cheeks. "Rendon Wakefield?"

Rising from the curb, I nodded. "That's me."

The man gestured toward the back seat. "Climb on in."

Once I was settled, I gave him directions to the dorm.

The sky was still overcast and I found it fitting for my mood. So stupid. Why hadn't I realized this would happen at some point when I'd accepted Nash's proposition? Running into people Nash had hooked up with had never crossed my mind and it should have.

The driver pulled up in front of my dorm and I paid for the ride before dragging myself through the dorm doors and up the stairs. The hall was abandoned with the exception of a few bleary-eyed students. Two girls, a blonde and brunette, dressed in tiny shorts and strappy tops giggled as one struggled to slide their keycard into the slot.

When I drew near, the blonde glanced at me and her blue eyes widened. "Hey, I know you!"

"Uh...hey?" If I sounded confused, it was because I *was* confused. We'd lived a few doors down from each other for a few weeks but had never interacted in any way.

"You were with Nash last night!" She sagged against the wall, giving up her fight with the lock.

My lips formed a tight smile as I ignored her comment. "You need some help?"

"Oh my god, please." She jammed the flimsy plastic into my hand.

I easily unlocked the door and handed back the card. "All set."

As I stepped around them to continue on my way, the one who said she'd recognized me latched onto my arm. "So, was it good? I hear he's amazing. I mean, the whole bi thing is weird, but he's hot and one of my friends hooked up with him last year..."

This was not happening again. I refused to listen to it.

Cringing, I jerked my arm away and she crossed her arms. "Do you think you could introduce us?"

Not a chance. "You'll have to introduce yourself."

She jutted her bottom lip out, but I ignored her and stepped away. Behind me, one of the girls cursed and then both giggled before the door slammed closed.

First hearing about Nash with other people and now a request to introduce them? Nash's reputation as the campus playboy wasn't a secret, but I didn't like the way she talked about Nash as if he was only good for sex. An object rather than a person.

A headache formed and my temples throbbed.

Letting myself into my room, I eased the door closed, grimacing at the creak it gave.

Tristan's sheets rustled as he flipped over to his back and I stood still. Once he stopped moving, I undressed and tossed the clothes that smelled like Nash's laundry detergent in the hamper.

"Not that I mind waking up to a naked guy in my room"—Tristan's half-asleep scratchy voice startled me —"but what are you doing sneaking in?"

"Sorry, I didn't mean to wake you up." Wearing only my briefs, I climbed under the covers on my bed and then removed my glasses. Rolling onto my side, I faced the wall and pulled the blanket up to my chin.

"Ren, what's the deal? Something go wrong with you and Nash?" Tristan's mattress squeaked as he shifted around.

"Everything's fine," I mumbled and squeezed my eyes closed.

"Liar," he accused with a gentle tone. "Tell me. Maybe I can help."

Reluctantly, I turned over and found Tristan sitting on the edge of his bed. His figure was nothing more than a blur so I reached out and snagged my glasses, bringing him into focus. A crease marred Tristan's brow as he watched me. Searching his gaze, I deliberated if talking about it might help. Maybe Tristan could give me some advice.

"People saw me and Nash leave the party together last night." Once I started, I couldn't stop as everything that had happened, minus the intimate parts of the night, poured from my lips like a broken faucet. "It's not even seven in the morning, and I've already had two people shove his past in my face. I can't deal with it. At least I don't think I can. It shouldn't be a big deal, right? When I agreed to this whole thing...I didn't think anyone would care, or even find out. And I definitely didn't expect to fall for him, so I...I—"

"Hey." Tristan held out his hand to stop my ramble and I sucked in a deep breath. "One thing at a time. What two people?"

Curling my legs up to my stomach, I hugged my knees. "Apparently, he slept with his neighbor last year."

He whistled low. "Well, that sucks. And this neighbor told you about it this morning?"

I nodded. "Jesse was on the back porch when I went outside. He was drunk and awful. Said I wasn't anything special and only a passing amusement for Nash." I relayed the whole conversation I'd had with Jesse, with every detail, hoping Tristan would have an objective point of view.

Tristan cocked his head while tapping his foot on the ground. "Did Nash hear any of this?"

Sniffing, I shook my head. "No, he was still asleep when I left."

"So, Nash doesn't know any of this happened?" he clarified.

"Nope."

Tristan folded his legs on the bed, crisscrossed. "Sounds like maybe this Jesse guy is hung up on Nash. Nothing else explains that, Ren. Everything he said was a bunch of bullshit spewed by a drunk, jealous dick. You have to know that."

"Maybe." Tristan was probably right, but I was too upset to simply shake it off. And Jesse was only part of the problem. I scowled as I recalled the second run-in. "And then a girl down the hall said something about him too when I was on my way back. She asked me if I could introduce them. Something about her friend sleeping with him. I don't know because I stopped listening. Why do these people think they can just walk up and ask me about him?"

"Maybe because that's been the standard so far." Tristan pursed his lips. "I don't really know."

"I don't think I can do this anymore," I muttered as I picked invisible lint from my sheets. "It's too much. All the people he's been with... What if this is only the beginning?"

"He was single, Ren." Tristan's voice softened. "You can't fault him for the things he's done in the past. These other people, well, his neighbor sounds like a jealous asshole and the girl... I'm not sure if she knew she was stepping on your toes. Know what I mean?"

"I'm not mad at him or judging him. But I don't think I

can have it crammed down my throat all the time either. Can you imagine how bad it would be if we continued to be seen together like that?"

He was quiet a moment. "You said you fell for him."

"I didn't mean to," I whispered as tears blurred my vision, and I blinked them away, only for one to roll down my cheek.

"No one means to. It happens when you least expect it." Tristan gave me a rueful smile.

"Did that happen to you?" I asked him.

"No, but we're talking about you." He worried his lips and tilted his head side-to-side. "So, what you're saying is you love him, but can't handle the baggage that comes with him."

"And stay sane," I added.

"Who says you were ever sane?" Tristan arched a brow. "Do you think Nash feels the same?"

Shrugging, I tightened my hold on my legs. "I have no idea. As far as I know, it's one-sided. But last night was…different."

Tristan drummed his fingers on his thighs as he eyed the wall behind me before flicking his gaze back to me. "I know I'm probably the last person to give relationship advice, but I think you should talk to Nash before you decide anything."

"What am I supposed to say to him?" The thought of bringing up what had happened this morning was enough to make me ill. I didn't want to tell him, not only because it had hurt me but I'd have to tell him why it hurt. And I was sure Nash was aware of how he was perceived around the school, but giving him a play-by-play on what I'd been told seemed cruel. My hands shook with anger just remembering the casual way people talked about hooking up with him.

"I don't know. The truth?" Tristan sounded unsure which didn't help. "What other choice do you have? It's that or walk away, right?"

And that was the problem. I didn't *want* to walk away, but why would I tell him how I felt? If I couldn't handle the gossip and comments that would come with any real relationship with him, what did it matter anyway? Whether I ended it because of my inability to deal with the fallout from his past, or he did because he wasn't interested in anything more than our agreement, my heart would get broken. It was a lose-lose situation.

Rolling back to face the wall, I feigned a yawn. "I'm going to try to catch a few hours of sleep and then I have a huge essay to write today."

Tristan sighed but left me alone.

Needing the distraction, I'd never been more grateful for homework in my life. Anything to keep my mind off Nash and the inevitable talk we'd have to have no matter how much I wanted to avoid it. The one thing about Nash that I both loved and had hated at one point was how persistent he could be. And there was no way he'd let me walk away without an explanation. Though once he got it, he may be the one to cut ties, and the thought squeezed my chest until it was hard to breath.

NINETEEN
NASH

YAWNING, I arched my back and stretched my arms over my head. The AC had run all night leaving the room chilly and I missed Rendon's body heat. I rolled to my side and reached for him only to find cold sheets. Frowning, I sat up. Blackout curtains kept my room dark, so I grabbed my phone from the nightstand to check the time. The screen lit up and I grimaced as my eyes adjusted to the brightness. It was three minutes past nine in the morning. While it was a late morning for me, I hadn't realized he was such an early riser on weekends.

I scratched at the scruff on my jaw and swung my legs over the side of the bed. As I stood it was hard to ignore my morning wood, so I reached down and squeezed my shaft. I groaned and stroked once as I remembered the second round from last night.

GROGGY, my lids cracked open as Rendon's ass pressed against my cock. My hands slid to his hips as I rocked against him. I didn't know how long I'd been asleep, but I was awake enough to know I wanted inside him.

Leaning forward, I pressed a kiss to his shoulder blade and he shivered.

"Rendon," I whispered.

"Hmm?" His sleepy reply made me grin. Was he even aware he'd been grinding on me?

My fingers dragged along his sharp hipbone to his front and wrapped around his hard cock. He hissed and thrust his hips. "Nash?"

"Yeah, babe?" I asked on a groan.

His hand curled around mine, encouraging me to stroke him and he squirmed as I slowly slid my fist up and down, circling his tip with my thumb on each pass.

"I want you." He sighed and reached back over his shoulder, gripping the nape of my neck and drew me closer to his neck where I placed open-mouthed kisses.

Ten minutes later, slicked with lube, I slid inside of him from behind and he moaned as I rocked slowly into him. There was nothing hurried about it. The soft sounds of need that slipped from his lips filled the hushed room and scalded me from the inside. A deep burn that filled my veins and made me hold him closer as I entered him with shallow thrusts.

When I came, it was a full body orgasm that blanketed me with warmth as I groaned into the crook of his neck. He whimpered and I eased from his body, rolled him to his back and trailed kisses down his stomach. Rendon hissed as I licked from the base to his tip.

"Nash, please," he said softly and I took him in my mouth, slowly bobbing my head over his cock, tasting him... loving him. The thought made me pause, but his hand gripping my hair encouraged me to keep going.

I wasn't afraid of my feelings. I was afraid he wouldn't return them.

Pushing my fears aside, I made him come with my mouth and only when he was fully sated did I release him. He tugged on my arms until I retook my place behind him. Burrowing beneath the blanket, he gripped my hand and draped it over his side, locking our fingers together. I held him until he fell back asleep moments later before I gently untangled myself to take care of the condom. When I returned, I'd wrapped myself around him and swore things would be different because I belonged to him now and he belonged to me.

"You're mine," I whispered.

"Mmm-hmm," he breathed out, surprising me that he'd heard.

I placed one more kiss to his shoulder.

A SMALL GRIN crept across my face as I recalled dozing off with his fresh linen scent mixed with sex surrounding me.

Wanting a morning kiss and possible swap of blow jobs, I grabbed a pair of boxer-briefs from my dresser and slipped them on before venturing out to find Rendon.

When I stepped into the living room, I paused. The open concept design let me scan the entire space but it was quiet...and empty. I searched the front porch and back deck. When I found him in neither place, I headed back to my room to grab my phone. He hadn't brought a car so where had he gone?

The mattress sank beneath my weight as I checked for missed calls and texts, but the only ones that waited for me were from people I no longer had interest in. I deleted them. Growing worried, I quickly pulled up my last conversation with Rendon and tapped out a message.

"Hey, where'd you go?"

As I waited, I stopped by the bathroom and then headed to the kitchen, snagging an energy drink from the refrigerator. I carried the can to the dining room and took a seat at the table. Chugging half the drink down, I tapped my fingers against the table. Why would he have left and not said anything?

When nothing came through, I bit the inside of my cheek and debated on sending another message. Had he asked Tristan to give him a ride? I would have taken him home. After five more minutes passed, I decided to knock out a quick shower and then dressed in loose blue shorts and a grey shirt. In the middle of brushing my teeth, my phone vibrated on the countertop. Leaving my toothbrush in my mouth, I snatched it up. Memphis.

"Heading to the sandwich shop for some biscuits and gravy. Want to come with?"

I spit and rinsed before answering. *"Maybe. Give me a minute."*

Switching back to my messages with Rendon, I typed as I strode back to the living room and plopped down on the couch. If he didn't answer again, I would have to stop by the dorm because I couldn't control the unease building in my stomach. *"Everything okay?"*

I breathed a sigh of relief when a reply popped up.

"Sorry, I had to leave early. I have a paper due in the morning."

"I would have given you a ride."

"You never get to sleep in. No worries. Sorry for not letting you know."

Disappointed, I twisted my lips to the side. *"It's fine. I understand. I'm going to head out to breakfast with Memphis. Want me to bring you something?"*

The dots bounced, stopped and bounced again as I picked at a loose stitch on the leather armrest.

"I'm good. We stocked up."

While I was reassured everything was okay, I was bummed I wouldn't be able to spend the day with him. But he had a good reason to head home, I reasoned. I could use the time to catch up on homework too, and without other plans, I decided after breakfast I'd knock it out. We could get back together tomorrow night I hoped, because I found myself already missing him.

"Okay, message me later." I sent and then switched back over to the conversation with Memphis. *"I'm in. Where you at?"*

Just then the loud rumble of a truck engine sounded in front of the house, so I sprang up and checked through the blinds and found Memphis's blue super cab, dings and all, parked by the curb. He knew like any good Texas boy, I was a sucker for biscuits and gravy. I grabbed my things and slipped on my shoes before heading out.

His windows were rolled down and he smirked as I approached the passenger side.

"I might have had plans," I said as I opened the door and climbed inside.

Memphis was wearing a white ballcap and his brown hair curled up beneath the edges. He peered beneath the rounded bill toward the front door of my unit. "Where's Rendon? I figured I'd be taking you both."

As I slid my belt over my chest and clicked it into place, I let a grin slip. "He snuck out before I woke up. Said he had a paper to write."

"Last night went well, I take it?" He gave me a smile that popped his dimple.

"Stop fishing for info." When I reached for the radio, he knocked my hand away and I scowled. "We going to get breakfast or what?"

"You know this whole thing with you two sucks. I'm going to miss all the juicy details." He revved the engine, a deep throaty growl, and then turned the truck around before heading toward campus.

"As if you don't have enough to keep you busy." I snorted and propped my elbow on the open window seal. "No one kept you busy last night?"

"Fuck no. Unfortunately, I had to drive that drunk girl home and decided to just head to my place afterward. Only thing I spent the night with was my hand and then a damn movie—an actual movie. No tits or dick. Fell asleep halfway through."

"Lame," I joked and his lips twitched.

"Whatever. Not all of us are in a super-secret sex arrangement and getting laid whenever we want."

"You *do* get laid whenever you want," I pointed out as he sped up on the main road and the cool morning wind whipped through the open window.

He gave a half-shrug. "It's getting old."

"Since when?" My brow rose.

He gave a non-committal grunt.

"Swearing off sex?" I probed because this wasn't the conversation with Memphis I expected this morning. I'm not sure I'd ever expected it with him. As far as I could tell, he enjoyed an endless stream of ass.

"Nah, but I'm tired of the random, you know?" He glanced at me from the corner of his eye.

I did, but only because of Rendon. "I get it."

"What are you going to do when it ends with Rendon?" he asked with a more sober tone.

My thoughts went back to the night before. "Actually, I'm not sure that's going to be the case anymore."

His head whipped in my direction, eyes wide, before studying the road again as we crossed into the busier part of town. "What do you mean?"

"Last night things changed," I hinted. I should have probably just told him but the comical confusion twisting his features made me laugh.

"Are you two together now?" his tone rose an octave as he slowed to let people across the crosswalk.

Chuckling, I sent him a wide smile. "Yeah."

"You are so whipped it's not even funny." He shook his head but his lips curled into a matching smile. "At least we don't have to worry about Shaw killing you now."

I hadn't even thought about Shaw and what it would mean to tell everyone I was in a relationship. A warm buzz filled my body and I realized I was actually excited to tell them. There was no fucking way I was admitting that. So I simply said, "Shut up."

"What are you doing today?" he asked, shifting topics as we neared the short strip of stores that catered to college students and staff for the most part.

"Homework, I guess. I have shit to get done I've been putting off. Might as well get it over with."

"Now who's lame?" He smirked as he pulled into the parking lot.

"What? It's gotta get done." I defended myself as he circled the lot and found an empty space. "Maybe you should do your homework for once."

"Already did." He popped his door and grabbed his

wallet from the center console. "Some of us aren't procrastinators."

"I'm not..." Well, usually I wasn't. Since Rendon came back into the picture, I had fallen behind and today really was the only time I'd have to catch back up. So it was working out for the best.

"Whatever, let's go stuff ourselves stupid," Memphis said and we hopped out.

Forty-five minutes later, I clutched my stomach as I climbed down from Memphis's truck and waved him off as I walked up the driveway. I made a pit stop by my truck to grab my book bag and carried it inside.

After I'd done my homework, I started a load of laundry, cleaned the kitchen and was mindlessly watching TV when I gave in and texted Rendon. He hadn't touched base all day. This relationship stuff was new to me but I thought he'd at least have sent me some sort of text or call.

"Did you finish your paper?"

No reply came back as I finished the episode of the show I'd settled on. I figured he'd crashed out and didn't want to blow up his phone with more texts if he was resting. Finally, I had to give up and lumbered down the hall to my room and then climbed in the bed. I had to get some sleep. Otherwise, morning practice was going to kick my ass worse than usual.

He'd call or text when he could. In the meantime, his scent lingered on my pillows and that would have to be good enough.

TWENTY

NASH

"STOP BEING A BABY," Memphis yelled from behind me.

It was early as hell when I met the guys at the athletic center. Mondays were the hardest after having a day off, but Coach liked to remind us what was expected of us, with a kick in the ass that started with steep uphill runs that made me, personally, want to curl up and die. Sweat drenched my shirt and rolled down my face and neck.

"Baby, my ass," I panted out as we made our fourth lap. "I'm beating you, aren't I?"

"No, I'm staying behind you in case your ass falls." His breaths wheezed and I smirked.

Once Coach had been thoroughly pleased with his cruel wakeup call, we were sent to get ready for our first classes so we made the trek back to the athletic center.

Memphis shoulder checked me as we entered the locker room that smelled like dirty socks and bleach. "How goes married life?"

"That escalated quickly." I cocked a brow. "We just

made things official. Might be too soon for a ring, don't you think?"

He chuckled as we peeled out of our soaked t-shirts and shorts.

"The rumor is you were spotted with my little bro Saturday night," Shaw said as he kicked off his shoes and started undressing.

Bishop stepped into my line of view and glared.

"Yup," I replied and Shaw peeked around his boyfriend.

"Guess you guys left before we showed up," Shaw said offhandedly, and when I grinned with a waggle of my brow, he cringed. "I don't want to know."

My grin widened as I chuckled and turned to grab my shower caddy from my locker.

He gagged. "Ah, shit. I really don't want to know."

The locker room filled with laughter, but one of the guys cleared their throat and attention swung to him. "Actually, that's not the only rumor I heard."

When I stepped into the giant stall, I found an open space and stood beneath the hot spray, cracking open my bottle of soap. "Oh, yeah?"

"Yeah," another of the teammate's answered from behind me. "What's the deal with you two? Rendon, right?"

"Rendon is Nash's boyfriend," Memphis said from some other part of the shower, but I recognized his voice. Fucker.

"Seriously?" Shaw asked as he and Bishop took up a corner spot. *Their* spot as far as Bishop was concerned. "You and Rendon are like together? As in boyfriends?"

"That a problem?" I asked as I soaped up.

"What the fuck, Sterling? You're dating Shaw's brother?" another teammate asked.

The questions came from all angles, so I held my hands

up. "Whoa, hold on. Yeah, we're together and yes, he's Shaw's brother. Anyone have an issue with that?"

"Well then you might not want to hear—" There was an oomph followed by a deep, "What the fuck, man?"

"Wait, did I just hear Nash Sterling is off the market?" Logan asked, brown eyes sparkling with amusement as he was last to the shower.

Giving zero fucks, I flashed him a grin. "You heard correct."

"I wonder why Rendon didn't tell me," Shaw wondered aloud.

Shrugging, I rinsed the suds from my body. "It's new. I'm sure he just hasn't had time. Did you talk to him yesterday?"

"No." His reply was drowned out by the taunts that started in earnest.

"Whipped." "Never thought I'd see the day." "He definitely hasn't heard..." "Can't blame him. The guy is hot."

The comments overlapped each other, but the last one caught my attention and my head whipped to the side. Fucking Logan of all people. He shot me a cheeky grin and I pointed at him. "You stick to your girlfriend."

He held his soapy hands up beneath the spray. "So touchy."

The room exploded, laughter echoing off the tiles and I glared at them all. "Fuck you guys. You wish you had someone like him."

"We're just messing with ya," Logan said but still the taunts persisted the entire time we finished up and dressed.

I was the first one done, and only once I shut the door behind me, did it get quiet again.

After I hurried through the indoor field, then out to my truck to exchange my gym bag for my backpack, I checked my phone. There wasn't a reply from Rendon yet, but it was early. Hell, the sun had barely risen thirty minutes ago, and between work and classes, he could be up to anything. We hadn't compared schedules and I made a mental note to do that. I shot off a text to Rendon again anyway.

"Want to grab lunch later?"

As I rushed across campus to my first class, I couldn't help glancing around, hoping for a glimpse of blond hair and whatever color button up shirt he'd pulled from his closet. The thought made me smile.

Once I entered the classroom, I claimed a seat toward the middle of the room and several rows up. I pulled out my phone as students filed in and filled the rows of seats, but there was still nothing. It had only been five minutes since the last time I'd checked, but I couldn't help it. I switched it on silent and stuffed it in the front pouch of my backpack.

After class let out and I still hadn't heard from him, a thread of worry crept into my mind. By the end of the second class, my unease had grown. He should have been at least able to check his message and hit me with a response by then. Shit, I'd never been bothered about a call back or text from any guy, or girl. Was I being too quick to jump to the conclusion he was purposely avoiding me?

I wasn't asking my teammates and giving them more ammo to mock me with. So I sucked it up and got through the rest of the day. But when practice ended that evening and the sun set low in the sky, there was *still* no response and real doubt set in.

I chewed on my lip as I made my way back to my truck. Though I wasn't sure how to handle the situation and knew I was likely overreacting, I decided to stop by the coffee house on my way home. I tossed my backpack on the passenger seat, cranked the engine, and then made the short drive to his work.

The chime went off as I stepped inside and joined the end of the long line. Instead of Rendon working the register, a girl with a blonde ponytail that stuck through the hole in the back of her red hat stood behind the counter. I glanced behind her and then scanned the rest of the packed shop. No Rendon. Still, I stayed in line, and when it was my turn, I approached her.

"Hi, what can I get you?" She smiled.

I tapped on the granite countertop. "Actually, is Rendon working?"

She frowned and leaned forward. "No, he called in."

My brow scrunched as my gut said something was definitely wrong. "Is he sick?"

"I have no idea. You might try calling him."

There was no point telling her I'd obviously tried to get in touch with him. But so I didn't seem like a crazy boyfriend, I ordered a blueberry muffin. My stomach growled once I received the paper bag to go and the baked sugar hit my nose. As I sat in my truck, I tore into the muffin. This time when I checked my phone, I wasn't surprised to find there wasn't a message from him, so I hit call. If he was sick, I'd run a few doors down and grab some soup.

After two rings, it went to voicemail. Stunned, I held the phone out and stared at it. He'd rejected the call.

More confused and concerned, I made the decision to stop by his dorm. I didn't care what it made me look like anymore. I wanted to know he was okay.

As soon as I pulled into the parking lot, I spotted his white hatchback and pulled into a space close by, tossed the rest of my muffin in the bag and climbed out. I stalked inside, then climbed the steps two at a time, weaving between students until I arrived at his door. Another wave of disquiet crept through me as I tapped on the cheap wood.

When no one answered after a minute, I knocked a little harder and the door cracked open. Tristan slid through wearing black pajama pants and matching black shirt, a faint scent of cinnamon clinging to him. He put his finger to his lips as he pulled the door closed silently behind him. He pushed me back until we were standing a few feet from the door.

I folded my arms over my chest. "What's going on, Tristan? Is Rendon in there?"

He swept his black hair from his eye and I noticed he wasn't wearing eyeliner. He scowled and hissed, "Lower your voice. The last thing he needs is to know you're here."

"What?" My voice rose rather than lowered. I tried to go around him, but he mirrored my steps. My teeth ground together. "I'm going in one way or another."

Tristan shook his head. "Listen to me for a minute before you go crashing in there. He's had a rough couple of days and hasn't slept well. He only fell asleep about an hour ago, so leave him be for tonight."

"Then tell me what's going on." My voice softened and I took a step back. "Is he sick? His work said he called in, and he rejected my call."

"You went to his work?" His eyes widened slightly.

"It was on my way so I popped in," I defended myself. "Stop stalling and tell me."

"Rendon didn't reject your call. I did. He was driving himself crazy not replying to your texts, so I confiscated his phone." He took a deep breath and moved to the side of the door, sagging against the wall. "He had an early morning run-in with your neighbor yesterday. Jesse was drunk and ran his big mouth."

Tristan gave me a pointed look and after a moment, understanding set in and I balled my fist. "What did he tell him?"

"The truth apparently." He folded his arms over his chest. "That you two hooked up."

I swallowed hard and my blunt nails cut into my palm. "It was over a year ago. I swear it."

"He knows, but that's not all." His gaze flicked to the carpeted floor before meeting my eyes again. "Man, I hope he's not mad that I'm telling you all this. He should be the one to do it, but I'm not sure he ever will. So...he isn't mad that you did all the people you did..."

"Tristan, this isn't funny," I warned. As much as I liked Tristan, this was serious and my patience was thin at best.

"Don't get mad at me, I'm just the messenger." He glared.

"Fuck, okay. I'm sorry, but please...just tell me what happened so I can fix this." I pleaded.

He relaxed again. "So, like I said, he's not mad about that. I mean obviously he's not happy either...know what I mean?"

I thought about running into one of Rendon's exes, if there had been one, and them spilling details about their sex life. My stomach clenched and I was glad I'd only eaten a small part of that muffin. "Yeah, I get it. So, I need to talk to him."

"But then," he continued, "when he got home after he left your place, some drunk girl down the hall said how she'd heard how great you were in the sack and asked him to introduce you two."

"What the fuck?" I practically shouted. "Tristan, let me

talk to him. He said he was writing a paper. I had no idea anything even happened."

"He did have a paper to write." He shook his head and sighed. "And I wish that was everything. But anyway, so he went to class yesterday morning and it happened again, and then again. All of a sudden everyone is in his business. He was blending in somewhere and after everyone saw you two at the party...I guess it opened a can of worms. I mean, I know you have a reputation, but I'd honestly never heard anything about you until this happened."

I had the urge to tell him to just give it time. It was early in the semester and at any given time there were so many rumors and talk behind my back, I didn't even bother trying to keep up. Some were true and some weren't. I should have realized Rendon would take some backlash once people realized he was with me.

Wishing I could get a list of names and knowing it wouldn't do any good because the whispers would only continue to spread, I said, "People need to mind their own damn business."

He nodded. "I don't understand it, but they think he's your boyfriend."

My muscles locked tight and my mouth went dry. I'd told the guys and it wouldn't surprise me if they'd been overheard talking about it or mentioned it their girlfriends. It wasn't a secret, but it just never occurred to me that Rendon would become a target because of it. *What the fuck?* I thought again as a mountain of guilt settled on my shoulders. But then... "Wait. Ren didn't tell you?"

Tristan's forehead creased. "Tell me what?"

It was my turn to be confused. "That we're together."

"Come again?" His expression stayed the same and I reared back.

"Of course they think we're together because I told my team this morning," I explained. "Fuck, I mean...Rendon and I didn't get a chance to talk, but relationships aren't a secret, right? And of all people, I thought he'd tell you. Shit, this is my fault because I didn't even think to warn him about it."

He held up his hand. "Hold on a sec, mister rambler. What are you talking about? You think...it's true?"

"Well, yeah. I told him he was mine and he said...he said..." I bit the inside of my cheek. Something about his response that night triggered a moment of hesitation.

Tristan moved to stand right in front of me. "What did he say?"

"He said...he agreed." Hadn't he? I thought back to that night as I wrapped him in my arms and he...fell asleep.

"Rendon has no idea why people think you two are together," Tristan said with a soft tone and grimaced.

I glanced down at Tristan with wide eyes. "Oh, fuck."

My head went fuzzy and the walls seemed to close in around me as my vision blurred at the sides. A crushing ache filled my chest beneath the weight of causing Rendon pain and the realization that he hadn't wanted to be with me. He had no idea it even happened. It felt like I'd lost him, but I'd never actually had him. Suddenly there were hands on my biceps, squeezing and shaking me out of my shock.

"Hey, big guy, calm down," Tristan coaxed. "I don't want to have to call an ambulance. Do you have any idea how many people it would take to load you up and get you downstairs?"

"I fucked up," I admitted on a whisper and then swallowed around the hard knot in my throat. "He was half-asleep, but I thought he was answering me when I told him he was mine."

It should have embarrassed me to admit it, but Tristan's eyes softened and he sighed as he stepped back, resuming his place against the wall. "Oh, fuck is right."

Slowly, I nodded in agreement.

He rubbed his temples. "Well, this is a clusterfuck and..." He lowered his arms and gave me a sympathetic expression. "You have to tell him and then clean up this mess."

I felt horrible. Worse than horrible. Tristan was his friend and a straight-shooter so I sucked in a breath. "Tell me the truth. Is this fixable?"

Tristan shrugged. "I honestly have no idea. But you'd be stupid not to try. It's pretty clear how you feel about him and he..."

"He what?" I grasped for anything he could give me. I was practically desperate for a way to make this right.

"You two give me a headache, you know that?" He closed his eyes before they snapped back open. "For once I'm going to shut my mouth. You need to talk to him and you need to tell him how you feel. Please."

My stomach dipped, knowing I'd have to admit what I thought had happened between us and my chest tightened once again. A derisive laugh bubbled up my throat. Of course this is what karma does to someone like me. It rips the best thing I *thought* I'd ever had right from my grasp. Feeling like a complete idiot, I gave him a curt nod. "I will and I'll put a stop to this shit he's being put through...somehow."

Tristan offered me a small grin. "There was never a doubt in my mind."

I stepped away and knocked into a guy walking down the hall. "Shit, sorry."

I hadn't even paid attention to anyone who may have overheard but a quick glance up and down the hall revealed he was the only person in sight.

"No problem." The guy went on his way toward the stairs.

I turned to go, but paused. "Thanks, Tristan."

He nodded, but right before I spun away, he said, "Nash, you should know that Jesse did it deliberately to hurt Rendon. Apparently, Jesse was pretty mean about the whole thing. He told Rendon that he wasn't different than any of the others and that he was just temporary. A passing amusement, I believe were the words he used."

Anger curled in my stomach and my fists balled. I gave him another curt nod. "I'll handle it."

He gave me a tight grin before I left. I jogged back downstairs, back to the parking lot and climbed into my truck.

Fuck! I hit the steering wheel, garnering the attention of a few students who were passing by. I glared and they scurried off, which immediately made me feel shittier than I already did. The smell of that blueberry muffin was making me sick, so I rolled down the windows, taking deep breaths of fresh air.

Feeling somewhat settled, I slipped my seatbelt across my chest and started my truck. There was one thing I could handle at the moment, so with a jerk on my gear shift, I spun my tires pulling out of the parking lot and headed home.

Jesse was usually home at this time of day. What the hell was wrong with him to do that to Rendon?

I seethed and white knuckled the steering wheel as I drove and when I turned down the street, I spotted his black muscle car in our shared driveway. My brakes screeched as I pulled in and slammed my truck into park before I jumped out and stormed up to his door. The door shook under the weight of my fists banging against it, and shuffling came from the other side.

The door cracked open and Jesse leaned his shoulder against the door frame. His jeans hung low on his hips and he crossed his tattooed arms over his bare chest. His dark eyes narrowed. "What the fuck, Nash?"

"What the fuck is wrong with you?" I gritted between my teeth.

He blinked. "What are you talking about?"

"Your conversation with Rendon yesterday morning." I checked myself before I punched him and had the police called. "Ring a bell?"

"Who?" He tilted his head and his eyes widened before he laughed. "That kid out on the back porch?"

"He's not a kid, Jesse. Why the fuck did you purposely try to hurt him?"

He straightened and scowled. "I didn't lay a finger on him."

"You know what I mean," I gritted out between my teeth.

"Oh, did he get his feelings hurt?" Jesse smirked. "Why do you care what I said? You banged him, right? One and done."

I took a step forward and lowered my voice until it was nothing more than a deep rasp. "You don't decide what I do with my sex life. You had no business saying *anything* to him."

"So, what? I was a dirty little secret?" he snapped as he leaned back, away from me.

"I wasn't trying to keep you or anyone else a secret," I bit out. "But to throw it in his face was beyond fucked up."

He shrugged and took a step back into his unit. "You're reaping what you sowed."

"What does that mean? I've never made anyone promises. I didn't cheat on anyone. What did I do that was so wrong that you had to step in and try to fuck things up for me with him?"

"So, what?" He blinked again and then his features twisted into an ugly mix of disgust and... jealousy. "The kid's different?"

Then it hit me and a sad laugh filtered through my lips as I shook my head. "This isn't about Rendon. It's about it not being you. Please tell me that's not right. That you didn't try to run him off because you were pissed it wasn't you in my bed."

"Your ego knows no bounds," he said through clenched teeth.

"Then why?" I folded my arms and stared down at him. "You apparently had a lot to say to him so spit it out."

"I didn't say you were wrong." His voice rose and his nostrils flared. "You just fuck anyone and expect not one single person to catch feelings or hope you might notice them more?"

"Not when I've been honest from the beginning about what I want and don't want. Even if he can get past this, you think he'll be okay with you being next door? This was your problem, not mine." If I was a violent person... I shook my head before the thoughts got away from me. I slowed my breathing and calmed myself as best I could. "Look, I never meant to hurt anyone. Hell, I go out of my way not to. I can't control whether you lied about being okay with a simple hookup, so why do it? Do you hate me that much?"

"I don't hate you, Nash. I just don't see what's so special about him." He shrugged and pursed his lips. "Like, what does he have that I don't?"

"It's not like that. You are...*were* a nice guy," I corrected. There was a side of me that didn't want to cause more pain to someone who was claiming I'd already done just that. But what he'd done to Rendon...it was unforgivable in my eyes.

He held up a hand. "Forget I asked. So, you like this one. Gonna keep him?"

It was my turn to clam up. It wasn't whether I was going to keep Rendon. It was if he'd keep me after I told him what I'd done. That I was the reason he'd been the subject of rumors and gossip.

"Oh, this is rich. You storm up here and for what?" He scoffed and crossed his arms again.

"What I do isn't your business. You overstepped. And, yes I do plan on keeping him if he wants to be with me and put up with people like you."

He nodded while a mean smile played on his lips. "And there will be more. You think he's not going to catch shit for being with you. You're delusional."

"Right." I laughed again. This time at myself. I'd made this damn bed and I was being forced to sleep in it. "Fuck you, Jesse."

"Did that already." He smirked.

"Wish I hadn't." I returned the expression, and what I said was the fucking truth.

"Fuck you, Nash." He slammed the door in my face.

Staring at the door, I balled my fist but forced myself to walk away and entered my unit. Pacing the living room, I wondered how I could fix the situation. Dropping onto the couch I leaned forward, elbows on knees and rested my head in my hands.

TWENTY-ONE
RENDON

"STOP JUMPING ON THE BED." I cracked open my lids far enough to glare up at Tristan and kicked at his legs as the mattress dipped beneath his weight.

"Rise and shine, buttercup." He beamed.

Groaning, I pulled the blanket over my head. "Leave me alone. I don't have class until this afternoon."

He hopped off the bed and hit the floor with a thud. And then the blanket was ripped away.

"Stop, Tristan." Holding on to a corner, I engaged in the game of tug-of-war that I eventually lost.

I sat up straight and scowled. "What part of *I don't have to get up* didn't you understand?"

"Well, for one, it's not morning." He cocked a brow and held up one finger. "And two, you have lunch plans with Shaw," he informed me with a second finger popping up.

"Okay..." I searched my memory, but I was sure I hadn't spoken to my brother recently about getting together. "And how did these plans happen?"

"He messaged while you were asleep yesterday. I agreed for you." He tossed the blanket back on my bed and made his way to his desk where he sat and turned the pedestal mirror light on. Only then did I notice he was fully dressed in his usual black skinny jeans and a black shirt with a red and white band logo printed on the front.

"Why would you do that?" I groaned as I snagged my glasses from the nightstand.

"Because I'm a good friend and you need to snap out of it," he said without glancing at me as he popped the lid off his eyeliner. "Get up. I have to leave or I'm going to be late for class and it's already eleven thirty."

I glanced at my nightstand in search of my phone and frowned. "Where's my phone?"

"Oh!" He sprang up and crossed the room before opening the drawer I wasn't allowed in and retrieved it.

When he held it out to me, I eyed it with disgust. "Seriously?"

"It didn't touch anything." He crossed his heart. "I swear it. I just didn't want you to find it and go back to being miserable when you saw all the missed texts and calls from Nash."

"Not cool." I took the phone while glaring at him. "And can you please not mention his name right now. If I have to go meet my brother, I need to at least look like I'm okay."

"You can't avoid him forever," he said as he took his desk chair again and applied the slim black lines.

I unlocked the screen and saw that I did have several texts waiting and a missed call, all from Nash. "I don't plan on avoiding him forever. Can't I figure out what to say first?"

"I don't know, can you?" He stood and grabbed his boots off the floor by the end of his bed before plopping down on his mattress.

Watching as he slipped them on and began fussing with

the laces, I considered his words. So far, I hadn't been able to decide what I even wanted to do, much less how to begin the conversation with Nash. How do you walk away from someone you love? I couldn't. And was I prepared for him to cut me loose? I definitely wasn't. And that left me in limbo. I wanted to tell him what had been going on, but if I did... I reached beneath my glasses and rubbed my eyes.

"Your silence speaks volumes, Ren," Tristan said as he stood and grabbed his backpack. "You didn't see him last night. He deserves answers...and I think you need to hear what he has to say. Between the two of you, you're going to drive yourselves crazy. And I hate to tell you this, but you are creating your own misery. Call him."

My spine went rigid. "You saw him last night? Where?"

"Oh." His eyes went wide. "Did I forget to mention that he stopped by?"

"What the crap?" I screeched and threw my pillow at him. "You don't think that should have been the first thing out of your loud, annoying mouth this morning?"

"Again, it's not morning." His brow rose and he popped his hands on his hips. "And also, I was prioritizing. You're going to be late to meet Shaw."

"You call that prioritizing?" I swung my feet over the side of the bed, ready to get up and strangle him.

He shrugged. "You act like I know what I'm doing." He scratched his chin. "Well, anyway you know now, so put your big boy undies on and call him. But *after* you get moving, because you have"—he tugged his phone from his tight pockets and studied the screen—"about ten minutes before you need to head out if you want to make it on time."

With those parting words, he walked out the door, shutting it behind him. I stared at the space he'd just vacated with a mixture of frustration and confusion. I was going to kill him. It was official, Tristan was my new nemesis. At least for today.

Pushing aside my issues with my roommate slash ex-friend, I stood and darted over to my closet, grabbing the first shirt and pair of shorts I put my hands on, luckily ending up with a green shirt and khaki shorts. After a five-minute shower and rushed morning routine, I threw my clothes on.

My phone chimed as I sat on my bed, lacing my shoes. It was from Shaw.

"On my way."

I had to scroll up through the exchanged messages he'd had with Tristan, though Tristan had never apparently let him know it wasn't me. I found that Tristan had helpfully suggested the local pizza parlor.

Rolling my eyes because I loved pizza but was still mad at him, I typed out a quick response. *"See you soon."*

After I finished tying my laces, I grabbed my backpack and slung it over my shoulder so I could leave from lunch with Shaw straight to class.

I opened the door and nearly had a heart attack when my nose came inches from running into a familiar broad chest.

"Jesus, Nash, you scared the crap out of me." I held a hand against my chest, heart pounding as adrenaline spiked through my body.

He reached for me but then dropped his arms to his sides. "Sorry, I didn't mean to scare you."

My breathing evened as I stared into his sober eyes. Taking a step back, I gripped the doorframe, using it as an anchor. "What are you doing here?"

He sighed and stuffed his hands into the pockets of a

pair of black mesh shorts. "Can we talk? I have something I need to tell you."

Adjusting the strap on my shoulder, I chewed on my lip as I considered what to do. "I'm sort of running late to meet Shaw."

His disappointed gaze locked with mine, but he nodded. "Yeah, okay. Maybe—"

"I guess he can wait a few minutes," I interrupted him and my cheeks heated. I fought the urge to cover them, fully aware they had stained pink.

Nash cocked his head. "You sure?"

"Yeah." I'd already committed to the decision. What Tristan had said piqued my curiosity, and when face to face with Nash, I found it impossible to turn him away. "Do you want to come in?"

He nodded slowly and followed me inside, closing the door behind him. Suddenly the room seemed to shrink to half the size as I sat on my bed and he took a seat at my desk, much like the first time he'd been to my room.

I let my bag fall from my shoulder to the floor and wiped my clammy hands against my shorts as I blew out a deep breath. "What did you have to tell me?"

"You've been avoiding me," he stated.

Caught off guard, I stuttered. "O-oh. Ah, y-yeah, I guess I have been. I'm sorry. I've just been dealing with...stuff."

He bobbed his head. "I stopped by last night and Tristan explained everything."

"What did Tristan explain?" A small sting of betrayal struck my chest as I realized Tristan hadn't explained squat to me. I was beginning to think he'd done it by design, which didn't come as a surprise.

"He told me about the girl down the hall...and about Jesse." Nash's hands fisted on top of his thighs.

I had to admit there was a brief moment of relief that I didn't have to tell him. But if he knew what had happened... why was he here? My stomach sank as I realized he could be moments from doing exactly what I'd feared and cutting ties.

"He told me everything people have been saying to you." His gazed drifted to the floor before meeting mine again. "Ren, I'm sorry this happened. And it's my fault."

"It's not your fault," I argued. Even if he was here to end it between us, I wouldn't allow him to take the blame for it. He'd done nothing wrong. "You didn't force those people to approach me and say anything. All of a sudden it seems like everyone has noticed me and not in a good way. Some people are saying we're...t-together. And I swear I haven't said anything like that to anyone."

"No, you don't understand, babe...Ren," Nash corrected himself and cleared his throat. "I know I can't control what people say, can't rewind time and undo things I've done, but the boyfriend rumor...that's my fault." He grimaced and confusion clouded my brain.

"How can that be your fault?" I wrinkled my nose and my glasses slipped. Pushing them back into place, I studied his guilty expression. "I don't understand."

Nash scratched at the back of his neck and then his shoulders slumped as he shot me an awkward smile. "Damn, this is hard."

"Just tell me what's going on." I grabbed a pillow from the head of my bed, pulled it into my lap and hugged it to my stomach.

"Okay, it's not only going to be hard...it's extremely embarrassing." He cringed and my brows scrunched together.

"Can you please explain? I have no idea what's going on."

"I know. Shit. Okay, here goes." He blew out a ragged breath and placed his hands on his knees as if bracing himself. "The last night you stayed over before all this happened... The second time in the middle of the night, you know when we...?" He rolled his lips together and I flushed at the same time pain sliced through my chest at the memory of how much that moment had meant to me. Still did, despite everything falling apart the next morning.

I nodded. "Yeah, what happened?"

"Well, afterward I was holding you and...fuck. Do you mind if I sit..." He pointed at the bed.

Hesitantly, I scooted over and made room for him to join me at my side.

He stood, slowly stepped close to me and sank onto the mattress. With him this close my nose filled with his scent and I soaked it up. I had no way of knowing if it would be the last time I would be permitted to.

Nash's gaze darted to me and then toward the poster on Tristan's side of the room. "I'm not sure I can look at you when I say what I'm about to say. But you need to know how bad I've fucked up."

"Nash, I'm getting worried." While one arm hung tight to the pillow, the other dropped to the bed and my fingers picked at bits of balled up threads.

"Right, okay, sorry...like I said, it's embarrassing." He shook his head. "No more stalling. So afterward we were lying there and you'd fallen asleep. At least I thought you had. In my mind what had happened was special. It was different and it meant something to me, you know?" He flicked a quick look in my direction before dropping his gaze to the worn carpet. "But I also thought maybe you had felt it too and we were on the same page. I told you that you were mine because in that moment I was filled with an absolute certainty that I belonged to you." This time when he looked at me, he held my gaze. "I *do* belong to you—whatever you choose to do with that information—I want you to know that."

My lungs had frozen in my chest and muscles refused to cooperate. All I could do was blink and listen as shock rendered me mute. This was not the conversation I'd imagined and I was having trouble grasping what he was saying.

When I didn't respond, he sighed. "I'd planned on talking to you about it the next day. About taking a step forward if you were open to it, but you surprised me when you answered me after I'd said it—and agreed. Well, I *thought* you agreed." He frowned. "I mean at the time, I thought you were half-awake, you know? Like dozing, but when I said something, woke up and sort of responded. When I think back on it, I'm pretty sure you had no idea what I'd even said and you just sort of hummed an agreement. Guess it was wishful thinking.

"God, that sounds stupid." He scrubbed a hand over his face. "I never want to admit that to another soul ever again. So, I thought we were together, and the next morning when you'd left, I thought it was weird... but I was mostly just disappointed. You said you had a paper to write and I guess, I wanted to believe that's all that had happened."

Nash glanced at me as if to gauge my reaction and my lips finally loosened. "I really did have a paper to write, but that's not why I left."

"I know that now and had I realized anything had happened, I would have headed straight over."

I had no doubt he would have. If anything, I could

count on Nash to be persistent. "Are we getting to the part about why people think we are dating?" I whispered.

He chewed on his lip and nodded. "I just want to make sure I leave nothing out. So...I told Memphis we were together. Man, I was stupid happy." He chuckled, the sound sad.

Forcing myself to not reach for him when all I wanted to do was comfort him was hard. Instead, I hugged my pillow again. Without knowing where this conversation would take us, my guard was still up, yet crumbling by the second.

"And then yesterday morning," Nash continued, "I figured you'd fallen asleep when you didn't respond to my text Sunday and would call or text when you woke up. No big deal, right? But I was excited...fuck I'm an idiot...but I told the team about us. I had no idea what a colossal mistake I was making. Someone must have overheard them talking about it or told their girlfriend. Who knows." He shrugged and puffed a breath. "But word got out, and that's why this is happening to you. And now, not only was I completely wrong, but you are catching shit for it. I feel like an idiot and a complete dick."

A niggling memory from that night tried to worm its way through, but I couldn't grasp it. But what I was beginning to understand was that Nash had wanted to be with me; my hands shook and stupid tears clouded my vision.

"This is on me," he continued and sniffed. "I know that. And I'll fix it, okay? I wanted you to know that and you deserved the truth. There, I said it." He took several deep breaths and then glanced at me. "How mad are you?"

"You...?" My mouth opened and closed. I wasn't mad. I was...stunned and having trouble getting a handle on my emotions while they twisted and ran circles around my mind, body and heart.

He nodded. "Yeah, I know. I messed up, but like I said, I'll fix it. I'm so damn sorry. I never expected people to treat you like that."

His eyes were slightly swollen, I realized, and my chest tightened as I reached out to touch the puffy skin.

"Ah, yeah. Little bit of a rough night." He shrugged as if it wasn't a big deal.

Nash had told his team we were together. Official. "Boyfriends?" The word tumbled from my lips.

"I know. The more I hear it, the more I realize how bad it is." He blew a raspberry and sniffed again. "At least the guys will get a kick out of it."

"You're not going to tell the guys," I muttered.

"Of course I am." His brows furrowed while he stared at me. "I told you I'd fix this."

Reaching out, I finally grabbed his hand. "No."

"No?" He frowned.

Shaking my head, I wove our fingers together. "Why did you tell me I was yours, and what do you mean when you say you're mine?"

Nash glanced down at our locked hands and squeezed. "If I say it, it's only going to hurt more and maybe make things worse."

"Say it anyway?" I asked.

He swallowed audibly. "If that's what you want."

I held my breath as he turned on the bed and faced me fully.

His gaze softened and those intense eyes of his bore straight into mine. "Ren, I love you. I'm not sure when that happened...but I think I knew you were different all along. As time went by, I knew you would be my game changer.

Somewhere in between, I fell in love, and now I've completely messed up. I know you weren't looking for that, and again this is on me. You've done nothing wro—"

"I love you." The words whispered from my lips.

Nash stilled and his mouth snapped shut. His chest rose and fell, a clipped beat as he closed his eyes. "Repeat that?"

He was being so open with me, it was only fair that I return the gesture. And I found myself *wanting* to like I'd never wanted anything in my life. "I love you. Already knew I did when I left that morning, and that's what made it so hard. I didn't want to lose you."

"God, I'm so damn sorry. Can I..." He reached for me but then pulled his arms back. "I'm not sure what this means." He gave me a small grin. "Help a guy out?"

As I stared at him, I had to wonder what this did mean. Having Nash admit he loved me was something I was completely unprepared for.

"I think...it means we give it a try?" A few minutes ago, I'd been upset and on my way to get pizza with Shaw. And now... "But..."

"What do you need from me?" His words rushed out.

Everything.

"It's not that. You're perfect." My cheeks heated. Shocker.

A trace of that cocky smile tugged at his lips before replaced with a sad smile. "It's not enough, is it?"

"Nash, I didn't say that." I gripped his forearm. "Not even close to what I was going to say. You know about all the things happening, about what people are saying. I was having trouble dealing with everyone talking about me and asking questions about you. Like things I don't want to hear, know or be asked. It's uncomfortable and I don't like it."

"I don't blame you. And that's a product of who I was. Had I known you'd step into my life, I wouldn't have—"

"I'd never hold that against you. I just want us to not be other people's business. As long as you are a star in this town, it will always be like this," I explained.

He turned and faced the wall again, resting his elbows on his knees as he rubbed his brows. "I understand."

Did he? Obviously I was doing an awful job of getting my point across. "Nash, I want to be with you."

He cast a wary glance at me. "But?"

I shook my head. "No buts."

He slowly turned his body toward mine once more. "No buts..."

I shook my head again. "I was trying to say that I will have moments of doubt and need reassurances. I might need to complain or rant and then ask you to hold me after. If you can deal with—"

"Done." He said the word so fast that I laughed, causing him to grin. "So, does this mean we're together this time? You know, I need clarification."

A chuckle of disbelief vibrated in my chest. "Yeah, I think it does."

"Kiss on it?" he suggested and I nodded.

"Good plan. There's no backing out afterward," I warned.

He tackled me to the bed. With a squeak, I sprawled out beneath him and he gazed down into my eyes. "It might be hard sometimes, you're right."

I nodded as my gaze searched his. "Life's not perfect, but before, I worried I'd be dealing with this alone."

"As long as we're together, that's not going to happen. Understood?" He pecked a kiss on my nose.

"You can't keep people from talking." I gripped his shirt. "You aren't that good."

He snorted but his expression quickly sobered. "I'll do everything in my power then. How's that?"

His face grew blurry as my eyes filled with tears and my nose tingled.

"None of that." Nash rolled on his side and pulled me against his chest as we struggled to fit on the small bed. "We do this as a team, okay?"

When I nodded and sniffed, Nash loosened his grip on me just enough to lean back. I wiped away the single tear that had fallen, and he dropped a kiss to my forehead.

"You said something about kissing on it," I choked out and the grin that split his face would be tattooed in my mind for the rest of my life. And then he swooped down and covered my mouth with his. Fast and hard, then slow and soft. Closed-mouthed, then tongues tangling. He promised me so many things with each kiss and without a word, I believed every one of them.

When we parted, we both struggled for breath. His lids hooded and he lowered his voice as he pressed his hard cock against mine, grinding and drawing a moan from my lips. "When does Tristan get back?"

My phone rang, causing me to jump and scramble from the bed. I checked my phone though I already knew it would be from Shaw.

"This pizza is fantastic. Feel free to join me."

"Crap," I muttered as I ran to the bathroom to check the damage. While I finger combed my hair Nash stepped in behind me and wrapped his arms around my waist.

"What's up?" he asked.

"My brother." I turned in his arms to face him. "I was on my way out and completely forgot. This is your fault."

"I'd apologize but I'm not sorry." His lips quirked and eyes sparkled with amusement. He leaned down for another kiss and muttered against my lips, "To be continued."

When he pulled back, I chased his lips and he chuckled, gave me a solid swat on my butt and stepped back. "You better get going. Can't have my boyfriend's brother too mad at me."

"Boyfriend," I repeated with a grin.

"It's a weird word, right?" He tilted his head and pursed his lips.

I shrugged. "I like it. I've never had one before."

He grinned, like I knew he would. He loved being all of my firsts. "Same. Boyfriend it is then."

My throat tightened and my smile widened as my heart skipped a beat. I was a massive mess of emotions, but the one soaring above the rest was relief, as odd as it might sound. Not only was I not losing Nash, I was gaining someone who loved me as much as I loved them.

Nash walked me downstairs and out across the parking lot.

"Are you walking or driving?" he asked.

"Well, I was going to walk but I'm late." I shook my keys I'd snagged on the way out. "I need to get going. Shaw's not known for his patience."

"Okay, text me later," he said.

"I will," I promised.

He pressed a quick kiss to my lips and then I jumped into my car. I grinned when I saw he was watching me, and he grinned back before he pulled a cherry sucker from his mouth, unwrapped it and popped it in his mouth. Then he turned around, presumably to head for his truck.

My gaze drifted down his body. My boyfriend had a really nice butt.

TWENTY-TWO

RENDON

"I'M SO SORRY I'm late," I said as I stuffed myself onto the red leather bench opposite Shaw. The smell of greasy perfection assaulted my nose and my stomach growled.

"I almost left," Shaw said as he plucked a black olive off the large pizza sitting in the center of the table. Two slices were already gone.

"I'm like ten minutes late. Calm down." I peeled a slice of cheesy goodness from the tray, forgoing a plate, and stuffed a giant bite in my mouth. "So good," I groaned.

"Ten minutes by whose watch?" He removed most of the olives from the rest of the slices because he knew I hated when he did that. "You're lucky I didn't eat it all."

"Whatever, where's my drink?" I asked after I swallowed.

"What am I? Your servant?" He took a long, exaggerated sip from his straw placed in a large red cup. "Get your own drink."

I rolled my eyes but scooted back out of the booth and fetched a cup from the counter. The restaurant was decked out in shades of red and dark green with white and black checkered floors. I spotted the soda fountain along the back wall and filled my cup with ice and sweet tea before returning.

"Jerk," I muttered as I slid back in my seat.

Shaw slouched in his seat, drink hanging from his fingertips. "So, how's school going?"

"Did Mom and Dad put you up to this?" I griped before I shoveled another big bite into my mouth.

He twisted his lips. "No."

"You're such a liar," I accused while glaring.

Shaw grinned causing wrinkles at the corners of his green eyes that mirrored mine. "You know how Mom is, but I wanted to catch up anyway. Someone's always too busy to hang out with me."

"I've had a lot going on." I shrugged. "And I have hung out with you."

"Twice." He held up two fingers.

"Sorry, I didn't realize you'd be able to detach from Bishop long enough to do this." I waved my hand around the parlor.

"Deflection is not a good look on you." He began picking the pepperoni from the tops of the pizza and I swatted his hand.

I confiscated two more slices he hadn't had the chance to destroy. "I hate when you do that. Maybe I actually want pepperoni on mine."

"Answer me and I'll stop." He reached across the table for my plate and I groaned.

"It's been fine, okay." I jerked my plate away from the table. "Jeez, you're annoying, you know that?"

He sat back and smirked. "Classes going well? Meeting new people? Friends? ...*Boy*friend?"

I paused with a slice half way to my mouth as understanding struck. "Mom didn't send you, you liar. You're just being nosy."

"Never said Mom sent me, now did I?" He smirked and I scowled.

"You think you're so smart," I grumbled as I picked up a napkin and wiped my mouth.

"Bishop thinks I am," he retorted and I choked on a laugh.

"Fine, yes I have a boyfriend." It was so new that I squirmed on top of the squeaky leather material. The words were still foreign. Jeez, my brother couldn't even give me thirty minutes to adjust. But I had to admit at the same time, the words made my heart speed up. Because it was Nash and he was everything I wanted. And he was mine.

"Anyone I know?" my stupid brother taunted.

I shrugged again. "I have no idea."

He scoffed and leaned forward, elbows on the table. "When were you planning to tell me you're dating Nash?"

"Um, never?" I offered.

Shaw feigned a pout. "You know when Nash told me he was going to pursue you, I laughed. I told him there was no way you'd fall for his shit...not in those words, but you get the idea. Way to make me look dumb."

"You look dumb already," I pointed out and it was his turn to scowl.

"You're lucky I love you." He flicked one of the pepperonis at me and I peeled it from my shirt, eyeing the stain.

"You too," I growled out as I dabbed at it with a napkin, zero success with removing it.

"Rendon," Shaw said and when I glanced up, he frowned. "I didn't want to bring this up, but I feel like I have to. Have people been...harassing you?"

How did he know? My hands balled around the napkin as frustration set in. "Did Nash call you?"

"Wait." Shaw's shoulders squared. "This *is* happening, and Nash knows?"

"I didn't come to lunch to get harassed. Can't we just hang out?" When I considered what might distract him I asked, "How's practice going?"

Shaw's eyes narrowed. "You don't care about football, so tell me what's going on. Don't make me drag it out of you, because one of the guys said he overheard a comment that was made to you yesterday in class. We have freshmen on the team, Ren."

"Order thirty-seven!" The shout drew my attention away. A guy with brown hair around our age stood behind the counter, glancing around expectantly.

"Ren," my brother snapped. "What's been going on? And why haven't you come to me?"

"Nothing has been going on," I insisted, but when he gave me the big brother stare I relented. "Fine. Some people have been coming up to me and saying stuff about Nash and things he's done and it sucks, okay?"

Shaw sighed. "Relationships are hard anyway. I can't imagine adding that to it."

"That's not the worst part of it," I muttered. "I keep having people ask me if Nash is really my boyfriend and there's always comments like 'how did *you* get him?'. It's the way they say it and look at me. Makes me feel bad I guess."

There was no reason to fill Shaw in about our situation prior to Nash showing up at my place. It would only cause problems and I wanted nothing to come between me and Nash.

"You guess?" Shaw said in a low steady voice, but when I looked up his jade eyes were practically on fire. He was mad. Like really mad and that didn't happen often. "How long has this been going on?"

"The boyfriend stuff just started yesterday morning, which made sense because Nash told me he'd told all you guys." Which had only registered that Shaw would have heard at that very moment. "He said he guessed someone overheard or one of the players told a girlfriend. Could have been anything. But it was like non-stop attention and whispers...and then blatant comments to my face, which I'm guessing is what your teammate heard."

When Shaw only tapped the table, staying mute as he turned his gaze toward the front door, I wondered if I'd made a mistake in giving him that much detail. I was glad I hadn't brought up Jesse because steam was practically oozing from my brother's ears.

"Shaw?"

My brother continued to drum his fingers on the table and gave a curt nod to absolutely no one. "People are now harassing you because you are with Nash and think they can..."

The question was rhetorical and unfinished. I could tell he was only thinking out loud, and my thoughts drifted to a particular moment in class yesterday. One of the many run-ins of the day.

I WAS PHYSICALLY present in class, but I couldn't follow the lesson at all. I was too distracted to pay attention to the Spanish teacher who was droning on about nouns while pointing at the projected image of their translations. Tristan sat next to me in the only class besides History that we shared.

I had wanted to skip classes today since I was still shaken up about the confrontation with Jesse and that drunk girl's request to set her up with Nash. I shuddered just thinking about it. Of course, Tristan had decided I was going and wouldn't stop poking me in the ribs until I got irritated enough to get up.

Tristan was being uncharacteristically quiet as I doodled on a spiral notebook, lost in my thoughts. Not even twenty minutes into the lecture, I was tapped on the shoulder from behind.

Turning in my chair, I gave the guy with cropped brown hair, brown eyes and wearing a black polo a questioning look.

"Are you really with Nash?" His assessing gaze took me in and he sneered. "Because—"

I held up my hand to stop him and spun back around in my chair, glancing up at the front of class. I'd had enough for the day. I couldn't understand why everyone thought Nash and me were together. Because we were seen at one party? Had we been spotted somewhere else? I just couldn't figure it out. But the entire morning had been that way. People coming up to me, asking if I was really with Nash. Some asked really personal questions and it was awkward. And then there were the looks of disapproval with the questions of why he'd pick me. Those hurt.

I'd learned giving them any kind of response only encouraged more questions and remarks, so I didn't bother. But now more than ever, I knew I had to talk to Nash. I didn't want him thinking I'd started that rumor, but I wasn't ready to face him yet because I had more I needed to confess.

While I stayed quiet, Tristan had plenty to say as he

spun around to face the guy. "Mind your own business, you nosy ass—"

I swatted Tristan's arm. "Don't even bother."

He gaped at me. "But I have an arsenal of interesting insults. Are you sure you don't want to hear them? They are hilarious."

Though I was tired and frustrated, my lips twitched. "I'm sure you do."

The guy behind us snorted. "Yeah, mind *your* own business, goth boy."

"Whatever, purple dicknose fuck box," Tristan sang.

My eyebrows shot up and then my nose scrunched. "Purple... Really?"

"What? I got it off an insult generator. Whoever created those are pure genius. I mean, I added the purple part...but yeah. Awesome comebacks and I don't even have to think them up."

He yawned and stretched his back as I just stared at him. He relaxed and winked. "I have more. Now do you want to hear them?"

I shook my head. "I think I'm good."

After we were dismissed, I parted ways with Tristan on my way to Chemistry. And it was more of the same, but I didn't have Tristan to back me up.

THE SLAM of Shaw's drink on the tabletop snapped me out of the memory and he shot out of the booth.

"Hey, what are you doing?" I asked.

"You said something at the sandwich shop that made me think high school wasn't a topic of discussion you cared to visit." He paused with flared nostrils. "Were you bullied, Ren?"

"I...ah..." My mouth hung open, because I wasn't prepared for that question and he seemed so angry.

He jaw ticced. "I wish you'd told me. I should have thought about this, but when I came out..." His stare turned dark. "I may not have protected you then, but I'll be damned if that happens here."

"What are you doing?" I asked again as he dug his wallet from his pocket and tossed some bills on the table.

"Look, relationships are hard work, Ren. More so with guys like Nash and Bishop." He shook his head and then held my gaze again. "But you shouldn't have to go through more hurdles just because people have an issue with you two dating. It's not their business."

"No, I shouldn't and neither should anyone else, but be serious, Shaw. What can you do? Nothing. You can't jeopardize your spot on the team and risk your scholarship. And anything you did wouldn't help because you can't stop people from talking." My voice had risen and he flicked his gaze to the tiled floor. I softened my voice. "I know you want to protect me. I get it. But I need to handle this. I've thought a lot about it...non-stop, actually. And...if things work out with me and Nash, this kind of thing could happen on a much larger scale. I can handle it. I have to because he means that much to me."

Shaw stood at the side of the table, nostrils flaring. "Rendon, I can't just sit by—"

"You can and you will. I'm a big boy now," I teased.

He growled. "It's not funny."

My expression sobered. "It's not, but it's life and I need to be prepared for it. I'm serious about Nash."

Shaw slouched back onto the bench. "You love him?"

I nodded. "More than anything."

"And he..."

"Loves me back." I shrugged. "Crazy but true."

He gave me a dopey smile. "Not crazy. The fucker is lucky to have you and you need to remember that."

"We are lucky we have each other," I corrected him and tossed a pepperoni at him.

He scowled as he peeled it off his shirt and I grinned when I saw the greasy spot it left behind. "Payback."

"It's hard to stand aside and do nothing," Shaw grumbled and I nodded in agreement.

"I'm asking you to anyway."

He gave me a long hard stare before he breathed out a sigh. "Fine, but I don't like it."

"There are lots of things I don't like, such as you picking off all the olives and yet you do it anyway."

"That's different," he said but laughed as he plucked off yet another one.

"You're such a jerk," I growled as he popped it in his mouth.

heard banging lockers and raised voices bitching about being tired and talking about their latest conquests. The usual. And the sudden thought that these guys, and even me at one point, had done the exact same thing. We gossiped about girls, and guys in some cases, the same way a fraction of the student body was doing to Rendon, and a wave of shame passed over me. It had never crossed my mind we could be overheard and hurt someone in the process.

As I stepped into the locker room, Memphis tipped his chin at me and stretched. "Shit, I'm tired."

I slipped by my teammates who were dressing for conditioning and headed for my locker.

Since I'd worn the clothes I intended to work out in, I attempted to toss my bag into my locker but the door stuck. In my frazzled state the more trouble it gave me the more my frustration grew.

"Fuck," I growled as I gave it a hard yank and it popped open and smack the locker beside it with a long clang. I threw my shit in and slammed it closed with equal force.

"Whoa, what's with the hostility?" Memphis said, and my gaze flicked his way as he approached my side with raised brows.

Sighing, I dropped my ass onto the metal bench and rubbed my eyes as my shoulders sagged.

"I just overheard some girls saying stuff about Rendon." I glanced up at Memphis. "I'm tired of it, you know? It's like I keep letting him down because I can't stop it. And I'm also dealing with trying to find a new place because of you know..."

I'd filled Memphis in on my neighbor situation and he'd called me an idiot which I couldn't argue with.

Memphis wrinkled his nose. "Yeah, that was just stupid."

"Yes, I know." I kicked at the floor and hung my head.

The door swung open and Coach scowled as he scanned the room with narrowed eyes. "Anyone planning on showing up today?" When everyone only stared, he shook his head. "Get your asses in gear and we'll add an extra lap for wasting my time. Anyone whining will see me afterward for additional community service."

Some of the guys groaned and Coach zeroed in on them. "It starts now."

The door swung shut as he left and we scrambled as one through the door. We were supposed to do hill runs and that was probably why no one was in a hurry to meet up with Coach. Well, we'd pay for that now. Just as I was about to step over the threshold from the locker room, my arm was snagged from behind me. I glanced over my shoulder and found it was Memphis who'd stopped me.

"Hang on a minute," he said and waited until the last person left. "I don't know what we can do about campus gossip. But I might be able to help with the neighbor issue because that *is* going to be a problem."

My brow dipped. "How can you help?"

"You know my parents are heavy into real estate. I know for a fact they have a few vacant houses in the area. Not as close to campus as your place but doable."

I shook my head. "I can't ask your parents to rent me something because it would be out of my budget. I'm lucky to be in the place I am." My parents made good money, but I couldn't ask them to pay extra rent on top of everything else they'd provided for me, including my tuition. The truck I drove had technically been my dad's, but since he didn't drive much anymore, he'd passed it down to me. They had

I needed a break from it too. I grabbed my phone from the side table and hit pause.

There were two missed messages from Rendon and I opened them as I continued to down my water.

"Tristan is rearranging his closet again while blaring some metal band that's giving me a headache. Since you said you were staying in tonight, I'm on my way over."

I checked the time the message was sent. Ten minute ago.

My eyes widened as I glanced around the living room. Most nights he spent with me, but occasionally he stayed in his dorm since Tristan insisted I share Rendon and *split custody*. His words. And tonight was Tristan's night. We hadn't had plans together and that was why I'd chosen to pack while he was away...because he had no idea what I was doing.

Was it okay to lie to your boyfriend and tell him you weren't home? Probably a bad idea, but I didn't want him to try and talk me out of it. And I wanted it to be a surprise. Resigned, I tapped out a reply. *"See you soon."*

Well, hell. The cat would be out of the bag soon, so I stood and grabbed one of the smaller flat boxes and unfolded it, taping one side shut before I flipped it over.

Using stack of newspapers, I began wrapping my picture frames from the mantle and gently placing them in the box.

I'd only finished packing three of them when a light knock on the door sounded and I held my breath. Here goes.

When I opened the door, Rendon bit his lip then his gaze darted next door and back to mine. I tensed. But then he grinned and my heart thumped hard in my chest. Despite him ruining the surprise, I couldn't stop the itch to grab him and hold him but refrained because I was pretty gross at the moment and smelled like cardboard and sweat.

When I stood there staring at him, he shuffled his feet. "Is it a bad time? I should have asked you first, huh?"

"What? No, Ren. You come over whenever you want. Get your cute ass inside." His grin returned and I stepped out of the way, ushering him in. When I turned to follow him, I ran straight into his back where he stood, frozen, and nearly knocked him on his face. Wrapping my arms around him, I steadied him and couldn't stop myself from taking a deep inhale of his fresh scent.

"What's going on?" Rendon whispered and only then did I notice his body was rigid.

Circling around him, I chanced a glimpse of his face. His brow was furrowed and he worried his lip as he scanned the room full of boxes and items laying around waiting to be put away.

"Ah..." I gave an awkward chuckle and scratched the back of my neck as a sudden sweep of nervous energy coursed through me. "I'm moving to another house?"

I hadn't meant that to sound like a question and he looked up at me with a frown. "Why? You didn't tell me you were moving. Are you...leaving?"

"No. I mean, yes, but only a little further out of town. Memphis's parents are huge into real estate." I couldn't remember if I'd ever had a reason to tell him that. I bit the inside of my cheek and then powered on. "They have a vacancy. It's a single-family home, completely updated. It's a little small, but we don't need much space and it has two bedrooms, a deck and fenced in yard. I think you'll like it."

"We?" His brows shot high.

"I'm totally fucking this up." I sighed. "I wanted to surprise you and didn't want you to try and talk me out of it.

It's a done deal. And you know what I mean. I'm not asking you to move in with me." *Yet.* "But you already spend a lot of nights with me so, yeah...we."

When he continued to watch me, I was the one who began to fidget. "You don't like the idea. Why?"

Rendon shook his head. "It's not that, but why are you moving? It's your senior year and you may not even be there for the whole spring semester."

"Any chance I can snag a quick shower before we continue this conversation?" I asked with a hopeful smile.

He shook his head *no* and my chest rattled with reluctant laughter. "Fine, but when you get close enough to smell me, that's on you."

"I can already smell you." Rendon cocked a brow and my laughter continued as he began wading through the mess until he sat on my couch. He frowned, reached under his ass and retrieved a roll of packing tape that had, somehow, been wedged between the cushions. I wasn't even sure how it got there.

He toyed with it, rolling it in his hands as his gaze latched on to mine. "So?"

A long breath rushed from my lungs as I sat on the cushion next to him and reached for his hands. He dropped the tape on the floor and wove his fingers with mine.

"We need out of here," I said while holding his gaze.

He tilted his head. "Okay. But, why?"

I gave him a pointed look. "Ren, you know why. You're not comfortable here. I'm not comfortable here."

He ducked his head. "I can handle him next door."

"Ren, look at me." I waited until he did and then continued as I squeezed his hand. "I know you can. You're stronger than I could have ever imagined, but I can't. It kills me that you don't use the back deck or front porch when I know you like it. I hate that stupid black car parked in my driveway and the way we both grow silent when we hear his engine coming and going. And when either of us have to see him... Hell, just knowing he's there bothers me, and more than anything, it bothers me that you *can handle it*. You shouldn't have to and I feel like we have this lingering black cloud over us while we stay here.

"You've managed the campus gossip and I wish I could do something to stop it other than give people the cold shoulder, ya know? But this? I can do something about this. So please let me."

As I'd spoken my piece, Rendon's expression ran a full array of emotions. Confusion. Understanding. Frustration. Happiness. But then his lips twitch. "Do I get the second bedroom?"

"Fuck no." I shouted, surprising us both and his eyes widened before he began laughing.

I pounced on him, maneuvering him sideways on the couch and laying him flat on his back. He spread his legs, one dangling off the couch, and I positioned myself between them as I stared down into his bright jade-green eyes.

"Nash," he breathed out as he searched my eyes.

"Yeah, babe?" I dipped down to kiss his neck and he hummed.

"You really do smell bad," he whispered.

I choked on a laugh and buried my face in his neck as my shoulders shook. When I lifted up to look at him, I grinned. "Too bad. I offered to fix that problem and you said no. Now kiss me."

Rendon sighed when I lowered my mouth to his and opened to me. I slid my tongue alongside his and tangled them together. He moaned and I grew hard. Fuck, I'd never get tired of his taste or the way he felt beneath me.

When I'd thoroughly devoured him, I sprang to my feet and pulled him up with me before I lifted him, my palms gripping his ass.

"Put me down. Why are you always handling me like a rag doll?" Rendon griped but despite his words, he wrapped his arms around my neck and legs locked around my waist. "When are you supposed to be done packing?"

"The guys will be here to help me move in the morning," I murmured as I placed another kiss to his lips.

"Shouldn't we finish then?"

"Oh, I plan to." I smirked and he rolled his eyes. When I grinded against him, he rolled them for a different reason and gasped as his legs tightened around me.

Without further questions from his cute mouth, I carried him to the bathroom and set him down on the counter while I cranked on the shower and shut the door.

As I stripped out of my dirty clothes, Rendon's gaze latched on to each part of my body I bared for him until I was completely naked. Under his scrutiny, eyes full of want, my cock pulsed and I stepped toward him. Slowly I started on his buttons, releasing them one at a time and his breathing sped up as I revealed inch after inch of flawless pale skin.

"Stop teasing," he whispered and I smirked.

"Tell me what you want then," I rasped out as the room filled with steam and the mirror fogged.

With a hand pressed to my chest, he pushed me back and hopped off the counter. Foregoing a slow tease, he tore out of his clothes and was on me in seconds. Standing on his toes, he pulled me down by the back on my head and, with a solid bite to my bottom lip, demanded I kiss him.

"Oh, fuck yes," I growled out and walked him backward toward the shower.

Rendon wrapped his arms around me and I lifted him by his ass again as I stepped over the lip of the tub and beneath the hot spray. Pressing his back against the tiled wall, I continued plundering his mouth with my tongue, twisting and sucking around his as I ground our cocks together. I pulled back and his chest rose and fell as he took heavy breaths.

"I thought we were showering," he panted out with a mischievous grin.

"Oh, we are." I smirked and lowered him to his feet. Grabbing the bottle of soap off my shelf, I squirted a dollop onto my palm and worked up a lather. With my eyes focused on his, I ran my hands all over his body, making sure not to miss an inch. I wrapped my soapy hand around him, jerking him off, and fondling his sac with the other.

"I like the way we shower," Rendon muttered and then moaned when I tightened my fist.

I smothered a laugh. He was so cute and smoking hot at the same time. And he was mine.

While I continued to stroke him, I moved my other hand, trailing my fingertips over his pale skin as I circled around his hip and gripped a handful of his ass and squeezed.

He gasped and rocked his hips, thrusting into my grip around his cock.

"Is there something you want?" I lowered my tone and then angled my head around to nip at his earlobe. At the same time, I slid a finger down his crease and applied pressure to his entrance. "Maybe you want me here?"

"Yes," he hissed and pushed back against my finger, trying to force me inside.

"How bad do you want it?" I rubbed and circled as his

hole softened. He rocked against my finger and my control was hanging by a thin tattered thread.

"Stop being a jerk," he whimpered.

I chuckled as I pressed in. He cried out and his head dropped back against the wall as the shower rained down onto his chest. I sank my finger inside him as deep as I could go and he rode it, moaning and chanting my name. With my other hand I worked him harder and he cursed. Hearing a dirty word slip from his innocent lips made my cock throb.

When his stomach contracted and he clenched around my finger, I knew he was moments from orgasm so I withdrew from him and released his shaft.

"No," he complained. "That was just mean. I was so close."

I nipped his pouty lip. "I promise to make it up to you. Turn around."

"Oh, okay." He eagerly turned and I had to bite back a grin.

He was so responsive to my touch and I loved how much he craved it because he did the same damn thing to me. I grabbed the lube and a condom I'd placed in the shower for these exact moments and suited up.

With slicked fingers, I entered him with one and then another. When he got close to coming, I pulled away until he calmed down, only to return with a third. Once he took three and tossed his head back, I'd had enough. I slipped free, but he didn't complain. Not when he glanced over his shoulder and saw that I was lubing my cock. His eyes hooded as he watched me stroke myself.

"Ready?" My voice sounded as if it had been dragged a mile through shards of glass.

"Always," he said while impatiently lifting his ass.

I smacked it and lined up my cock to his hole. Our

drastic size differences made the position difficult but not impossible. With bent knees, I leaned over Rendon and with one shove bottomed out inside him.

His moan met my groan in a long drawn out chorus that echoed off the bathroom walls.

"Fuck, you're so damn tight. I'll never get enough of the way you clench around my cock. Fucking never," I swore and dropped my forehead to his shoulder as I bathed in the pleasure shooting from my cock to every inch of my body. I shuddered and gripped his hips.

"Me either. Now move," he demanded and rose higher on his toes.

"Bossy." I grinned and lifted my head, eased back and snapped my hips forward. "*Fuck.*" My shout vibrated off the tiles and I began a ruthless pace that he kept up with, demanding more and harder.

The bathroom filled with grunts, groans and moans. And the sound of skin slapping against skin drew my balls tight as I filled him over and over. He was so sensitive that I didn't even have to touch his cock to make him come. Ass play alone was always enough to get him off, but it drove him crazy when I jacked him at the same time, and I wanted him completely out of his damn mind when he came for me. So I reached around him, gripped his cock tight, stroked him fast, and bit his shoulder.

"Oh, god," he shouted. "Nash, please."

I wasn't going to last. Not when his needy moans set my blood on fire and orgasm racing from my balls. My cock was ready to explode in his snug ass.

"Come for me," I demanded and he shoved back, meeting me thrust for thrust. "Fucking come, or I'll blow first."

His head dropped forward as his come shot from his tip and dripped onto my hand, warm and sticky. "Fuck yes."

I thrust once more and came so hard my knees buckled. I caught myself and flopped down against his back, breaths heaving from my lungs. "Give me a minute."

He laughed, which made him clench around me again and I groaned.

He laughed harder and I straightened, easing from his body and spun him around.

Pressed his back to the tiled wall, I gazed down into his unfocused eyes and smirked. "You think making me come so hard I can't think straight is funny?"

"Yes, but I also think it's hot." He puckered his lips and I wasn't ever going to deny him.

I kissed him slow and deep as he placed his hands on my chest, trailing his fingers over my skin with featherlight touches. The love in that kiss was potent. I couldn't imagine ever sharing the connection I had with Rendon with anyone else. I didn't want to. He was my other half and I was thankful for him every minute I had him in my arms. I could only hope I'd never have to go back to a life without him in it and I poured that hope into the kiss.

Reluctantly, I pulled back and then disposed of the condom before rewashing the both of us. After we'd dried off, he tied the towel around his waist and I tugged him into the bedroom. "The rest of the unpacking can wait. I just want to lay with you."

He dropped his towel and climbed onto the bed beneath the covers and I followed him. I tugged one of his legs over my thigh, and fitted him closer to my side. We lay in silence as I stared into his emerald-green eyes that were sated and lids heavy.

He yawned and struggled to keep his eyes open.

"I love you," I whispered and he gave me a sleepy grin.

"I know you do, Nash. And I love you too. With my whole heart," he murmured. When he closed his eyes, I leaned forward and kissed his forehead. Contentment like I'd never known washed over me as I fell asleep with him wrapped around me.

TWENTY-FOUR
NASH

MY TRUCK ATE up the miles to my parents' house, the only home I'd known growing up. Thanksgiving was something we always celebrated together, even if I only had a short time with them before I had to rush back to campus for practice or load up onto a bus to an away game.

It was always a small affair with just my parents, twin sisters and me. But this year Rendon sat in the passenger seat, complaining about his ass hurting from sitting so long. As comfortable as I'd grown with him, we were still learning new things about each other. A few hours into the drive I'd discovered he didn't do well with long road trips and had to get out and walk often.

Rendon shifted in his seat, drawing my attention to the way he twisted the hem of his shirt in his lap. He was always fidgeting and I was forever saving clothing from his clutches. Reaching out, I wrestled the wrinkled fabric from his hands and wove my fingers between his.

"You as nervous as me?" I asked with a smile.

"Yeah. I guess I am." Rendon's voice shook. "I've never

done this before and have always spent the holiday with my parents."

"Neither have I, but we'll do it together." I pulled his hand in mine to my lips and placed a kiss on his knuckles. "As far as your parents, we'll learn to make it work. We promised to spend Christmas with them so that will be new for me too."

"I can't believe you've never taken anyone home to meet your family," he said, and when I glanced over, his brow was furrowed.

"There hasn't been anyone I wanted them to meet." I flashed him a quick smile and he bit his lip.

"No pressure," Rendon muttered and I chuckled.

Rendon looked out the window at the large homes that fronted the beautiful lake in East Texas where I'd grown up. It was just beginning to look like autumn in late November. A few leaves were turning brown and blowing across the road with the slight breeze coming off the water that shimmered as we drove by.

"Stop worrying, Ren. My family is going to love you," I assured him.

As I pulled into a neighborhood, his hand clamped around mine and I ran my thumb over his knuckles, attempting to calm him.

The houses were spread acres apart and set far back from the road. I turned into the third driveway and parked behind my mom's maroon sedan, shiny as usual from a fresh wash and wax. The large rustic ranch style house was surrounded by a beautifully manicured lawn and backed up to the lake. The front yard boasted shrubbery that stayed green year-round and artistically placed flowers in red, purple and white. My mother had been blessed with a green thumb and coming home was bittersweet. Sugar

Land, or anywhere else in the world for that matter, just couldn't compete.

When I cut the engine, the quiet was jarring. There were no sounds of cars driving by, busy sidewalks or students crowding into open areas, talking and laughing with friends. All the sounds of a bustling town had been left behind.

"Wow, this is amazing." Rendon's eyes widened as he surveyed the area.

"It is," I agreed, not taking my eyes off him.

Rendon's cheeks flushed as he ran his free hand through his hair. Leaning over the console, I traced his jaw with my fingers before tipping his chin until he was forced to look at me. "I love you. No matter what. You're with me and we got this."

A slight smile lightened his face and I breathed a sigh of relief as I freed his hand. He reached to open the door and we climbed out, meeting in front of my truck's hood.

Before I could gauge his expression, two identical ten-year-old giggling beauties, wearing matching blue long-sleeved dresses, came racing across the yard. Each caught their breath as they latched onto my legs and squeezed tight. "Bubba! We missed you."

"I missed you too." I ruffled their short dark curls and grinned down at them.

They quieted as they peeked at Rendon who stood awkwardly with his hands tucked into his pockets.

"Is he your boyfriend?" Jordan whispered, glancing up at me with yellow-green eyes.

"He is. And he's really nice. Promise." I squeezed their shoulders. "This is Rendon. Rendon, meet Jordan and Brooklyn, my baby sisters."

Brooklyn, the one with the most attitude, huffed. "I'm not a baby."

"Hi," Rendon said and a nervous smile crossed his face.

They both loosened their hold on me and appeared to size him up which made me chuckle.

"You don't look like I thought you would." Brooklyn tilted her head and Rendon shuffled his feet. She lowered her voice and tapped on my side. "He's cute."

"Brooklyn," Jordan scolded.

"What? I like his glasses." She crossed her arms over her chest and turned her attention back to me. "Mom said I'd need some pretty soon but not Jordan."

"All right, no fighting. Let's go inside and say hi to Mom and Dad." Nudging their shoulders in the direction of the house, I urged them to go ahead. "Let them know we're here, *baby* sisters. We'll be right behind you."

With a glare from Brooklyn and a pout from Jordan, they turned and took off hand-in-hand.

Facing Rendon, I gripped his shirt and tugged him toward me. He'd have lost his balance if I hadn't wrapped my arms around him. "Trust me, that was the worst of it. They're a handful but you can't help but love them."

He grinned up at me. "They're cute and call you Bubba."

"Cute but vicious. Keep an eye on Brooklyn," I teased. "Now, we better head inside or they'll come back out and march us in there."

His gulp was audible but he gave a sharp nod. "Let's go before I chicken out."

Leaning down, I pecked his lips and wove my fingers between his as I tugged him across the lawn and climbed the steps to the dark wood porch.

The heavy hardwood front door swung open just as I

reached out to grasp the knob and a tall, graceful woman stepped into the doorway. My mom had only gained beauty as she'd aged. Her skin was several shades darker than mine and her black hair was pinned back on one side while the rest fell in long curls over her shoulder. Amber-brown eyes sparkled as crow's feet formed at the corners because of the wide smile that stretched across her face.

She opened her arms and I released Rendon so I could wrap my arms around her slender frame and give her a proper hug. "Missed you, Mom."

She pulled back and pushed me aside gently as she stepped out onto the porch. Rendon's eyes widened as she leaned in to hug him too. "Bless you. I never thought he'd bring anyone home."

"Cut it out, Mom." I chuckled as Rendon eyed me over her shoulder. "Rendon this is my mother, Alicia Sterling. Mom, Rendon."

When she loosened her arms and stepped back, she kept her hands on his arm and considered him. "You done good, baby," she said to me and released him.

"I think so." I shot Rendon a wink and tucked him under my arm. His shoulders relaxed under my touch and I squeezed him to my side.

Mom's smile was warm as she stared at the two of us. "Sorry, Rendon, ignore me. I really thought I'd never see the day." She glanced away, but I hadn't missed the mist in her eyes. "Come on in and introduce your guest to your father."

We stepped through the door and the scent of the vanilla candles my mother always burned was buried beneath the smell of honey-glazed turkey, stuffing, rolls and my favorite—apple and pumpkin pies.

The walls were painted cream and decorated with family portraits and modern artwork. If I was lucky, I'd

"Maybe."

Rendon elbowed me and both girls scowled their disapproval at me before turning to Rendon. But surprisingly it was Jordan who spoke to Ren. "You could probably do better, you know."

I choked. "What the fu...crap? My sisters are turning on me."

Both matching noses tilted up in the air, but Brooklyn sassed, "You aren't supposed to say that word and we were just being honest with him."

Rendon made a weird snort slash cough sound and took a gulp of lemonade before clearing his throat. "Probably," he agreed and glanced at me, mischief in his eyes.

I smirked at him before turning back to my nosy sisters. "I do love him. Now stop giving us a hard time or I'll show him your pictures from when you two got into the cabinet and covered yourselves in chocolate and flour. I believe one of you lost a tooth prying the lid off the bottle."

"See if we care." Brooklyn shrugged as she bit off another piece of roll. Calling her bluff, I stood and she held up her hands. "Wait! Okay, I'm sorry. We'll stop." She shot a wide-eyed Jordan a meaningful look. They did some weird twin communication I'd gotten used to over the years and both nodded in agreement, pretending to zip their lips.

Mom's head was ducked over her plate but her shoulders shook as she laughed. My dad was watching us all with a grin as he sat back and let us bicker.

Glancing around the table, my chest tightened. All the people I loved sat together, laughing and smiling. Talking smack about me. Teasing Rendon. I felt like a big baby, trying to get a grip on the emotion clogging my throat.

When we finished eating, my mom offered up dessert.

I shook my head in protest. "I'm stuffed. Rain check for a few hours?"

Rendon and my dad patted their stomachs and groaned. Make that three rain checks.

"It's there when you guys get ready. Girls, do you want some now?"

They nodded enthusiastically and as she cut them small slices of pumpkin pie, I leaned over and whispered in Rendon's ear. "I want to show you something. Are you up for it?

He eyed me quizzically but a small smile crept over his face. "Sure."

"Rendon and I are going out on the dock," I told everyone and my mom paused as she placed the second piece of pie on Brooklyn's plate.

Her eyes softened. "Let's take this inside," she suggested and herded the girls inside before coming back out to help Dad.

"Let me help." I reached for Dad and he puffed his chest.

"I can handle this." He sucked in a breath as he stood. I shot Mom a concerned look and she mouthed *stubborn*.

He made his way through the door and she hung back. "Nash, don't worry, baby. We have a doctor's appointment first thing when they open after the holiday. It's not usually this bad but they refused to give him his cortisone shot at his last appointment. It's always something with those doctors." She sighed. "Now off with you two," she insisted as she slipped inside, sliding the door closed.

"You think she means it? He's usually better?" Rendon asked with a worried brow.

"I know she does, but...it's just hard." I blew out a deep breath. It would never end. His illness, while not life-threat-

EPILOGUE
RENDON

"OH, COME ON!" Nash yelled at the flat screen mounted on the wall. He leaned forward, elbows on knees as he glared at the TV. It was even bigger than the massive one he'd had back at his duplex in Texas. The movement dipped the couch and I slipped further against his side on the new white leather couch.

From Denver, Colorado, we watched the Saints' first game of the season. Both Nash and I had been curious about not only who his former coach would put in as starters to take his and Shaw's vacated wide receiver spots, but also how Memphis meshed with them.

The offense was on the field during the second quarter. So far they'd pushed the defense to the fifty-yard line with one first down after the other. The camera scanned the home stadium with rows of fans in black and gold. Nash had even changed into his old, worn Saints t-shirt in support.

Though Nash had moved after he'd made the overall number three draft pick, I'd hung back at my parents' house for the summer. While Nash making the final roster for the Eagles was pretty much a given, we'd decided to hold off on me applying for a transfer until it was set in stone two weeks ago. We'd seen each other as much as possible and exchanged video calls every night, but the separation had nearly crushed me.

I split my attention from the screen to the large tablet perched in my lap.

"What's he griping about now?" Tristan muttered as he shuffled around his bedroom in his new off-campus apartment. "Five minutes ago he was grumbling about a dropped ball."

"No idea. I didn't catch it," I said as his screen suddenly bounced and jerked around.

"Yellow monkey's ass fucktwat," Tristan cursed and then all I saw was a massive blue eyeball lined in black before he jerked back away. "Shit, sorry. Tripped over a bag and almost smashed my face into this damn phone. Stupid crap laying around everywhere."

"You still haven't unpacked?" I asked with a raised brow.

"You act like I've lived here a month. It's only been two weeks and I have *stuff* now." He exaggerated the word. Tristan had also gone home for the summer and then moved into an off-campus apartment for his sophomore year. "I only had clothes, a mini fridge, a mirror and stupid shit at the dorm, but now I have like furniture, bathroom stuff and dishes." He sighed. "It's a lot, okay. Stop judging."

I glanced at the TV. The Saints offense was still on the field at their own twenty-yard line now on second down.

"I'm surprised you're not watching the game," I said as I returned my attention to Tristan.

"Why the hell would I watch the game?" Tristan's eyes bugged. "Also, I can see up your nose."

Made in the USA
Las Vegas, NV
16 February 2024

85883998R00204